I0668524

SNPGRDXZ
AND THE TIME WARRIORS

BOOK 2
OF THE SNPGRDXZ SERIES

PAUL R. LLOYD

Paul R. Lloyd

Snpgrdxz and the Time Warriors: Book 2 of the Snpgrdxz Series

Copyright © 2014 Paul R. Lloyd. All rights reserved.

Published by
Paul R. Lloyd Books
P.O. Box 638
Warrenville, IL 60555

No part of this book may be reproduced in any form or by any electronic or mechanical means, including information storage and retrieval systems, without permission in writing from the author, except by a reviewer who may quote brief passages in a review.

This is a work of fiction. The characters, events, locations and names appearing in this book are products of the author's imagination or are used fictitiously. Any similarity to real persons, living or dead, or to actual events or locations is coincidental and not intended by the author.

Snpgrdxz illustration used on the cover: Justice Carmon. The cover design was a gift from someone who wishes to remain anonymous.

THANK YOU

Thanks for choosing the Snpgrdxz series.

Purchase more of my books by searching Paul R. Lloyd on www.amazon.com.

CHAPTER 1

CURIOUSER AND CURIOUSER

In the speediest move I ever saw her make, sixteen-year-old Jennifer Hawkins opened fire with her M16 and charged down the long, grassy slope. I never loved her more than at this moment as she protected me against a horde of three-foot tall troll-zombies.

Jennifer sported long, straight brunette hair tied in a ponytail that bounced as she ran. Her fair complexion reddened the harder she raced. Fat ruby lips and high, sweaty cheekbones complemented her beauty. She was a bit on the skinny side but tall. Like me, she wore twenty-first century blue jeans and a t-shirt. Our brown leather boots were sourced from a shopping spree in nineteen twenty-three so they were brand new. I turned my attention back to the troll-zombies before I accidentally pointed my rifle at the back of the beauty I admired.

The troll-zombie horde split to go around our rifle fire. Yes, by this time I had worked up the gumption to support Jennifer with my M16 without shooting her in the back. The malodorous critters were not as attractive as the zombies we had seen in the movies, and I doubted they would do well on the SATs. But they knew the nearest path to brains wasn't through a hail of gunfire.

At the bottom of the hill, Jennifer smiled but punched me hard on the right shoulder. "Bryan Ganarski, you almost got us killed."

"I'm sorry, but the sight of those creatures made my head hurt." I had my skull fractured by a glancing bullet wound about six months earlier. Stress brought on headaches, and our time travels kept us under constant strain.

"No excuses. We have to catch up." Jennifer shouldered her rifle and headed across the field towards the woods.

"How will we find the others?" I hurried to match Jennifer's pace.

"Follow these footprints." Jennifer pointed to the grass.

I didn't see anything at first, but eventually noticed slight disturbances and color differences in the grass about the size of a boot. I lost the trail in the woods. "Now what?"

"This way. They moved in a straight line." Jennifer continued in the lead as we headed deeper into the trees to catch up with our friends.

Like our world, the land of the trolls had its share of mosquitoes, flies, spiders and other tiny creatures that lusted for our blood. "Hold up," I said.

"Bryan, we can't stop."

"Mosquito repellent won't take long." I rifled through my backpack but found none.

"Don't be a teenage wuss." Jennifer messed around in her backpack. "Here, hold these." Out popped her hair dryer, clips of silver bullets, makeup kit, clips of lignum vitae bullets, personal lady supplies, case of Diet Coke which I dropped, two hand grenades and mosquito repellant.

While she repacked, I sprayed the goop on my clothes and exposed skin. I lacked the muscle to qualify for high school athletics despite my six-foot frame. Instead, I hung out with Gilbert in the pursuit of academic excellence and girls. I found the young lady of my dreams in Jennifer Hawkins while Gilbert prowled in vain. Although if we ever find the long missing Maria Gonzalez, Gilbert's luck could change. Or not. It was hard to tell with Maria and her imitation Goth ways.

Jennifer placed one arm around my neck, swiped her mosquito stuff back and kissed me square on the lips. She backed away, sprayed and returned the repellent to her backpack. She passed a bottle of ibuprofen to me along with a canteen of water. "This is for bravery in action. Keep up your courage and we'll be fine. And remember, you did not see that box of personal items."

I was about to thank her when we heard Frank say, "Sound advice."

Frank Bronson meandered in our direction from twenty feet away where he must have been hidden in a stand of buckthorn. He possessed the broad shoulders of a football player but on a small college team due to his five-foot-ten-inch frame. In his mid-twenties, his athletic career had ended in favor of firefighting in our hometown of Wheaton, Illinois. Like us, he carried an M16 rifle and a backpack stuffed with ammo, grenades, rations, clothes and first aid gear.

"Where is everyone?" Jennifer shouldered her repacked backpack.

"Tony led the team along a trail up ahead. I volunteered to stay behind in case you guys survived the troll-zombie horde."

"We did, no thanks to Bryan," said Jennifer.

"Cut your boyfriend a break, Jennifer. He's walking wounded."

Jennifer placed her right arm around my shoulders and kissed me on the cheek. "I did. And Bryan, you were wonderful charging down that steep incline with me. I didn't know you had the guts. Too bad you tripped earlier at the top of the hill when the others took off."

"Who knew a root stuck out of the ground? There wasn't even a tree nearby, but you were awesome staying back with me. You saved my life." I awarded Jennifer with a kiss.

"Let's catch up with the gang," Frank said.

Jennifer and I followed Frank through the woods until we reached the trail five minutes later.

"This way." Frank pointed out the uphill path to the left of us.

"Downhill is the other way," I said.

"Zombie-troll village is downhill. Our friends trudged uphill."

About fifteen minutes later, we began to smell rotten eggs mixed with baby excrement. We heard the troll-zombies stagger out of the woods onto the trail.

"Run," Frank yelled.

We clambered up a rise in the path. At the top, we followed a right turn. The troll-zombies moved slowly but they were the most persistent of creatures.

Jennifer hollered, "Halt."

I stopped while she and Frank bent over to catch their breaths. I scanned the trail behind us with my rifle locked and loaded.

"We better take off," Frank said once his breathing returned to normal.

I opened fire on a group of troll-zombies that came into view at the curve behind us.

"Hurry," Jennifer yelled.

We sprinted another fifty yards where CJ jumped out of the bushes. "You guys okay?"

When traveling in time, you risk the unlikely possibility of bumping into another version of yourself, and Jennifer had. Now we journeyed with two Jennifers, including my girlfriend, the original or "young Jennifer." The guys sometimes called her "that Ganarski girl" as if we were hitched, which we are not. We're still teenagers after all. Tony, our art teacher and basketball time keeper from back at Lincoln High, was the only one who got away with calling her "Wild Thing."

We named the second version of Jennifer "College Jennifer" or "CJ" because she was college age, five years older than my Jennifer girlfriend. The age difference had to do with CJ ending up in nineteen eighteen and having to wait five years for the rest of us, including herself (don't ask) in nineteen twenty-three.

What would we do if a third Jennifer Hawkins showed up? How many ways can you refer to the different versions of a girl named Jennifer? And don't even think about how College Jennifer was no longer my girlfriend while her high school same-self sister was. CJ matched my Jennifer in every way except for a few extra pounds and her age. And today they dressed differently. While my Jennifer sported her blue jeans and t-shirt, CJ wore a house dress purchased in nineteen twenty-three. Like Alice in Wonderland, time travel became curiouser and curiouser.

"We're fine, but we won't be for long." I opened fire with my M16. The others fired on the troll-zombie horde bearing down on us with no signs of stopping or reversing course.

***

Unlike human zombies, troll-zombies retain enough intelligence to know it doesn't make sense to attack rifle fire with your teeth and outstretched arms. After dropping ten of the troll-zombies with head shots, the remaining monstrosities reversed course and disappeared into the woods down the hill from us.

"Let's catch up with the others," said Frank.

"They aren't too far in front of us," said CJ.

We met up with Gilbert, Tony and Snpgrdxz twenty minutes down the road. They had discovered a large rock outcropping by the side of the trail and used it as a bench to take a break.

"You guys thirsty?" Gilbert held out a canteen. Gilbert Armstrong was my best friend from Lincoln High. He stood half a head taller than me with the broad shoulders and barrel chest of a football linebacker. However, he tackled math, not athletics.

"Bryan has a headache," Jennifer said.

"So what else is new?" asked Tony Romano, our leader who was responsible for us becoming lost in time. He sported the shoulder-length salt and pepper hair older guys grow into. On the skinny side, Tony usually needed a shave.

"I don't think we should remain here long," said Snpgrdxz. As you may have guessed, Snpgrdxz was not your usual teenager. Instead, he was our shape-shifting, space alien comrade. He had survived a flying saucer crash back in our world decades before we met him. Despite his years on earth, he still considered himself a teenager.

Most of the time, Snpgrdxz appeared as Daniel Brickmaster, making him both the easiest and hardest friend to describe. The easiest because he appeared as a nondescript teenage boy with brown hair and eyes. Everything about Daniel smacked of average such as his height, weight, clothing choices, lip thickness, nose size, and teeth color. The difficulty of describing him stemmed from his averageness, but he believed "average" was the secret to keeping below the radar of the men in black.

His alien culture did not use vowels which made his name a nuisance to pronounce. The easy way was to insert the letter "I" everyplace you thought a vowel belonged. So it was pronounced "Snip-grid-ix." We went back and forth calling him "Daniel" or "Snpgrdxz."

Frank passed a bottle of ibuprofen to me. "You guys realize we have an army of undead sleepwalkers between us and the only way out of the troll world."

CJ handed the canteen to me and paced with her arms flying above her head. "If you guys would take a moment to reflect on our conversation way back in nineteen twenty-three, which was back this morning, we agreed to cross the troll world in search of another exit."

"CJ is right. We move out in this direction." Tony headed down the trail away from the Wheaton When Portal, the place of our crossing into this strange but beautiful underworld.

"Wait, the horde turned around," my Jennifer said.

"Run," Tony shouted.

Troll-zombies moved at the speed of overgrown snails, but running rarely succeeded in losing them. Persistence and general stupidity kept them on your trail. Sooner or later, you tired and they didn't. Think ugly used car sales people here. We scurried, but we were tired.

To fight off the pesky brutes, Snpgrdxz transformed into a giant troll-zombie master who commanded them to go away. Snpgrdxz spoke in his own version of the troll language. When that didn't work, he switched to zombie speak, a set of meaningful groans, moans and undead body noises. When he mixed the undead noises with basic troll, the troll-zombies paid attention. To make sure the troll-zombies understood, Snpgrdxz transformed into an even bigger zombie.

The transformation process scared the bejeebers out of the meandering automatons. They took off leaving their giant master behind and the forest trail to us. Snpgrdxz returned to his Daniel Brickmaster form and put his clothes back on.

"We have to save Maria Gonzalez," Frank said.

Maria Gonzalez instigated our time journey through no fault of her own when a troll kidnapped her out of Lincoln High. Our group would head home immediately and abandon the search for Maria to the professionals if we could. But once we crossed the Wheaton When Portal the first time, we learned we knew no way to control it. Returning to our home time involved as much guesswork as a multiple choice test in Miss Throngbottom's English class.

"I'll go." Snpgrdxz mutated into a giant troll-zombie again as he lumbered off in the direction of the troll village. The last time we travelled this way, the territory was in the possession of small three-foot tall forest trolls commonly known as *Huldrefolk*. The trolls must have been involved in a zombie apocalypse since our last visit and now we faced all the joy of dealing with trolls combined with zombies.

The rest of us hunkered down to wait while Snpgrdxz learned if we timed our entry into the troll world perfectly to meet up with the captured Maria Gonzalez. If so, we could rescue her before the trolls boiled her. This made no sense since one of the trolls kidnapped Maria before the zombies invaded. If you think about time travel, it will make you crazy so instead we prepared ourselves for anything without regard to proper time placement.

Our journey began about a year ago when Tony swore we would find the missing Maria Gonzalez alive and return home in time for dinner. So far, we had discovered Maria's boiled and chewed bones in a troll encampment, and our parents must have stopped holding dinner for us months ago.

While Frank Bronson and CJ Hawkins intertwined fingers, Gilbert parked against an oak tree.

My high school sweetheart, Jennifer Hawkins, stood over me. "Bryan Ganarski, why aren't you securing our perimeter?"

"I'm busy with more important things." I stretched my lanky body along the ground, yawned and stood up.

"Like what?" Tony asked.

"Making out with my girlfriend." I kissed Jennifer.

"I like your ideas." Jennifer snuggled close.

"We better stay locked and loaded," Gilbert rubbed his Black, shaved head before he assumed a defensive position by the oak tree, rifle at the ready.

"Retreat," Snpgrdxz shouted from fifty feet down the trail.

"This way." Tony took off away from the troll-zombies.

"Don't we have to stay and fight?" CJ asked.

"It's safer to escape along this troll path to where it meets the werewolf trail. We'll sneak past the vampire cave and the werewolf village undetected." Tony hollered over his shoulder. We followed.

Snpgrdxz yelled, "Lock and load. Here they come." He snagged his clothes and backpack as he passed by us.

Tony stopped us. "I guess CJ was right. It's too late to run. Take up positions behind these trees and wait for my signal to open fire."

We didn't have much of a time lag before Snpgrdxz dressed again and the troll-zombies struck. For some reason, they didn't send their army after us the way they had the first time we arrived in their territory.

A hunting party of twelve troll-zombies meandered down the path toward our position. Tony waited longer than I would have before he shot the first troll-zombie in line.

The rest of the troll-zombies dragged their buddy with them as they beat a hasty retreat. Troll-zombies aren't used to modern firearms so you could startle them with a little instant death.

"Remind me to never walk point," said Gilbert.

"This way." Tony headed in the direction of the vampire cave. This may start to sound like a dumb horror story to you, but the last time we found ourselves in the troll world, we ran into vampires and werewolves. To cross the troll world, we had to pass by their hangouts.

"How will we sneak past the vampires?" Frank asked.

Tony scratched his head. "The nosferatu will be asleep and the werewolves will be regular people. They'll think we're werewolves from another village."

"Let's not forget about the troll-zombies," my Jennifer said.

"You're right, Wild Thing. We could run into another of their hunting parties, or these guys might become brave again, but at least we're away from their village now. I suspect they'll spend the remainder of the day in search of easier pickings." Tony pointed in the direction of the troll-zombie community in the valley below.

The two suns in the western sky shouted mid-afternoon so we needed to make time passing the twin monster lairs. The shadows stretched a long way by the time we reached the cave of the vampires.

We would have passed by safely if it weren't for the trap we fell into. The vampires had dug a hole in the ground and covered it over with sticks hidden under a layer of dirt. The trap held our weight until our entire group traipsed on it. A cracking sound provided the first hint of trouble. We dropped through sticks and bellowed the universal oomph as we hit bottom.

***

My head hurt and my knee ached. Gilbert grasped his Black, bald-shaved cranium where our heads had collided.

"Everyone okay?" Tony asked.

"No, Bryan bashed my head in," said Gilbert.

"He bashed my head, too," said my Jennifer.

"He bashed both your heads?" Daniel Snpgrdxz Brickmaster asked.

"My head hit Gilbert and my knee must have hit Jennifer. Are you okay, honey?"

"Yes, dear. Just be more careful next time," my Jennifer said.

"Anyone else injured besides Gilbert and the old married couple?" Tony asked.

"Somebody scraped my shin with their boot," said Frank. "I think it was CJ."

"Hey, you know we aren't married yet," said my Jennifer.

"Yep, it was me. I just can't get close enough to you." CJ clutched Frank's arm to pull herself up.

"I'm okay and so is Daniel. Everyone else suffered minor injuries. Does that about cover it?" Tony asked.

"What about Bryan's bullet-shattered cranium?" my Jennifer asked. Tears streamed down her cheeks so I figured she was remembering the months I spent in nineteen twenty-three recovering from a bullet that grazed my head during an attack by a bootlegger gang.

"My head hurts but not so bad that I have to worry about a fracture," I said. "Besides, I clunked the other side of my skull." I didn't have the courage to ask Jennifer why she said "yet" in the same sentence as "marriage."

Tony messed around in his backpack to yank out a rope with one of those hook devices you see in the movies when somebody needs to scale a high wall. "Stand back as far as you can."

We smushed together into a corner, but the hole was tiny so there wasn't much room. I felt my Jennifer's body heat against me so I hugged her from behind. She pushed against me more so I kissed her on the neck.

Tony threw the rope.

"I got it," a voice said from above. "You fell into Glimtuckmucker's troll trap. And there's not much time before Glimtuckmucker and his band of hearty nosferatu wake up so you better scramble up here."

"I'll go first to see if this guy is safe." Tony pulled a pistol out of his backpack. "Silver bullets." He shouldered his backpack and an M16. "Lignum vitae bullets." Tony climbed the rope and disappeared over the top.

Tony reappeared with another person peeking over the edge. "Guys next so we can pull the ladies up," Tony said.

Gilbert climbed the rope followed by Frank.

Snpgrdxz said, "Plastic Man can go last."

My Jennifer and CJ clambered out of the hole next. Neither of them needed any help. Daniel stretched his arms up to the top of the hole and pulled himself out of the trap.

We recognized Growlpucket from our last visit to the werewolf village.

"You better leave us alone or we'll shoot you full of silver," said Tony.

"Do you think you'll have time to shoot all of us?" Growlpucket clapped his hands once and a crowd of people scampered out of the trees and bushes. Our only escape was the vampire cave so our choices included having our blood sucked or serving as werewolf meat.

CHAPTER 2

WEREWOLF MEAT

"We could shoot our way out of the village for a head start," said CJ.

"What about the vampires?" Gilbert asked.

We sat in a circle in the visitor's hut which was a large, single room. The cabin was constructed from pine boards taken from the forest nearby. The floor was bare wood.

"This will be a dangerous night," Tony said.

"No kidding," said Frank. "We'll have a pack of werewolves on the hunt for us."

"Vampires?" I asked. And yes, my voice shook.

"Load your M16s with silver bullets because the werewolves will be the immediate danger." Tony checked his M16.

"Wood bullets in the Glocks?" CJ asked.

"Yes," said Tony. "I have a supply of specialty grenades for the grenade launcher. We'll start with silver grenades, but I have some grenades loaded with wood pellets for our nosferatu friends. "

"Grenade launcher?" Gilbert asked.

"Yeah and I have a flame thrower in the backpack someplace. Here's the grenade launcher." Tony dragged a big rifle thing out of his backpack that was longer than the pack. It had a huge revolver mechanism that allowed for the rapid fire launch of multiple grenades.

"What is that?" Frank asked.

Snpgrdxz shook his head. "I don't believe it. You fit a South African MGL in your backpack?"

"What's an MGL?" Gilbert asked.

"It stands for Multiple Grenade Launcher. See the revolver mechanism? It allows for the rapid fire of grenades. The men in black like to carry them in the trunks of their cars in case they run into people like me." Snpgrdxz locked and loaded his M16.

"I'll handle the grenade launcher since I have experience with it," said Tony.

"You do?" my Jennifer asked.

"Ah, Wild Thing, what you don't know about me." Tony searched around in his backpack again. "Here it is." He pulled a flamethrower out of his backpack.

"How do you keep pulling things out of your backpack that are bigger than it?" I asked.

Tony smiled in my direction, but didn't answer. He handed the flamethrower to Frank. "You're a fireman so you should be able to handle one of these."

"Tony, I put out fires for a living. I don't start them."

"Not even in practice?"

"I used one once so I guess I'm more qualified than the kids."

"Kids?" Gilbert asked. "How long have we been on this road trip, Frank? Kids. These kids will be killing vampires and werewolves tonight. That makes us men and women no matter how old we are."

My Jennifer stood up. "We are men and women. And this road trip has been way too long so I say let's kick butt while these werewolves are still human. Then we can high tail it before the vampires wake up."

"And you have a right fine high tail," said Gilbert.

"Shut up," said my Jennifer.

Gilbert laughed.

"Shut up or we'll find out if you're vulnerable to silver bullets" my Jennifer stamped her foot. I snagged her hand to make her sit, but she yanked out of my grasp and stepped back.

"Cool it, Wild Thing," said Tony. "Gilbert's just trying to lighten the atmosphere. And you are right. Let's blow this joint while we're fighting humans. We'll high tail it, like you said, before the vampires wake up. Frank, you take the lead with the flame thrower and don't hesitate to burn this forest to the ground when we come under attack. Monsters can't take flame. That little tool of yours will work against lycanthropes as well as nosferatu."

Three very attractive ladies entered our cabin. "Hungry? We want you nice and strong for tonight." The ladies smiled.

My Jennifer plugged them with her M16. "We're out of here."

Tony led us out of the cabin. Even werewolves have day jobs so the village appeared empty except for some scattered children playing and a few women doing domestic chores.

We ran in the direction of the setting suns. At the edge of the forest, we heard a deep voice yell, "Hey, stop them."

Tony dropped to the back of our little group and fired three grenades at the crowd that began to form. "Posse is right behind us. Vamoose."

As planned, Frank led the way. Tony's grenades stopped the werewolf crowd so we placed another hundred yards between us and them before we heard the yells of the angry crowd. Tony's grenades killed another bunch of the werewolf people. My legs shook as I ran with my friends to get away from an angry crowd that would turn into werewolves as soon as the moon came up.

***

Werewolves, even in their human form, run as fast as horses if not faster. We made another hundred yards into the woods before the shouts of "There they are," rang out close behind us. Tony emptied his grenade launcher in an attempt to slow down our pursuers while killing as many as possible before the moon came up.

"Circle up," Tony yelled.

Seven people don't make for a very large circle or perimeter of defense. Our advantage was our advanced weaponry compared to the unarmed werewolf people. But the suns had set and soon the moon would rise.

The werewolf people yelled at us, but didn't attack. "We're coming for you, food."

"Don't let their yelling get to you," Tony said. "It's propaganda. We're not food. We're children of the living God. He will protect us as we pray."

While praying, the bats descended from the tree tops. The good news was the bats showed no favoritism. Werewolf people blood was as tasty to them as our own. Frank let loose with the flame thrower while Tony distributed three hand grenades to each of us. The grenades were stuffed with lignum vitae and oak pellets.

Frank succeeded in setting the tree branches on fire above us. The flames formed a protective halo of light and fire that the bats avoided. Instead, they chose the easy pickings among the unarmed werewolf people. The sound of people screaming and blood sucking frightened us but encouraged us as well. It was better for werewolves to die at the hands of vampires than us.

We could tell when midnight arrived for the moon rose. The people screams became deeper right before the wolf howls and growls began in earnest. The bats screamed and fluttered away from the werewolves. The trees that had offered us protection under the flames, burned out.

"Retreat," Tony yelled.

We ran deeper into the woods. The path led us up hill. At the top, Tony yelled, "Regroup into a defensive perimeter."

Vampires fly faster than werewolves run so they arrived first. Frank's flamethrower worked best, but we needed three or four of them to keep all the bats away and we only had the one. Tony fired his reloaded grenade launcher which proved to be a decisive weapon, unless a bat got too close. We couldn't very well blow ourselves up or burn our little bodies to a crisp. Actually we could, but we chose not to for now. Why waste ourselves until the ammunition ran out.

Tony tossed the grenade launcher to Gilbert. "Keep firing. And all of you toss your grenades as soon as you see the werewolves."

Within seconds, the werewolves sprang out of the woods. By the time our grenades exploded at their feet, many of the werewolves were too close to burn or blow. Snpgrdxz and I resorted to our Glocks with the silver bullets. These proved effective at close range until Tony opened up with another flame thrower.

"Wild Thing, take this flame thrower from me and burn those puppies," Tony yelled.

My Jennifer wasted no time grabbing the second flame thrower and letting loose with the close in werewolves. The burning animals fell at our feet. CJ put them out of their misery with pointblank silver bullet shots from her Glock. This proved important because even a flaming werewolf can scratch you and turn you into a lycanthrope.

Tony opened up with a third flamethrower which succeeded in driving the vampire bats and werewolves back. It also succeeded in starting a major forest fire.

CHAPTER 3

HELLFIRE AND DAMNATION

Turpelator strode out of the flames. "Cease fire."

The creatures of the night halted their attack. The werewolves sat like puppies waiting for a treat from their master. The bats fluttered above the burning treetops.

Turpelator raised his index finger in our direction which I took to mean to wait one minute. He turned to his minions. "Fools, why do you attack when these humans and this alien have you out armed and outfoxed? You cannot win here tonight. Return to your homes. We shall feast another time, my friends."

Have you ever heard a bunch of bats and werewolves grumbling at their master? The noise filled the woods, drowning out the sound of the flames which spread like, well, wildfire. What else would they spread like?

"Go!" Turpelator shouted. The bats arose as one and flew into the night. The werewolves vanished into the woods.

Turpelator faced us. "Another time, perhaps." He clapped his hands and a wall of flames flared up between us and the night creatures. Turpelator vanished into the flames.

"Guess he's familiar with hellfire and damnation," said Snpgrdxz.

***

The fire burned out in the rain and morning mist behind us as Tony led the way across a wide, shallow river into the deep woods the next day. "We should be safe from attack now that we're far away from zombies, troll-zombies, trolls, werewolves and vampires. They are territorial, more or less. And we'll have plenty of game for our food in the deep woods."

We couldn't see far into the ancient oaks and evergreens around us. Troll hunting parties, if trolls still existed in this world, weren't likely to spot us under the cover of the trees. I felt safe for the first time since entering the troll world.

My Jennifer sidled up to me on the trail. "I'm so glad we left the evil Turpelator behind."

"Me, too." I kissed Jennifer.

According to CJ, this was the twenty-eighth time we crossed out of nineteen twenty-three in her time loop trap, but the rest of us didn't remember any of those past crossings. As far as we were concerned, this was our first attempt at returning home while breaking CJ's time trap. Are the rest of us caught up in our own time traps and unaware of it?

More likely, CJ was the only one of us trapped in time, and she repeated the same experience multiple times, while the rest of us passed this way but once. This will come as no surprise to you by this time, but you can see why I thought I was crazy. How do you explain these weird phenomena?

According to CJ, the last twenty-seven times we crossed the Wheaton When Portal, the zombies attacked, and Jennifer was pushed accidentally through the Wheaton When Portal by herself. She said we encountered zombies, never troll-zombies. They were something new.

She always landed in nineteen eighteen with her body restored to age fifteen. Then she waited the five years for us to arrive in nineteen twenty-three which explains why she was five years older than her same-self sister.

Among the many mistakes we made on the trail that day were feeling safe, thinking Turpelator was behind us, and not remaining alert for troll hunting parties.

***

The arrow struck Fireman Frank in the left shoulder with a loud splat and spurt of blood. He tumbled down an embankment we were about to cross before the trolls spotted us. The arrow snapped off when Frank rolled over a rock, leaving the point and a bit of the shaft embedded in his shoulder.

CJ yanked her skirt up a little and ripped a chunk of her slip off at the bottom. "Don't standby gawking at my legs. Yank the arrow out of him."

Tony checked Frank's wound. "Better to push it through. The arrow head has flanges in the design that will tear his flesh up if we pull it back."

"Where'd you learn about that?" Gilbert asked.

"Grew up on Gabby Hayes and John Wayne. They always snap off the arrow in the movies and push it through." Tony pressed on the arrow.

Frank screamed and the arrow stayed put.

"Shucks, in the movies, the guy always has a flesh wound. This puppy is embedded in your shoulder bone," Tony said.

"Shoulder bone?" Snpgrdxz asked.

"Whatever bone," Tony said. "We have no choice." He yanked the arrow as Frank screamed again. The arrow head and shaft popped loose.

Frank's shoulder gushed more blood. CJ applied her torn piece of slip material to the wound.

"Little sister, hold this while I make more clean bandages." CJ guided my Jennifer's hand to cover the wound. "Press hard to stop the bleeding."

Tony grabbed a sewing kit and a bottle of alcohol out of one of the backpacks and played doctor while Frank chewed on a stick to keep from screaming. When Tony finished, he dumped more alcohol on Frank's wound.

CJ raised her skirt again, but first checking to make sure Frank had a great view. He appeared in too much pain to appreciate the show.

After tearing off more slip material and folding it into a pad, she handed it to my Jennifer who used it to cover Frank's injury.

CJ lifted her skirt yet again, about half way up the birthmark shaped like a reverse map of Italy on her left thigh this time, to tear off another piece of cloth. She folded this piece to make a wrap she tied around Frank's shoulder to hold the bandage in place. And yes, my Jennifer had that same birthmark on her thigh.

"Can he travel?" Snpgrdxz asked.

Frank rose to his feet. "Yes."

He sat back down. "No."

***

"Dizzy?" Gilbert asked.

"Yes." Frank rubbed his arm below his wounded shoulder.

Snpgrdxz transformed into a shorter version of Daniel Brickmaster but with a huge right arm. "I'll carry him. Let's move out. I may seem strong this way, but I'm not as powerful as I appear. Shape shifters are about looks not feats of strength. I have strong muscles in this arm, but they won't last as long as they would if I was the Snpgrdxzanator."

Snpgrdxz hauled Frank as we headed into the heart of the deep forest along a troll trail. The trail wound through a river valley so we were never far from fresh water. High mountains surrounded the valley, much like the vistas you see along I-80 in Pennsylvania. We travelled a green world where animals chirped, birds swooped, mosquitos buzzed and trolls roamed. We kept our M16s at the ready.

23

While we had no way to know which direction we traveled because we were not on the earth anymore, we followed the path of the two suns as they crossed the sky. The trail meandered along the general direction of the river. We named this direction the west of this world because we faced the setting two suns, but the main thing was we were on a line traveling away from the Wheaton When Portal and the trolls and troll-zombies who lived there.

Hikes left you with too much time to think. Was I still crazy? I hadn't had one of my hallucinations in months since we left home. I meant the kind of hallucination that makes real bullet holes in your crucifix and authentic dead bodies of people who have an extra body running around someplace else. Did you follow this? I wasn't sure I did, which was why I kept questioning my sanity. But I remembered a dead Jennifer and a live Jennifer at the same time. Neither one of them was my real Jennifer. So what kind of fakes were they?

If we had two Jennifers in this time and strange world of two suns with live trolls, could two Jennifers also exist in our home time back in Wheaton? Or even three Jennifers when you count the one who was home in bed that night while her two twins ran around my house? One twin ran around. The other was a dead body that some other Gilbert and Jennifer hauled away to burn with the help of a wrong Snpgrdxz.

Would I have to also deal with two or three Gilberts and Snpgrdxzs? Were my insane hallucinations actual events where I encountered time travelers who are with me right now in these woods? Was it possible they had no memory of their visits to me because those social calls were still in their futures?

With multiple time travel futures, would they show up in our home time more than once? And could I meet a few Bryan Ganarskis when I returned home? Was I home already and this hasn't happened yet? And if I'm not, would I have been instantly home if my hard head hadn't stopped that bullet? Were we a fatal bullet to the brain away from home?

And was our home place still the twenty first century? Jennifer's base time place seemed to have shifted somehow to nineteen eighteen for some strange reason I didn't understand.

Did time move forward for the people in the twenty-first century in the same way it did for us now? It must.

Did time always move at the same speed? Or did time move slower or faster depending on the year you were in?

Time travel threw off my concept of aging. Was I still sixteen or were we gone long enough that I turned seventeen? And if I was seventeen now, would I have to return to being sixteen when I arrived back home?

What about Jennifer, my Jennifer, I mean? She began our journey at age fifteen, but CJ was more like twenty when we met her. How did that work? Every time CJ ended up back in nineteen eighteen, she found herself returned to age fifteen. It was a form of eternal youth unless she could break the time loop. One day, she was twenty and the next, she was fifteen. What would happen if she moved forward in time until she died of old age? Would her life end, or would she wake up back in nineteen eighteen at age fifteen?

If I returned to my original time would I still have this scar on my head and these headaches? I didn't tell you about the scar before because I figured you knew I must have one. I kept it under my hair which I wore longer than usual.

But none of these thoughts had anything to do with my main concern of the moment which was whether we would ever find another portal to take Jennifer safely out of the troll world. And if we did, would we come out on planet earth or somewhere else in the universe? That we would pass through to another time and place was a given, but would we land in nineteen eighteen to become stuck in Jennifer's time loop? And how many times did we need to visit the troll world before we found Maria Gonzalez?

The three-foot tall woodland trolls attacked late that night.

***

Trolls hated noise so they didn't hang around long once my Jennifer chased them off with her M16 blazing. She was lucky the trolls were not the best archers in the dark.

Our fire had died down to a few coals. I worried about running out of ammo, which was something you do when you wake up with a splitting headache from the loud gunfire. We had no way to refill our supply if it ran out. Fortunately, Tony packed a lot.

When the trolls retreated, Tony asked for a head count.

CJ and Fireman Frank were missing.

My Jennifer screamed her name.

Tony called, "Wild Thing Number Two, where are you?"

"Don't shout. We can hear you." Wild Thing Number Two, I mean, CJ's voice came from around a large tree.

Gilbert and I aimed our flashlights so we were able to see the tree when CJ poked her head around it.

"We're here," CJ said.

Fireman Frank crawled past CJ and waved his good arm. He had one of those long, skinny smiles like the kind dogs flash when you catch them swiping a hamburger from the picnic table.

"How do you feel?" Snpgrdxz asked.

"Never better." CJ had the same sheepish guilty expression I've seen on Jennifer's face whenever she got caught doing something she wasn't supposed to since she was in kindergarten.

"He meant Frank, Wild Thing Two," said Tony.

"You didn't waste any time getting over Chauncy, big sister," my Jennifer said.

"I loved Chauncey and I miss him, but right now I love Frank." CJ said. "It doesn't make sense to miss out on a new love just because your old love died."

"If you're finished with the hanky-panky, let's move out." Tony was all business as he waited at the edge of the darkness beyond flashlight range.

"Shouldn't we wait for morning?" my Jennifer yawned.

"Trolls know where we are. They'll return." Gilbert checked his handgun and shoved it into his belt.

"How do we decide which way to go?" Frank sat up.

"We keep on the path." Tony headed into the darkness.

"We can't see you, Tony." Snpgrdxz stretched his arm about twenty feet to snag Tony on the shoulder. "Okay, found you. I'll guide the others."

Snpgrdxz took my hand and then we all held hands and followed him as he reeled his arm into a normal Daniel Brickmaster arm length.

"I'm not like her," my Jennifer said.

"You mean CJ?" I asked.

"Yes. I'm a one-man woman. If I'm not with the one I love, I go out and find him. I don't like having multiple partners in my life."

"I only have eyes for you, my dear." I flashed my peepers in my Jennifer's direction.

"Good, then we're the same. That means a lot to me."

"Frank, will you make it?" Gilbert asked.

"I'm a little feverish and sore. And dizzy, but I can travel."

"Let me know when I need to carry you again," said Snpgrdxz.

The night beast roared in the distance.

"No full moon tonight," Gilbert said.

"Ain't our world," said Tony.

"Yeah, we're playing by a different set of rules," said CJ.

The roar came again, much closer this time.

The black furry beast charged out of the darkness. It snagged CJ and dragged her off. Snpgrdxz managed to stretch his arm out to hang onto the beast, but the fiend bit him. Well, the creature tried to nibble Snpgrdxz. Instead, Snpgrdxz shape shifted his hand away from the fur ball, but it allowed the critter to escape with CJ.

Don't ask me what the thing looked like. The night was black and so was the monster. He was gone as was CJ.

CHAPTER 4

THE WEREWOLF
OF TROLL LAND

Gilbert paced back and forth. "CJ's disappearance proves Mr. Turpelator's fourth law of time travel. We're making things worse the more we travel in time. First, we lost Maria Gonzalez, and then we ended up with two Jennifers, one young and one old. Then we almost killed Bryan. Now, we lost CJ."

Tony burped. "Dude, losing CJ puts us back in the right with only one Wild Thing. We love CJ, but does the universe need two Jennifers?"

My Jennifer sulked, "My new sister may still be locked in time. We can't know unless we rescue her and make sure she gets home. If she's stuck in a time loop, then so am I."

"Where is CJ's home?" Snpgrdxz asked. "She is the product of a time loop we're attempting to break. Once we rescue her, where do we drop her off?"

"We talked about this before, remember? My older twin sister will return home with me," said Jennifer. "I love her. And my parents will, too. After all, she is their daughter as much as I am."

"And I care for her," said Fireman Frank. "Let's rescue her."

"I'll become a hound dog. Great sense of smell, but no ability to speak. Try to keep up everyone." Snpgrdxz's transformation produced one big hound on a leash.

I grabbed the lead. "Stay together."

Gilbert snagged his clothes.

Snpgrdxz the hound dog barked three times and plunged into the woods yanking me along. The tether had a soft, bumpy feel like warm leather.

The night brute roared. Snpgrdxz barked again. He kept his nose to the ground and headed straight for the rumbles of the beast.

**

When the monster leaped from a hilltop above us, Snpgrdxz saved our lives. First he shrunk his hound dog body into a regular-sized mouse. He transferred his bulk to his head. This he morphed to triple the size of the beast's head but with the same werewolf good looks. With fangs triple the size of the werewolf's, Snpgrdxz drove off the beast which vanished into the darkness of the nighttime forest.

We ran to the top of the hill where we found Jennifer passed out next to a patch of flowers.

"Dudes, Dudette, be careful." Tony stretched his arms out to block us. "That's aconitum."

"What's that?" my Jennifer asked.

"Wolfsbane." Tony picked a flower. "It'll kill you if you're not careful."

Snpgrdxz shape shifted into a giant lightning bug. He fluttered above the scene and blinked his butt to light our view.

"When did you learn how to light up your butt?" Gilbert asked.

"She's injured." Tony said.

"I hate to be the one who notices such things, but this is not CJ." Gilbert pointed at the prostrate maiden.

"Looks like my Jennifer," Fireman Frank said.

"My older sister self did not wear those, those, what are those things?" my Jennifer asked.

"Buckskin," said Tony.

"Maybe the werewolf changed her clothes for her to make her look more like him," said Gilbert.

"Wouldn't he tear her limb from limb and eat the pieces?" Tony asked.

"Ewww," my Jennifer said. In the dim glow of Snpgrdxz's butt light I could see my Jennifer turn green.

"She's bleeding. If a werewolf scratches or bites you, doesn't it mean you'll turn into one?" Fireman Frank asked.

"Yes, but we can prevent that," said Tony.

"How?" asked my Jennifer.

"Poison her with wolfsbane?" I asked.

"Exactly." Tony kept a straight face.

"I was kidding," I said.

"Won't she die?" asked Fireman Frank, his voice cracked.

"Most likely. Unless we get the amount right. Give her the right dose, she's cured. Too much, she'll die. Not enough, she transforms on the next full moon and slaughters us. Of course in this world, all bets are off on the rules of Weredom. She could change any time as far we can tell."

"How much wolfsbane is the right amount?" I asked.

"No way to know," said Tony.

"Then what do we do?" my Jennifer's voice cracked and she hugged Fireman Frank.

A buggy sounding Snpgrdxz said, "Hrmpphy ewwp, mmm bah urts."

"Was that Snpgrdxz?" asked Gilbert.

"What did he say?" asked my Jennifer.

"No idea," I said.

Tony chuckled. "He said to hurry up because his butt hurts."

Paul R. Lloyd

Tony grabbed a handful of wolfsbane and stuffed it into the wounded Jennifer's mouth. He poked her several times in the ribs.

Jennifer's eyes popped open. She grabbed her side and swallowed. "What the heck are you guys up to?"

"We saved you from turning into a werewolf," my Jennifer said.

"Or we killed you. We're not sure which," said Gilbert.

Fireman Frank hugged Jennifer and dragged her out of the wolfsbane patch.

"Let's take more of the wolfsbane with us," Tony said.

"In case someone else gets bit?" Fireman Frank asked.

"In case I run out of stuff to smoke." Tony tucked the plants into a plastic bag he inserted into his backpack.

"I feel sick," the new Jennifer said before she passed out in Fireman Frank's arms.

***

"Why is he holding me?" the sick new Jennifer asked.

"I love you," Fireman Frank said.

"You're cute, but we don't have time for love crap. We have to get out of here."

"But... but... we... behind the tree... earlier this evening."

"In your dreams, pal. You think I'd cheat on Bryan after I waited five lonely years for him to show up in nineteen twenty-three? And that's after I passed through my time loop twelve times so it's more like sixty years though I'm not sure they count because I repeated the same years over and over and never aged a day, but it feels like sixty to me. And on this pass through, I spent three more years dodging trolls, werewolves and the things that scare away trolls and werewolves in this world. Hard to keep track of time here. I notched the days on my wood bow. The one good thing about the whole deal is every time I pass through the

32

Wheaton When Portal, I come out as my old fifteen-year-old self and meet up with Bryan in nineteen twenty-three. "

I admit it. The new Jennifer astonished me. She didn't sound like CJ. Her voice had a husky, earthy quality of someone who spent a lot of time in the open air.

Snpgrdxz was back as Daniel Brickmaster. He nudged me. "Ain't her."

"What?" I asked.

Daniel said, "She isn't CJ. We saved the wrong one."

"What are you talking about?" Fireman Frank pointed a flashlight on the prone Jennifer.

"Snpgrdxz doesn't think she's our CJ," I said.

"No kidding," said Fireman Frank.

"I didn't go to college guys, so how could I be?" asked the new Jennifer.

"Hold on," Gilbert shouted. "How can CJ not be CJ?"

We stared at him in hope of any words of wisdom he might share to clear this thing up. He handed a stack of clothes to Daniel.

Before the new Jennifer could answer, a previously human type of zombie popped out from behind a tree and grabbed hold of Daniel Brickmaster whose pants were still down.

CHAPTER 5

ZOMBIES ON THE MARCH

Daniel morphed his left arm into a spear and stabbed the zombie between the eyes. The zombie ceased moving, but a hundred of his friends stumbled out of the night-blackened trees.

Daniel had given us time to shoulder our M16s and open fire. Even my sweetheart Jennifer pasted a dozen or more brain eaters.

The problem with a zombie horde was they didn't understand how to target a goal. Any other army would have fought us until we were dead or some general ordered a retreat. The zombie horde scuffled away through the forest like we were a mere snack left behind on the way to a bigger feast.

"Are they skipping out on us because they smell a bigger feast behind us? Is there another army of unknown creatures sneaking up on us?" I asked.

"Not anymore," said Gilbert.

My darling continued to shoot zombies in the back of the head after they abandoned their attack on us.

"Save your ammo," Tony cried.

I placed a hand on Jennifer's arm to get her attention. She dropped her arm to her side but didn't let go of her M16.

"You okay," I asked.

"Yeah, we Ganarski women are tough." my Jennifer nudged my arm.

"Ganarski women?" asked Gilbert.

My Jennifer screamed and ran off into the trees in the opposite direction of the zombies.

***

Tony cleared his throat. "Older Jennifer, how many times did you say you cycled through this time warp?"

"What about the zombies?" Gilbert asked.

"They ain't our concern," Tony said.

"Won't they return, like the troll-zombies," Frank asked

"If they come back, they'll become our concern. Until then, no worries, children." Tony paced in a circle, hand rubbing chin. "Listen up. If you think about a battle after the action, you'll end up with combat fatigue, and you'll be worse than useless to the rest of us. If that happens, some of you may find yourselves left behind."

"What about whatever army of monsters the zombies attacked behind us?" I asked.

"Stop worrying about zombies and trolls. There are worse things awaiting us in this world, so let's focus on how we find that next When Portal and leave this world behind."

"Let's find Jennifer," I said.

"Which one?" Gilbert asked.

"Both of them," I shouted.

"You want to know how many times I recycled through the time loop?" the new Jennifer asked.

"Yes, but first let's find the missing Jennifers before something eats them."

Tony divided us into two teams. Daniel and I served on one team with Frank as the leader. Tony led the other team which included the new Jennifer and Gilbert. Tony's group continued along the trail while the rest of us circled around our location.

We wore our cave dweller head lamps last used in the tunnel system under Lincoln High School, but we couldn't see far. We took turns calling Jennifer's name. Daniel morphed a long hound dog nose and sniffed ahead for us. He found her trail, and we followed it.

"What?" my Jennifer called after we had searched for a few minutes.

"Where are you?" I hollered.

"I'm busy," she yelled.

"Busy?" asked Daniel.

"Busy with girl stuff. Leave me alone," my Jennifer said.

Daniel and Frank laughed. I smiled as my face warmed up.

"Not to worry," said Frank. "She's okay." He patted me on the back.

"Explore the cave while you wait," called my Jennifer.

"What cave?" Frank asked.

Jennifer joined us. She stuffed her shirt tail into her blue jeans. "Follow me." She led us to a cave entrance. Without the lights we either would have missed it completely or wandered into it without realizing we had entered a cave.

Frank fired his M16 into the air. In the distance another rifle resounded. "Let's head back to the trail to meet up with Tony's group. Daniel, can you lead us with your nose?"

We arrived back on the trail about the same time Tony's group joined us.

The two suns broke the horizon one after the other about an hour apart for a dazzling display of light. We built a new fire and Tony cooked a hot oatmeal breakfast for us to share. We used powdered milk and boiled river water for the liquid.

"Do you still want to hear how many times I've cycled through the time loop?" asked Third Jennifer.

"We know you are keeping count because our CJ told us she was." Tony patted older Jennifer's shoulder.

"Let's get this straight. You guys have already visited me in nineteen twenty-three, and you are now back in the troll world? And on this cycle you brought older me with you, so you have two Jennifers, the nineteen twenty-three Jennifer and the person you think of as the original Jennifer?"

"Yes." I almost shouted.

"Okay, didn't I tell you this was my cycle twelve? I didn't travel with you guys this time because we agreed you should leave without me. I tried to cross the land of the trolls in search of another exit to a time other than nineteen eighteen."

"You found another exit in the thirteenth time loop cycle?" Frank asked.

"I don't know yet, do I?" Older Jennifer asked.

"This is too much for me." Gilbert sat down. "We're going around in time circles here. We've got to find a way to save Maria Gonzalez, who, may I remind you, was a stack of well-boiled bones the last time we saw her."

Tony wrapped an arm around Gilbert's shoulders. "Calm yourself, dude. We'll find your Maria if we hit the Wheaton When Portal right."

"And if we don't?" asked Frank.

"Be cool because we will sooner or later. But first we have to break Wild Thing's time loop." Tony picked up his backpack.

"Is that possible?" asked older Jennifer.

"It better be because I'm headed into it," said my Jennifer.

"Let's break it this cycle," said Frank.

"We will as soon as we find CJ," said Gilbert.

"We found her," said Frank. "Except she's the wrong one. Can we throw this one back and trade her for the other one?"

Snpgrdxz chuckled. "I like the way you think, Frank. But let's keep our new old Jennifer and find our CJ. Where do we begin?"

A woman screamed nearby.

CHAPTER 6

ANOTHER JENNIFER

"Over here," cried the woman who sounded like CJ but with a deeper voice than my Jennifer's teenybopper high pitch.

"Who's there?" asked Snpgrdxz.

"Me, I've been here for a while." CJ appeared out of the trees.

"Guess we couldn't see the CJ for the trees," snickered Tony.

"I'm CJ, the one Frankie loves."

"Yeah, what cycle are you on?" asked Gilbert.

"I told you back at the house. This is try number twenty-eight for me."

"How did you get away from the werewolf?" Frank wrapped CJ in his arms.

"Easy. Once the sun came up old fur ball shifted into the ugliest human ever. I asked his name and he said, "Master." He wandered off into the woods. "Why would he want to be called 'master?'"

"Are you people coming or what?" The new Jennifer stumped down the hill. We called her "Third Jennifer." She looked like CJ's twin sister except for her tougher, meaner appearance.

We first distinguished her as a new Jennifer by her smell. The river close by didn't mean she bathed as often as we did in the twenty-first century. She may have formed the once-a-week routine common to an earlier era and then slipped into a monthly or longer pattern while living alone in the deep woods.

We couldn't miss Third Jennifer's tough voice. "Okay, we'll rest here and move out at noon. Find a spot to hide. I said hide. HIDE! HIDE! HIDE!"

"Yes, drill sergeant." Tony sounded more than half serious to me.

We continued to call College Jennifer "CJ" and my Jennifer continued as either "Bryan's Jennifer" or "your Jennifer." Gilbert sometimes called her "that Ganarski woman," which turned her face red and pissed me off.

The good news for me was my Jennifer jumped into my arms on the second "Hide" from Third Jennifer. Or was it Snpgrdxz up to his old tricks? No. He promised. "Snpgrdxz, where are you?"

Silence. Not good. That's when someone yanked my shorts about out of the back of my pants while I still carried Jennifer in my arms. I spun around and knocked Third Jennifer to the ground with my Jennifer's feet during the spin cycle.

No one was behind me, but Daniel Brickmaster laughed. You can always tell his laugh because of the alien click.

"You can put me down now," my Jennifer said, her voice a tad husky.

"Kiss me first," I ordered. She did. We fell to the ground laughing.

"Quiet, you two." Third Jennifer had taken command. Jennifer and I moved to a nearby tree and sat on the ground together.

I fell asleep with my arm around Jennifer and her head on my shoulder. When I woke up, the two suns of the troll world hung near the top of the sky. The rest of the sky remained pale blue like ours on a clear day back home. Fireman Frank's foot tickled my ribs on the side opposite my Jennifer. She snored.

"It doesn't get any better." Frank pointed his foot at Jennifer.

"I know. Isn't she sweet?" I could feel the smile creep across my face.

"I mean the snoring," said Frank. "It doesn't get any better. CJ is even louder."

"Move Out." Third Jennifer barked orders loud enough to wake a sleeping Jennifer.

My Jennifer smiled at me. "Good morning, handsome."

I leaned down for a kiss. She pulled up into the kissing zone and it was good. Real good. You know you love someone when you are willing to kiss them before they brush their teeth.

We moved out in single file formation behind Third Jennifer. She carried a wooden spear, a solid metal spear, a quiver and a bow. Her weapons were large so I assumed she stole them from the large mountain trolls, which if you think about it, was a feat for a young maiden.

While Third Jennifer marched point, I took up the number two position with my Jennifer behind me. "Where did you learn to use the spear and arrows?"

Third Jennifer gave me a cold stare. "I've been stuck here longer than you wimps. A girl learns a few things or a girl becomes troll stew. I chose to learn."

"How come you carry a metal spear?" I asked.

Third Jennifer stopped and cold stared me. And cold stared me some more.

I could feel my IQ drop like a rock.

Third Jennifer said, "Did you or did you not see a werewolf during the night?"

"Yes," I said.

"You do know silver is about the only thing that will kill a werewolf, right? That and wolfsbane."

"Oh, but why would the trolls have silver... oh, I get it. You stole their anti-werewolf weapons." I could feel the triumphant smile cross my face as my IQ returned to normal. Well, my version of normal.

Third Jennifer continued to cold stare me as she shook her head and moved up the trail. I followed next and everyone else tagged along behind me.

The trail at this point narrowed into an old animal path widened by wandering woodland trolls so we had a lot of cover from vines and trees.

"Let's be tent mates tonight, okay? Us Ganarskis have to stick together," my Jennifer said.

Everyone could see my face beam, and they understood my Jennifer and I were in love.

"I can't believe I said that." My Jennifer covered her face with her hands. Her M16 fell to the ground.

"Are you two like secretly married?" Frank asked.

"No, but we're in love," I said.

"I'm so sorry, Bryan." Jennifer hugged me.

"Sounds like a Freudian slip," Tony said. "In your heart of hearts, you two are married. At least Wild Thing is. It's part of what makes her wild."

"Will you forgive me?" My Jennifer stared into my brown eyes with her deep green peepers.

"Nothing to forgive. As far as I'm concerned you are a Ganarski woman."

"Does that mean we're married?" my Jennifer asked.

"I guess I mean you're a future Ganarski woman so go ahead and call yourself one. We're a tad young for marriage, don't you think?"

"You mean we should go home, finish high school, earn a college degree, find jobs, and have a career first?" My Jennifer batted those soft green eyes of hers at me in a way that said she had no intention of waiting that long before we mingled our bits. "I don't think so. I'm focused on becoming a Ganarski sooner rather than later."

My Jennifer kissed me, but she had opened the box called "matrimony", and there was no way to close the lid. I loved her, but a wedding? I needed to think about it. Long and hard. Mostly long as in a long, long time from now.

Whenever time this was.

"Let's go cave diving," Tony said.

CHAPTER 7

THE DARK CAVE HORROR

"To the caves, people. We have a long way to go." Tony marched into the cave. We stared at his back for a short time and then followed.

Outside the world was clear, warm and bright in the double sunshine. We could have rambled around the hill, like I wanted to, but no, Tony insisted we learn about caves in this other when world.

Snpgrdxz the space alien shape shifter was all for exploring new worlds. "We may discover this cave leads to another portal. We have to explore it."

"I'm in favor of seeking an escape portal right here, right now." Frank tugged CJ by the hand.

The cave offered nothing but darkness and damp coolness. It was about ten feet high at the entrance and went straight back like a mine shaft or like a tunnel dug by a rock eating worm giant. The ten-foot width and height made our passage easy enough until we crossed the twenty-five foot mark from the entrance. The idea of a worm giant made me wonder what kind of creatures waited for us inside.

The cave opened into a huge black chamber. We couldn't tell how high the ceiling was, but fifty feet was a conservative guess. With our lamps and flashlights we could see rock walls, dripping water, and in the ceiling crevices, bright white blobs. Stalagmites covered the floor of the chamber while stalactites hung like darkened lanterns from the ceiling.

With their built in radar and vampire sense of smell, the white giants spotted us. The pale blobs descended like dive bombers in an old war movie.

The one advantage of the ceiling height was to give Tony time to pass around the oak stakes and load some wood shafted arrows. The group formed a circle and opened fire on the bats, except for me and my Jennifer. She noticed me drop and followed suit. I was after the lignum vitae bullets. Tony had placed a stack of M16 clips in my backpack way back at Lincoln High. I handed five to Jennifer and slapped number six into my M16.

I opened fire while Jennifer passed around the clips, reserving one for herself. She opened fire and dropped several of the white monsters. I noticed an extra-large one I took to be the alpha of the tribe. I aimed but held my fire as the thing morphed into Turpelator.

"Greetings, chums." Turpelator waved his hands over his head and the rest of the bats left the cave.

"Turpelator?" Gilbert asked.

My Jennifer opened fire on Turpelator. He vanished but reappeared in the dark distance of the cave. "Hold your fire. I won't hurt you."

"Yeah, but I want to hurt you," cried my Jennifer.

"Cool it, Wild Thing," Tony ordered.

My Jennifer held her fire and relaxed her hold on the M16. "Let me know when it's okay to kill him."

"You're hurting my friends," Turpelator said.

"Your friends are blood thirsty vampires," Daniel said.

"You are correct, old boy, but if you spare the rest of them, they will spare you. You cannot leave this cave alive unless I order your safety."

"What do you want in exchange?" Third Jennifer asked.

"CJ," said Turpelator. "If she will sacrifice herself to me, I will assure the safety of the rest of you."

"You expect us to allow you to kill our sister?" asked my Jennifer.

"I promise not to kill her. She will have the privilege of joining us."

"I'll take a pass on that honor, if you don't mind," said CJ.

Turpelator's sigh was loud enough for us to hear. "Sooner or later you'll join with me, my dear. You already are a werewolf, but I'll make you a vampire and more, much, much more."

"What makes you think she's a werewolf?" Daniel asked.

"She was bitten." Turpelator crossed his arms in the beams of our lamps.

"How can you be sure? She seems fine to me," said Tony.

"I bit her." Turpelator laughed.

"He didn't look like you when he turned back to human in the morning," said CJ.

"Who among us appears their best the first thing in the morning? Let's say I clean up well, shall we?"

"If you bit her, wouldn't she become a vampire?" my Jennifer asked.

Turpelator made the mistake of laughing at Jennifer. She opened fire.

From another part of the blackness of the cave, Turpelator said, "Okay, you win. Promise to hold your fire in this cave, and I'll keep my minions at bay. Do we have a deal?"

Tony asked, "What about our CJ."

Turpelator said, "She is free to make her own decisions. I am patient and have all the time in the world, both of them." Turpelator's laughter faded away in the darkness.

"Wait. How come you're not dead and buried in our world? Jens Wurzburger shot you with wooden bullets and the coroner cut your heart out," said Gilbert.

Turpelator laughed. "Do you think I'm a mere vampire or werewolf you can kill with your trinkets?"

"You looked mighty dead to me," said Gilbert.

"I am Daemon, fools. You can never kill me." Turpelator's laugh extended for a full minute after he vanished.

"What's a daemon?" CJ asked.

Tony said, "A human who evolves into a demon. He's not a true demon, but he has all their powers including immortality."

"So we can't kill him?" Young Jennifer asked.

"We can kill him. We already have. It's just that he will keep coming back to life. If we destroy his body, he'll create a new one out of the dirt. He's a daemon, an evil spirit with a body. We don't have the power to destroy him," said Tony.

"Who does?" Frank asked.

"God. Now, let's move out" Tony led our group in what we hoped was the right direction to the nearest exit from the giant black chamber. After a half hour of hiking in a more or less straight line, Tony found the wall to our giant chamber. With his right hand on the wall, he began the search for an opening. We found it fifteen minutes later. Tony kept his right hand on the wall and continued into the next section of the cave. Like the entrance, it was ten feet wide and ten feet high.

After three hours of trudging through the darkness, I fell into a deep shaft.

CHAPTER 8

A DEEPER CAVE

When a bump to the head knocks you unconscious, you don't realize you are out. It's not like falling asleep. Instead, you simply don't exist. It's as if you are a computer and someone shuts you off. When you reboot, you are disoriented with no sense of how much time passed.

My Jennifer cradled my head on her lap while the rest of me lay sprawled across the cave floor. She held a wet cloth to my forehead. Someone had lit a half dozen of those glow sticks people use on Fourth of July picnics.

"Did we pack glow sticks?" I asked.

"My backpack," Tony said. "I keep a lot of stuff in here you don't know about. Remember the penicillin I gave you the last time you bumped your head?"

"You mean when I was shot?"

"Yeah, that bump."

In the soft green glow, the cave had grown to about twenty feet wide and high.

"How did you get me out of that shaft I fell into?" I asked.

"We didn't," said Frank.

"We climbed down, buddy," Gilbert patted me on the shoulder.

I sat up which made me dizzy. I checked the ceiling for the shaft and found it. A rope dangled out of it.

"So we have to climb back up?" I rested back on Jennifer's lap.

"Tony wants us to explore this cave," said Snpgrdxz.

"Can you stand up?" Third Jennifer asked.

"Good question." I pushed up off the ground with my Jennifer's hands lifting me under the shoulders for as high as she could reach from her sitting position. She allowed her hands to slide down my back as I rose up. When she reached my butt, she gave me a good push before executing a perfect squeeze play.

"Yelp!" I said.

My Jennifer giggled.

The pain in my left hip was intense. My right knee hurt. It felt soft and swollen. I lifted my pant leg and exposed the swollen knee joint. "This doesn't look good."

"Can you walk?" Tony asked.

"I'll try." I took a few steps. The left hip forced me to step gingerly on my left foot. My right knee made it hard to put weight on my right leg. "Not very well."

"We can't wait here." Tony rummaged in his backpack.

"I won't leave him," my Jennifer said.

"Try this." Tony held a foot-long aluminum stick. When he flicked his wrist, the stick shot out to the length of a cane. He handed it to me.

The cane made it possible to not place all my weight on my right foot as we hiked into the depths of the cave. Snpgrdxz half carried me by placing his right arm around my back and boosting me as I stepped. My Jennifer held my right arm while I worked the cane. Gilbert carried my backpack along with his own.

"Halt!" Tony yelled. He held his arm up.

"What is it?" Third Jennifer asked.

"Something doesn't smell right." Tony moved his flashlight around to examine the ceiling, walls and floor of the cave. "Aha. Up ahead about five feet."

We gathered around Tony to see what he was pointing out.

"Is that a trip wire?" Frank asked.

"Believe so," Tony said. "You people wait here." Tony stepped forward until he reached the fine wire. It appeared to be a fishing line strung across the width of the cave about six inches above the floor. Tony flashed his light around again. "There it is. Stand back, people."

We backed up a few feet. Tony scrabbled around in his backpack until he yanked out another short stick like the one he turned into my cane. He flicked his wrist to enlarge the stick to match the one I leaned on.

"Give me your stick, Bryan." Tony inserted my stick into the top of the new one.

"Back up everyone." Tony pushed with his hands to indicate we should reverse course. "A little more, children."

He demoted us. We were people a minute ago, now we were children like back in Wheaton.

Tony smiled. He turned to face the fish line in front of us. He stepped forward a few feet to get within stick range of the wire. Tony lay down and pushed the stick against the wire which resulted in a click followed by a swoosh and the sound of something big smash into the right side of the cave. In the dull light of our lamps, we saw a brown blur.

Tony approached the object crushed against the wall. It was a wood board about a foot square. Long spikes had been driven into it. If Tony hadn't spotted it, at least one of us would be wearing a hole-some smile or a perforated brain.

"How'd you know it was there, Tony?" Third Jennifer asked.

"I have a gift for these things," said Tony.

"Who placed it?" CJ asked.

"It could have been anyone." Tony examined the spiked board. "There's blood on the nail ends so this weapon has been in use before."

"Turpelator did it," my Jennifer said.

49

"Could be," said Snpgrdxz. "Or perhaps the trolls use this little trick to hunt dinner."

"Let's stay alert people." Tony led the way but at a slower pace this time. I was happy with the new speed after Tony remembered to return my cane.

We walked for another two hours without incident.

"We need to take a breather," Gilbert said.

"A little walking too much for you?" CJ asked.

"I'm carrying two backpacks and I'm worried about Bryan. He keeps falling behind." Gilbert pointed his thumb over his shoulder in my direction.

"Frank needs to rest his shoulder," CJ said.

"It is becoming sore," Frank said.

"Okay, people, let's take a break for dinner. Maybe we'll sleep here tonight." Tony dropped his backpack to the ground.

While Snpgrdxz joined the others in meal preparation, Jennifer gave me a giant hug.

"How are you holding up?" she asked.

"I have to pee," I said.

"Me, too." Jennifer led me by the hand back down the cave the way we came.

When we were far enough away for pitch black privacy, I said, "Ladies room here. Mens room farther back."

I traipsed another twenty feet into the darkness to do my business. When I finished, I started back to join up with Jennifer.

"Wait," she yelled. "I'm not finished yet."

I leaned against the stone wall of the cave for Jennifer to signal me. The cave was a silent place except for the voices coming from the rest of our group. I heard rocks falling behind me so my ears were perked. A funny shuffling sound suggested that something was in the cave behind us.

"Jennifer, can you hurry?" I asked.

"Give me another minute, Bryan. Ladies are worth waiting for."

The shuffling sound came closer.

I waited another minute. Then two minutes. Then three. The shuffling grew louder. A second sound came from the shuffler behind us. This noise made me glad I had already emptied my bladder. It sounded like teeth grinding together from something with extra large teeth.

"Time to go, Jennifer," I said.

"I'm going as fast as I can. Okay, you can come forward now. Thanks for your patience."

I limped up to Jennifer. She zipped her blue jeans as I approached. She smiled when she saw me checking her out. She placed her arm around my neck and kissed me. She whispered in my ear, "White."

"White?" I asked.

"I saw you trying to check out my panties when my zipper wasn't zipped. They're white today."

My breath escaped. "Oh, okay, white."

Jennifer took my arm and led me back to the gang.

Meanwhile, the shuffling noise drew closer.

CHAPTER 9

THEM

The spider was as large as a pickup truck with the V8 engine and plenty of room for passengers in the back seat along with a shotgun in the rear window. Jennifer and I returned to our friends in time for me to say, "Something's coming."

Something came.

Tony opened fire with his M16 while the rest of us dug out our rifles. We laid down a steady stream of fire, but the spider seemed to appreciate the bullet massage. He stood and watched us with his dozen eyes.

Third Jennifer wrapped a cloth around her aluminum spear and soaked it with a bottle of vodka. She set the rag on fire with a match and chased the spider down the cave with it. When she returned without the spider, CJ asked, "Where'd you get the vodka and do you have more?"

"You have to be creative to survive the troll world. I snagged it from Tony's backpack." Third Jennifer lifted the vodka bottle and drank the last inch in the bottom of the bottle.

"That was for medicinal purposes," Tony said.

"And a little on the side for yourself, Tony?" Frank asked.

"My mouth is filled with germs, so I have to kill them somehow," Tony explained.

Tony found some Sterno containers by rooting around in his backpack. Third Jennifer used her torch to light the

Sterno. Our dinner consisted of Army surplus MREs, the little food packs the military uses in the field. I had roast beef and gravy with potatoes. My Jennifer had chicken. Once the food was hot, everyone felt better.

"Let's spend the night here," Tony said.

My Jennifer unrolled her sleeping bag next to mine. She handed me two ibuprofen tablets.

I took the pills with water from a bottle I had in my backpack. The rock floor was bumpy but I was too tired to care.

We didn't mind the werewolves howling in the distance except for CJ of course who yearned to join them in a cave romp. We tied her to a rock outcropping in the wall of the cave. A group of friendly vampires passed through our area around one in the morning. They seemed nice enough except they were still stuck in their previous lives as real estate agents. Instead of attacking us, they spent a quarter hour trying to convince us that we would benefit from a little bloodletting. We refused their offer and they meandered away into the darkness.

The pesky cave ghosts gave us the most trouble. At first, they floated above us and howled, but as we ignored them due to our need for rest, they took more drastic action. A group of cave ghosts appeared as regular people and re-enacted their death scenes. Since most of them died horrible deaths at the hands of monsters and deviants, their antics kept us awake until Tony pulled his guitar from his backpack and we sang praise songs. Ghosts, goblins and demons don't like to hang around religious music and praise.

With ghosts of the departed departing, we slept until morning. Jennifer and I held hands.

We spent the morning traipsing through the cave. We were about to stop for lunch when we spotted a dead end. Tony kept his right hand on the wall of the cave and followed the dead end around to the opposite wall.

Frank said, "Wait." While we rested, he shined his flashlight around the dead end. "We might spot a tiny opening that will take us out."

There wasn't one.

After lunch, we followed Tony back the way we came, but about an hour into retracing our steps, he found an opening in the wall. We had missed it because we were following Tony along the opposite wall. We turned down that tunnel.

Two hours later, the tunnel opened into a new chamber. It was smaller than the previous one we had visited. This one had a ceiling about thirty feet above the floor. Shiny white bats covered it. The chamber was small enough for us to see the entrance to another passageway across the chamber. We headed straight for it.

Twenty paces into our trek, the split tail rattler appeared. It was a good eight feet high and just as wide as it was high. The back end of the snake divided into two tails about thirty feet behind the head. Each tail had its own rattle. While we took in the enormity of the beast, the snake snagged Tony in its mouth. Before the creature could clamp down on him, Tony opened fire with his M16, shooting into the snakes cranium. Tony pulled a grenade off his belt and tossed it down the rattler's throat. As he ran away from the snake, he waved his hand to indicate that we should back up fast. We all dove to the cave floor when the explosion went off.

The grenade separated the rattler's head from its body.

"Fresh meat for dinner," Tony said.

I expected the Jennifer triplets to protest, but they didn't. Instead they fired up the sterno while Tony carved snake steaks from the rattler's side. The flock of white bats descended on the snake body to drain its blood.

After our mid-afternoon snack or early dinner, we headed across the chamber. The bat voices began when we approached the center of the cavern.

"We will suck your blood later," said a bat.

"Turpelator promised safe passage until you leave the caves," claimed another.

"Don't worry about your blood spilling on the ground outside the cave. We'll lick it up."

"Jennifer, is it that time of the month? We can smell you?"

The three Jennifers raised their M16s, but I stopped my Jennifer while Frank corralled CJ, and Tony and Gilbert took on Third Jennifer. Meanwhile, Snpgrdxz sang *Silence is Golden* by the Four Seasons. He may have been a teenager, but he was a well-aged teenager to remember that oldie.

Snpgrdxz had a good voice. I would have joined him if I knew the words. Tony might have known the words, but he didn't sing. My parents might have known the words, but for sure, my grandparents knew them.

Snpgrdxz polished off a few Bee Gees songs by the time we spotted the cave exit as a blacker shade of dark in the distance. At least, I think it was the Bee Gees. The sound was definitely disco. Tony liked it.

The chamber led to another dark cave tunnel. We followed it for an hour when we saw tiny sparkles in the distance. The tiny lights grew as we approached until they were about six inches tall. The creatures were tiny fairies with filigree wings.

"Lock and load," Tony yelled.

***

The idea of mortal combat against six-inch fairies didn't appeal to me. Aren't fairies immortal? Doesn't that make them hard to kill?

I felt relief when one of the fairies greeted us, "Welcome to Fairlight. I am Hyminia, queen of our clan. And this is Princess Mincheah, my sister. Welcome. We enjoy company."

Hyminia wore a tiny silk gown and sparkling jewelry. A tiara that would have been too small for a Barbi doll covered her head. Her sister Mincheah also wore silk but her jewelry was not as elaborate as Hyminia's. Mincheah wore a short skirt while Hyminia's full length skirt seemed appropriate to the head of the fairy state.

"Aren't you the fairy I met in the tunnel under Lincoln High School in Wheaton?" I asked Hyminia.

"Hyminia has not travelled beyond Fairlight in one thousand years. You perhaps are confused? You look injured. Shall I fix you?"

"Sure," I said.

"Follow us into our chamber." Hyminia fluttered ahead of us followed by her sister. Her entourage of half a dozen fairies lit the way. We shouldered our rifles as we continued along the path of the cave. It made a gradual dogleg right turn followed by a sharp left turn.

When we made the left, we stepped into the land the fairies called Fairlight. A bedazzling white light in the ceiling lit a chamber many miles across. Small green hillocks covered the chamber floor. Trees looked full and mature at six feet high. Lush flowers grew everywhere. The land wasn't cultivated. Tiny lights buzzed about the entire chamber.

Hyminia led us to an open field where she invited us to sit. She flew into the forest. I checked the small woodland where tiny houses stood among the trees and carved mushroom houses scattered about the ground.

Hyminia returned with a short stick. She waved it about my body while she sprinkled me with fairy dust. My knee and hip no longer hurt. My near constant headache vanished. I danced about in an imitation Irish jig. I pulled Jennifer off the ground to entice her to dance with me. She hopped about with me before she stopped and laughed.

Frank said, "Hyminia, can you heal my shoulder?"

"Hyminia try." Hyminia performed the same ritual over Frank. His shoulder healed as we watched.

"Queen Hyminia! Queen Hyminia!" shouted a fairy fluttering about with its legs and arms waving as she flew. "Somebody stole your scepter."

CHAPTER 10

THE CASE OF THE MISSING SCEPTER

"Pineliah, whoever possesses the fairy scepter becomes our king or queen. We must find it now." Hyminia pressed her hands to her temples.

"We'll launch an investigation," said Pineliah, the fluttering fairy.

"Is there anything we can do to help," Tony asked.

"No, you are our guests. We will make you comfortable and feed you until you are ready to travel," said Hyminia.

A nine-inch tall creature flew into the meadow where we sat. In addition to its larger size, the creature wore a brown outfit. Its complexion was darker than the fairies. "What's all the excitement?"

"Woodchuck, I'm so glad you're here. Somebody stole my scepter," said Hyminia.

"I meant who are all these big people? Are they a band of thieves?" the tall critter asked.

"They are new friends," said Hyminia.

"I don't think you should count strangers as friends when your scepter has gone missing," said Mincheah.

"The thing was taken before they arrived, Mincheah," said Hyminia. She introduced us to the tall winged brownie named Woodchuck.

"Why don't you conduct a search for your scepter?" asked Gilbert.

"I'll organize a search party," said Pineliah.

"You're conducting the investigation. Mincheah, you organize the search," said Hyminia.

"Yes, my sister," Mincheah flew away.

"I should help Mincheah," said Woodchuck.

"You didn't tell us yet where you've been," said Hyminia.

"As conductor of the official investigation into the loss of the fairy scepter, I need to know where you were on the day of the theft," said Pineliah.

"I believe I said that," said Hyminia.

"So the day of the theft, let's see. That would be today, right?" asked Woodchuck.

"Elementary, my dear Woodchuck," said Pineleah.

"I woke up in Brownieland, ate breakfast, second breakfast, elevenses and lunch. Then I flew to Fairlight to join my girlfriend for an afternoon snack."

"Aha, the plot thickens," said Pineleah.

"It does?" asked Hyminia.

"Indubitably," said Pineleah. "Woodchuck thickened the plot by eating so much before he arrived. And it still doesn't explain where he was when somebody stole the scepter. Where were you?"

"When was it stolen?" Woodchuck asked.

"I already told you. Today," said Pineleah.

"Well, if you told me today, what time did you tell me?" Woodchuck asked.

While my mind wandered to the insanity of the evening adventures before the start of my junior year, Pineleah said, "About five minutes ago."

"Someone stole the scepter five minutes ago?" Woodchuck asked.

"No. I told you about it five minutes ago."

"So when was the scepter stolen?" Woodchuck asked.

"A little while ago," said Pineleah.

"Can you be a little more precise?" asked Gilbert.

"'A little while ago' is precise fairy timekeeping," said Pineleah.

"Ahhhhhhh!" screamed CJ. "What kind of investigation is this?"

"A precise one," said Pineleah.

Mincheah interrupted this train of pursuit, "I just remembered. I saw Woodchuck holding the scepter."

"When was this?" Pineleah asked.

"A little while ago." Mincheah flew off.

"I don't know what she's talking about, but that comes as no surprise since she is my girlfriend." Woodchuck fluttered in the air above Hyminia.

"She was talking about you holding the scepter. When was that exactly?" asked Pineleah.

Woodchuck rubbed his chin. "The only things I held today were bagels, bagels and cream cheese, toasted bagels with butter, cinnamon buns for dipping in coffee, a box of donuts of mixed variety, fifty-six cups of brownie coffee, two dozen fried eggs. Have I forgotten anything? Let's see, oh yes, a rasher of bacon. Two rashers now I think on it, including the one at Elevenses. This reminds me, when do we eat?"

"So you deny holding Hyminia's scepter?" Pineleah asked.

"I did not hold Hyminia's anything today, although I'm not sure where the donuts derived from. Hyminia, had you sent a dozen donuts to the brownies?" Woodchuck asked.

"If I had sent anything to the brownies, it would have been brownies. I know how you people love chocolate and anything brown," said Hyminia.

"There were three chocolate donuts in the dozen," said Woodchuck.

"I may have sent those," said Hyminia.

"People, people, people, this is getting us nowhere," said Gilbert.

"What are people?" asked Woodchuck.

"The big giants, aka humans," said Pineleah.

"Oh," said Woodchuck. "That explains everything."

***

"What do we know so far?" asked Gilbert.

Pineleah poked around Snpgrdxz's foot with a tiny magnifying glass. "Only that her majesty's scepter is missing, and Mincheah saw Woodchuck holding it earlier today while he consumed bagels, donuts, bacon and eggs, and coffee at his first several meals of the day."

"So what can we conclude from that?" asked Hyminia.

"We have to go shopping for food and the game's afoot." Pineleah glanced up from Snpgrdxz's shoe.

"My foot is not a game," said Daniel Snpgrdxz Brickmaster.

"If we're playing footsies, I'm all in." Woodchuck flopped on top of Daniel's shoe in a most provocative pose.

"What I mean is we know the fairy scepter must be in brownie land," said Pineleah.

"We do?" asked Gilbert.

"How did he figure that one out?" my Jennifer asked.

"I'm not sure. Maybe it was hidden in the donuts." I yelped out "donuts" because CJ punched me in the ribs.

"Elementary, my dear human. Elementary. The brownie spent the morning in the consumption of his many breakfasts —"

"Don't forget Elevenses," said Woodchuck.

"—His many meals, then, in brownie land. Since he was in brownie land and Mincheah saw him with the scepter, she must have seen him in brownie land. Ergo, the scepter is in brownie land."

"Unless, of course, Woodchuck brought it with him when he flew to fairyland just now," said Daniel Snpgrdxz.

"Yes, well, I hadn't thought of that. Have you the scepter in your possession now?" Pineleah asked.

Woodchuck said, "I've already told you I haven't seen your royal scepter. It's not likely something you're going to hand to a brownie to peruse at his leisure, is it?"

"But you could have stolen it," said Pineleah.

"But I didn't, did I? The only perusing I've done lately in fairyland was the perusal of Minicheah who everyone, including you, already knows is my girlfriend and thus ripe for perusal."

"Are you planning to peruse me?" Jennifer asked me.

"But of course, my dear, but I think we should marry first before we peruse our brains out."

"Is that a marriage proposal?" Jennifer asked.

***

The bomb exploded as my Jennifer locked lips with me. At first, I naturally assumed the earth's movement was a result of the kiss and my previous overeager peruse of Hemingway's *For Whom the Bell Tolls* last year in lit class, "last year" being a relative term for us time travelers. It wasn't a huge movement, but then we only kissed and hugged while our hands maybe edged over the line a little, but not far enough below the belt to truly move the globe.

In the end, the explosive power had all the impact of a cherry bomb. It blew up a mushroom house near Hyminia causing her to perform a half dozen somersaults before she settled down.

"Only brownies make bombs that large," said Pineleah.

"Actually we make our pizzas about that size. We don't make bombs as far as I know," said Woodchuck.

"As far as you know isn't much beyond food, is it?" Pineleah asked.

"Speaking of food, what time is lunch?" asked Woodchuck.

Mincheah flew to the tiny group of fairies. A half dozen warrior fairies armed with spears and shields accompanied her. They had swords attached to their belts.

"We found Woodchuck's fingerprints on the royal scepter pedestal," said Mincheah.

"My dear, don't your remember our date last week? You said the pedestal would be perfect for –"

"Don't bring up our mating habits," cried Mincheah. "The important thing is you were definitely at the scene of the crime."

Woodchuck folded his arms. "But you said the pedestal was the perfect shape to –"

"Our private life has nothing to do with this investigation. You were at the scene of the crime. Where did you hide the scepter?"

"What could they possibly do with a tiny six-inch fairy pedestal?" my Jennifer asked.

CJ whispered in her ear.

"Oh." My Jennifer blushed as she turned to me. "Maybe we'll get one as a wedding present, my one true love."

"We're not engaged," I yelled.

"I'm teasing, Ganarski." My Jennifer raised steam from my ears with another earth shaking kiss.

"And I already told you where the scepter was," said Pineleah.

***

"I saw him steal it. I saw him steal it. I saw him steal it." A new fairy flew to our group, crashed into CJ's... well, I don't want to go there... well, I would go there if it were my Jennifer, but it was CJ and the very concept of... well, you get the idea. The fairy bounced twice in that location and spit a few times before it bounced off Frank's head. It fluttered to a halt in front of Queen Hyminia. "I saw him steal your scepter, my queen."

63

"That settles it. Case solved," said Pineleah.

"What exactly did you see?" Gilbert asked.

"Yes, Oakeniah, tell us the precise fairy truth," Hyminia asked.

Why did I have the feeling that "precise fairy truth" was somehow not as truthful as say a Baptist minister testifying in court.

Or a Jewish rabbi.

Or a Buddhist monk.

Or any other normally truthful person in our world.

It could be as truthful as a history teacher, however.

Oakeniah waved her hands. "The truth is I spotted Woodchuck carrying a duffel bag as fast as his giant wings could flap in the direction of brownie land. He had something in that satchel for it sagged so much and weighed him down so. But he flew as fast as he could away from fairyland."

"When was that, exactly?" Pineleah asked.

"Exactly a little while ago," said Oakeniah.

"Okay, I confess," said Woodchuck.

CHAPTER 11

WHODUNIT?

"Woodchuck did it!" cried Pineleah. "Off with his head, but first torture him until he reveals the location of the queen's scepter. Then you may return his head and send him back to brownie land."

"I meant I confess to stealing the queen's donuts." Woodchuck burped.

"I wondered why there were no donuts at breakfast, second breakfast or Elevenses," said Queen Hyminia.

"Place him under arrest," Pineleah shouted.

"I'm out of here." Woodchuck flew as fast as he could away from the area. His speed was roughly that of a small caliber bullet or about eight hundred miles per hour.

"Obviously, he wasn't weighed down by a dozen donuts," said Mincheah.

"Shouldn't make a difference whether the donuts were in a satchel or in his belly," said Pineleah. "Perhaps his speed had something to do with aerodynamics."

"Prepare for war with the thieving brownies," cried Mincheah.

***

The fairies dug trenches at each of the two cave entrances into Fairlight. The brownies staged their armies just beyond Fairlight in the two cave passageways.

"Why do they need trenches when both armies can fly?" my Jennifer asked.

"I have no idea," I said.

"They must enjoy ground combat," said Tony.

"Shouldn't we skedaddle before the war? Let's face it, they're immortal and we're not. They could be tossing bombs, bullets and artillery shells for a long time before either side tires of fighting." Frank stood up.

"Hold on, Frank," said Tony. "We're supposed to be peacemakers. Let's see if we can restore a little order here before we continue on our way."

"But I want to go home," my Jennifer said.

Seven fairies joined us on the lawn of Fairlight. They wore high hats similar to what bishops wear, but with little crowns on top. Their robes trailed several inches behind them such that they needed to remain airborne to maintain a proper attitude of seriousness and respect as we soon learned this little group was the Fairy High Council.

"We call this emergency session of the High Council to order," said the bearded fairy in the middle of the group.

The high council members lined up in a row facing the other fairies. Queen Hyminia scolded the council, "What is the meaning of this? You're not to meet unless I call a meeting and I haven't."

The high council fairy in the middle said, "My queen, we are your loyal subjects, but we must meet now to urge you to find peace with the brownies. They are taller than us and likely to win any combat. While we are immortal, they may still inflict mass quantities of pain upon our people."

"War is war," Queen Hyminia said. "Steal yourselves for victory."

"But you have no authority to declare war, my queen," said one of the council members.

"How dare you. I'm the queen."

"The queen – or king – of the fairies is the one in possession of the royal scepter. As no one is in possession of it, we will have no choice but to declare the throne vacated and the high council will serve as regent until the scepter is found and placed in the possession of the rightful heir to Fairlight." The head high council fairy pounded a fist in the air.

"But I'm the queen. You have no power to remove me?"

The leader of the high council said, "Ah, but there is no need to remove you, my queen. You have lost the scepter and so you have removed yourself."

"But it's only a tiny tad missing. I'll have it in my possession in a little while." The queen stamped her foot in the air.

The council huddled. We heard lots of mumbling and rumbling noises. After a "little while" the council returned to order. The leader said, "We grant you until lunch time tomorrow to show the council that you are in possession of the scepter."

"But I may need a little more time."

The high council leader said, "We have spoken. At lunch time, we will declare the throne vacated until the scepter is found. The person in possession of the scepter will be declared our king or queen."

***

"You're under arrest," shouted Mincheah. "Guards, take the former queen Hyminia into custody.

"How can you arrest me? I'm your queen and you're my baby sister?"

"Take her away," said Mincheah.

One of the guards said, "Where shall we take her? We haven't had a jail in Fairlight for a very long time."

"Really?" Mincheah asked.

"Truly, ma'am. The last time we had a prisoner was more than two thousand years ago," said the guard leader.

Mincheah smacked a fist into her palm. "Since we have no jail, place her under house arrest. Hold her in the throne room."

"Wait!" Gilbert shouted.

"Now what?" Mincheah asked.

"You can't arrest Queen Hyminia," said Gilbert.

"Why not? She's the one who lost the scepter." Mincheah glared at Gilbert.

"She didn't steal her own scepter. Someone stole it from her. We have to figure out who did it," Gilbert said.

"We already know Woodchuck did it," said Mincheah.

"He's a suspect, yes, but you don't know he did it for sure," Gilbert said.

Mincheah paced the lawn. "I saw Woodchuck holding the queen's scepter. His fingerprints are all over the pedestal, and Oakeniah saw him fly off with a duffle bag weighed down by the weight of the scepter. What more evidence do we need to prove Woodchuck stole the scepter?"

Gilbert rubbed his jaw.

CJ said, "Gilbert, what evidence can you offer to prove Woodchuck is innocent?"

Gilbert stood up to speak but quickly realized he was ankle to eyeball with Mincheah so he sat back down. "Mincheah, isn't it possible that Woodchuck told the truth when he said he carried a dozen donuts in the duffel bag?"

"But he had the scepter in his possession," Mincheah stamped her foot.

"But holding the scepter doesn't mean he stole it. Maybe he just wanted to look at it," Gilbert said.

"Maybe he just wanted to borrow it," said Mincheah. "But I don't think so. He's our thief. And we have to steal our scepter back from him."

"I thought he was your boyfriend, Mincheah," Gilbert said.

"Yes, he was up until a little while ago. Now he's nothing but a dreaded enemy. The brownies started this war by

stealing our scepter, but we'll finish it by stealing it back."
Mincheah flew into the air and circled over the heads of the
council.

"Mincheah is right," said a member of the high council.
"We must prepare for war. Tony, dispatch your troops to the
cave entrances."

CHAPTER 12

WAR

"Retreat to the castle," shouted a fairy with a long spear. "The brownies have broken our lines."

"This way," shouted Hyminia.

We followed Hyminia to a castle at the edge of the large fairy meadow. The fairies had carved the castle in the cave wall. The lower level included an entrance large enough for our group to squeeze through. Inside, hundreds of tiny candles lit a great chamber, or at least, great by fairy standards. We had to squeeze close together to fit. We sat with our knees up. Various fairies occupied our knees.

"I've been thinking," said Gilbert.

"Amazing," said CJ.

"No, seriously. I've been thinking," said Gilbert. "Queen Hyminia, have you ordered the castle searched?"

"Why would I want to search the castle?"

"She's no longer the queen," said Mincheah.

"I am until lunch time tomorrow," said Queen Hyminia. "And beyond lunch if we find the scepter."

"There's no need to search the castle for something the brownies have in their possession in brownie land," said Mincheah. "We must all charge into the breach and stop the brownie invasion."

"If you haven't searched the castle, how do you know it's not here?" asked Gilbert.

"We haven't searched the church or the cheese factory or the milk shed or the egg loft or the corn crib. Shall we search them all during the middle of an invasion or are we going to defend ourselves?" cried Mincheah.

"Before we charge off against the brownies, who by the way, are not at war with us, let me ask a stupid question," said Gilbert.

"We've no time for stupid questions," shouted a foot stomping, hand waving, jumping-up-and-down, Mincheah.

"If the brownies have the scepter, why have they invaded Fairlight when they simply could walk in and declare one of their own king of Fairlight?" Gilbert asked.

Mincheah stopped in midflight towards the exit and fell on CJ's head. She sat up in CJ's hair and glowered at Gilbert.

"Search Mincheah's quarters," ordered Queen Hyminia."

***

The brownies defeated the fairies with their size advantage. At nine inches tall, they towered over the six-inch fairies.

Woodchuck broke into the main chamber of the castle where our group took shelter with Queen Hyminia. "Aha," said Woodchuck, "We win."

Queen Hyminia said, "Okay, we'll supply the blueberry pies at next week's victory celebration. Do you also want peach?"

"That sounds great, Hyminia," said Woodchuck. "And don't worry. We'll let you guys win next time."

"Hey, we're going to learn judo and kick brownie butt next time," said Queen Hyminia.

"That's what you said last time and we set the record for speed conquest by conquering Fairlight in just a little while."

"Okay, stop your bragging. We have a mystery to solve. Someone stole my scepter."

"You're not still mad about the donuts are you?"

"Naw. Keep them as the spoils of war."

Gilbert jumped up, hit his head on the rock ceiling of the castle, and sat back down. "Do you mean to tell me you guys fought a war and the winner gets donuts?"

"Would you like some?" Queen Hyminia asked.

Gilbert waved his arms. "No. I thought you guys went to war. You know, bombs and weapons of mass destruction, body parts, blood and that kind of stuff all over the place."

"Where does this guy come from?" Woodchuck asked.

"Wheaton, Illinois," said Gilbert.

"Wheaton, Illinois, must be one scary place," said Woodchuck. "Here, we just run around and yell a lot. Then we declare victory and the loser feeds us donuts or pies."

"Sometimes we eat your bagels," said Pineleah.

"And ice cream in the summer," said Oakeniah.

"Oooo, donuts and ice cream," said Mincheah.

"That does sound yummy. May we have some also?" asked CJ.

"What about the scepter?" Gilbert asked.

"Oh, it'll turn up," said Woodchuck. "It always does."

"I think you should search Mincheah's room," said Gilbert.

"I already dispatched my troops to search her room," said Hyminia.

"You can't search my room. I'm the sister of the queen," said Mincheah.

"You will want to search Mincheah's room because the scepter is located there at the moment," said Gilbert.

"How can you tell?" asked Queen Hyminia.

Gilbert scratched his nose, rubbed his chin and tweaked his ear. "First off, Woodchuck didn't take it and the brownies don't have it. If they did, a brownie would claim the throne of Fairlight, especially since they just won the war, even if all you get is donuts."

"Don't forget the ice cream," said Frank.

"But Mincheah has a motive. She wanted to take over the kingdom. And she didn't mind having her boyfriend accused of stealing it."

"Someone had to have done it," said Mincheah.

"She enticed Woodchuck to visit the throne room with her and checkout the scepter and its stand," said Gilbert.

Woodchuck scratched his belly. "He's right, you know. Mincheah invited me into the throne room for a make out session, and she asked me to move the scepter stand because it was in our way, even though we had plenty of room to begin with."

"That's not true. Why are you lying?" demanded Mincheah.

"Enough, Mincheah," said Queen Hyminia. "Pineleah will hold you here until my warriors complete their search of your room."

We ate donuts and ice cream while the search team completed the search of Mincheah's room.

Gilbert's expression went from passionate love of chocolate and peach ice cream to instant oh crap. "Queen Hyminia, if one of your warriors finds the scepter, won't that make her queen?"

"She's a loyal – wait. I'll be right back." Hyminia charged down the corridor after her warriors. We heard a scuffle accompanied by some high-powered fairy cursing.

My Jennifer asked me what the curse about finding a perfect mate meant. "Wouldn't that be a blessing?"

"No, it's a wicked curse. Imagine you met your perfect soul mate, say me, for example. Then we, ahem, make love for the first time with your bit and my bit the perfect fit for each other. Then let's say I die. Yech, not for real, just for the sake of the story. Such a mating and separation would mean you would never be satisfied by any other mate for the rest of your life."

"I wouldn't want to mate if it wasn't with you." My Jennifer breathed funny, but so did I.

My Jennifer and I were about to become engaged and married, or we were about to do the deed without a wedding. Either way, I was about to explode which wasn't good for your blue jeans.

More scuffling noises followed which took me out of my reverie.

The silence of the caves followed.

Five minutes without sound, except for the heavy breathing of my Jennifer and me, led to Oakeniah shouting, "Long live Queen Hyminia."

Queen Hyminia possessed the scepter, a torn and tattered dress, one black eye and a large scratch across her right cheek.

When she appeared behind Queen Hyminia, Oakeniah possessed two black eyes, several bruises and a dress torn and tattered beyond repair and revealing more fairy flesh than Oakeniah intended. She pulled and yanked at her gown to cover places in need of less exposure.

The fairies gathered around their queen to honor her with their bows, scrapes and shouts of "Long live the queen."

Even Mincheah joined in the celebration as did the fairy high council. Several of the council members sighed. I assumed they were disappointed not to serve as regents.

"Mincheah, step forward," Queen Hyminia ordered.

"Oh, you don't have to honor me for saving your scepter from theft by hiding it in my room, dear sister. You would have done the same for me."

"Dear sister, you stole the scepter. You intended to replace me as queen. There is but one punishment fit for you."

"Punishment? But Hyminia, I'm immortal, like you and all fairies. You cannot hang me."

"There are but two punishments fitting for you, Mincheah. One is hanging you from a tree for a few centuries."

"I think I will prefer the other punishment, whatever it is," said Mincheah.

"Then you are hereby sentenced into exile for the next one-thousand years. I will personally escort you to the land of the humans where you will live among them."

"No, not humans. They smell. They have big feet that step without looking. They invent things that fly and roll and move about without consideration for tiny creatures. They expect gifts from us. And have you ever seen one of them eat. Oh, and worse, have you ever been asleep under an oak leaf when one of them cuts loose in the woods?"

"I'm so glad you remember your last thousand year exile, Mincheah. And not to worry, for I shall cast a spell to make you appear as one of them. We leave immediately."

Pineleah shackled Mincheah's hands and feet. A group of about half a dozen fairies joined behind Queen Hyminia to make an entourage with Mincheah at its center.

"We go now for the land of the humans. Do you humans wish to accompany us to what you call the Wheaton When Portal?" Hyminia asked.

"We're headed the other way," said CJ.

"Yeah, we're trying to avoid the Wheaton When Portal because Jennifer Hawkins keeps ending up in the year nineteen eighteen."

"Suit yourselves. Follow that cave over there where the brownies live. It will lead you to a stairway that will take you up to the first circle where you will see the cave exit into the world of the two suns," Hyminia said.

We found the steps after an hour of hiking and without finding the well-hidden brownie land. The stairway curved up and around the cave wall into a shaft that veered off out of sight so we had no idea how high we had to climb to reach the top. Or what new dangers awaited us.

CHAPTER 13

ESCAPE FROM THE VAMPIRES

Hobgoblins live forever but that didn't stop a hobgoblin ghost from descending the stairs as we climbed up. This happened about an hour into our climb. The correct form may be to say that the hobgoblin appeared in spirit form rather than physical body. He looked just as ugly in spirit as in life. The hobgoblin ghost muttered to himself and seemed angry about something.

Human ghosts descended in pairs and threes. The first two frightened us as we backed against the wall to let them pass, and we hoped, not harm us. By the end of hour two, we were engaging the ghosts in conversations as they floated by. Some were friendly and chatty.

"You think you're so good as to climb these stairs, eh?" asked an attractive teenaged girl escorted by a teenaged boy. They looked alive except for their slit throats and red eyes.

"Are you having a bad day?" my Jennifer asked.

The teenaged girl ghost huffed. "Wait until you get kicked off the first circle and see how you like it. Oh, wait, you are climbing out of the pit. How'd you earn a pass? I thought there was no hope."

"We're just climbing the stairs," I said.

"Are you people dead?" the teenaged boy asked.

"No," Snpgrdxz said.

"Explains everything," the girl said. The teenaged ghosts continued down the steps.

"Hey, what happened to your necks?" Gilbert asked, but the ghosts ignored him.

"Somebody or something slit their throats and we're headed that way." Frank rubbed his throat.

We reached the top of the steps after a three-hour trek that left us exhausted. The steps stopped in a cave passageway. One direction led deep into darkness with a pinhead of possible light. A faint but larger light appeared in the other direction.

"Can we rest here?" Gilbert asked.

"I don't think so." Third Jennifer indicated the pinhead light as it grew.

"Run!" Tony yelled.

"You're kidding, right?" CJ asked.

"Go, go, go!" Tony screamed.

I snagged my Jennifer's hand so we could hobble toward the cave exit together. Running was beyond us after the three-hour stair climb, but we stumbled along at a gait faster than walking. The others passed us but we kept moving.

At the cave exit, we gathered in a circle to pray.

"Lock and load," my Jennifer ordered which if you think about it was a stronger close to a prayer than the usual "Amen." She didn't add the "in Jesus's name" part which may have been best since I'm not sure you should lock and load in Jesus's name. I doubt Snpgrdxz was a Christian, but you never know about alien shape shifters.

We flashed our lights down the cave behind us. Our beams bounced off thousands of Turpelator's white bats.

"Run," Tony cried.

***

We sprinted while Tony jerked three grenades from his backpack, pulled the pins and dropped them at the cave entrance.

We slammed onto the ground as the explosion sent a shock wave over our heads.

The grenades blew the mouth of the cave closed.

"That won't hold them long, will it?" asked Frank.

"They're vampires, Frank. They can turn into vapor and leak their way through the rock pile," Gilbert said.

"Time to skedaddle." Tony headed into the trees as the rest of us jogged behind him as best we could.

The woodland was not much different than forests in the Appalachians back home. Most of the trees were oaks but we came across maples and other hardwood trees. Once in a while, a pine grove would join the crazy quilt of trees and mountains.

The animals were either the same or similar to those back home. We spotted rabbits and squirrels but some had long fangs. The raccoons looked like raccoons. Bobcats and some strange critters I had never seen before played among the leaves and underbrush. Prides of small wild cats practiced sneak attacks on wary raccoons and squirrels. We assumed these were feral cats, but they could have been a breed of the wild variety never tamed by man or monster.

We stopped for breakfast with the two suns in the eastern sky enough above the horizon to bring us into full daylight.

By mid-morning we left the trees behind for a flower-strewn mountain meadow. The path through the field appeared as though it had been in existence forever. It led downhill where the land flattened and a large blue lake nestled in the midst of the meadow.

Near noon, we spotted a man in the distance traveling toward us. As he approached, Mr. Turpelator, our high school physics teacher, appeared as a regular human guy rather than a vampire, werewolf or other monster. How many Turpelators lived in this world of time travel and running into various versions of yourself?

"Greetings, fellow Dragons," Mr. Turpelator said. The dragon was the Lincoln High School mascot, despite its having nothing to do with Wheaton. Or had something come out of the caves under the high school back when it was built in the eighteen nineties? Were there real dragons in our past – or future?

"Why are you here in the middle of the troll world?" I asked.

"I should ask you folks the same question. I was enjoying the sites and this lake is particularly invigorating. But as you must have observed by now, this is the wrong time for finding the missing Ms. Gonzalez," said Mr. Turpelator.

We had stopped by the lake so Tony could cook lunch over a tiny camp stove. CJ invited Mr. Turpelator to join us. My Jennifer kicked me in the ankle.

"What was that for?" I asked.

"Why'd my stupid sister invite the bastard for lunch?"

"Don't know, but he ain't the Turpelator who molested you back in nineteen twenty-three."

"How can we be certain when death itself doesn't stop a person from showing up again? At any rate, he is the Mr. Turpelator teacher person who kissed me against my will back at Lincoln High School. An incident you witnessed without so much as a peep of protest."

"Do you forgive me?"

"Yes, because I love you, and you will never, ever let that monster near me again."

"You got it, Jennifer."

As it turned out, my Jennifer didn't have to worry this time. In the middle of chewing a reconstituted Army surplus MRE, Mr. Turpelator leaned over to CJ and started a make out session that she returned.

"Thank you," CJ said when Turpelator broke off.

"What the…" Frank said an actual word rather than the three little dots.

***

"He's the alpha and I'm his beta so don't worry, Frank. Mr. Turpelator honored me with a kiss of affection. I returned it with a kiss of loyalty."

"What about me?" Frank asked.

"I love you, darling, but that's different."

"What do you mean?" Frank asked.

CJ frowned as her face went from pale white to sunburn red in an instant. "I have no idea." CJ shook her head as though to clear it. "What did you say?"

"I asked why you thought it necessary to make out with your friend, Turpelator." Frank threw his dinner plate to the ground.

"I did what?" CJ looked astounded.

"We all noticed, CJ," said Gilbert.

Mr. Turpelator marched quickly in the direction we had come.

"Hey, Mr. Turpelator, why'd you kiss CJ?" Gilbert hollered, but Turpelator didn't respond.

As we cleaned up dinner, Snpgrdxz sidled up to me. "I know what's going on."

"What?" I asked.

"Take a gander down the path at Mr. Turpelator."

I followed where Snpgrdxz pointed. Mr. Turpelator was no longer visible, but I spied a large dog, "Where'd he go?"

"You're gazing at him."

"You mean the dog?"

"It's a wolf."

"You think Mr. Turpelator is a werewolf?"

"And he bit CJ. That's why she made out with him and then didn't remember. She's his sex slave now."

***

Tony ordered us to set up a perimeter defense around our campsite. "We'll setup along the edge of this lake and post guards to stay alert for signs of trouble. It's afternoon, but we need the extra rest. The lake will protect us from land creatures. This meadow goes on for miles in every direction, so we should see, hear or smell trouble a long way off."

Tony and Third Jennifer took the first watch. Gilbert and Snpgrdxz had the second watch, and my Jennifer and I handled the third watch.

Tony said, "We'll let Frank and CJ rest so they can take first watch at our next rest stop."

When Snpgrdxz shook me awake, embers from our campfire provided the light. The starless sky was somewhere above us, but we couldn't see it.

I woke my Jennifer with kisses. She slept in her yellow sleeping bag which she had setup next to mine. My Jennifer took watch by holding her M16 at the ready while she sat upon her backpack at the edge of our campsite. I stood watch about twenty-five feet away on the other side of our pup tents.

"Hear that?" Jennifer asked in a soft voice.

"Hear what?"

"Listen."

The chirr of mosquitos floated across the prairie. "The fire attracts them," I said.

"It took all afternoon for the mosquitos to find us?" Jennifer asked.

"Good point. Maybe in the troll world mosquitos don't come out until the sun goes down."

"They sound louder."

"I don't think those are airplanes," I said. The chirring had transformed into what sounded like a fleet of old fashioned, prop-driven aircraft.

"If they're planes why is it taking so long for them to fly over?" Jennifer asked.

"Good question."

We listened without speaking for a few minutes before the sound evolved yet again.

"Do I hear people singing?" Jennifer asked.

"Sounds more like humming," I said.

As we listened, we made out a distinctive "zom... zom... zom." It sounded like hundreds of voices chanting in unison.

"It's creepy, Bryan."

"Zombies!" I screamed. I kicked the tents and screamed loud enough to wake the undead.

"Shoot them in the head," Tony shouted. He arranged us in a semi-circle by the lake.

"Do zombies cross water?" Gilbert asked.

"We'll find out," said Frank.

My Jennifer snuggled against me. She shook. Acid rose in my throat and my heart fluttered in my chest. I broke into a sweat.

We couldn't see the zombies until Tony shot a flare into the air, but by then we were too late.

CHAPTER 14

ZOMBIE ATTACK – WHAT AGAIN?

"Fix bayonets!" Tony shouted as the zombie army approached.

"How?" my Jennifer responded.

"Stick the handle of your bayonet on the end of the damn rifle until it snaps into place." Tony demonstrated for us. I felt bad for Tony who had forgotten to teach us bayonet drills. For that matter, he hadn't taught us how to fire an M16. We simply slapped in an ammo clip and fired. We were happy to learn the bullets came out the end with the hole in the barrel rather than the end with the shoulder rest.

"Into the lake!" Tony splashed a hasty retreat as the rest of us followed.

Twenty feet from shore, we were in water up to our knees, but the zombies didn't follow us. Instead, they danced the zombie march along the shore and sang the "zom... zom... zom..." lullaby.

"Hold your fire," Tony ordered. "We have to conserve our ammo."

The wind rustled above us. I took a gander where the sky should be and spotted an endless darkness. Then leathery wings appeared out of the dark. I gawped as they flapped in a circle above us. The creature dove to force us to duck our heads as it passed by.

"Is that a giant bat?" Gilbert asked.

"Not sure but here come the zombies." Tony pointed with his M16 to shore. A bunch of zombies waded into the water in our direction.

The sky creature landed by our campsite on shore while scattering and knocking over zombies. In the glow of another flare launched by Tony, we spotted our new adversary, a dragon. The creature breathed fire that lit up the shoreline of the lake and forced the zombies back.

I wasn't the only one who was happy we were in a lake because some of us, me included, were about to pee our pants while the dragon morphed into a man.

"Greetings, pals," said Turpelator. I'm certain it was Turpelator but which one? Was it our high school physics teacher or the dead bootlegger? I know what you may think. How could it be the dead bootlegger? At this point, I wasn't sure about how dead was dead. I mean this troll world was enough to give you the heebie-jeebies. We had three versions of Jennifer so why not a couple of versions of Turpelator, especially because he can morph into a dragon and control an army of zombies.

The zombies reversed direction and marched into the darkness away from our camp.

"Sorry about the inconvenience, chums," said Turpelator. "A zombie horde tends to march in the direction of fresh meat and you passed between them and a herd of cattle on the other side of the lake. Enjoy your walkabout." Turpelator followed his horde into the night.

"We defeated a zombie army without firing a shot," said Tony. "Nice job, kiddoes."

"Uhmmm, my pants are wet. I'll change them now," said Snpgrdxz.

"Yeah, me too," replied the rest of us. We didn't wait to setup our knocked-over tents as we stripped bare bottom in front of the entire troop. Our privacy came in the form of the distance apart from each other and the remaining blackness of the night.

My Jennifer came up to me, placed her arms around my neck and planted a tongue-tickling zinger on me. "You're my hero."

Oh, by the way, she wasn't wearing pants or anything. Neither was I.

***

In the morning, the blazing hot desert started about two hour's walk beyond the other side of the lake. Instead of a clear break in terrain, the desert and prairie melted into each other. As we progressed, the meadow yellowed away from green. The open spaces between plants increased in size and changed from dark brown to baby poop tan. Its consistency went from firmly packed top soil fit for the plough to squishy sand. Once we entered the beach, the plants appeared about every five feet. Instead of grass, flowers and the occasional small bush, we found various types of cactus.

We trudged along until the two suns reached the middle of the sky when Tony announced siesta. We pitched tents and crawled in without the benefit of shade. My Jennifer helped me setup my tent and crawled in with me. We spent the afternoon snuggling. We didn't do anything, honest, except for good, old-fashioned teenage cuddles.

After our nestle time, we peeked out of the tent to see if the others were up yet. Instead of friends, we spotted a giant black spider several stories tall.

The width of the spider's abdomen stretched twelve feet. Its legs added as much as double the space the spider took up as it trudged closer to our camp on a furry body.

Jennifer and I watched from inside my pup tent on our stomachs with our M16s at the ready.

The two suns in this crazy place sank below the western horizon as black nothingness stepped in for the night shift.

"Come out and play, old chums. It's dinner time," said the spider who glared through twelve eyes.

"Aren't spiders supposed to have eight eyes?" my Jennifer asked.

"You grow as big as that puppy, and you'll have twelve eyes, too," I said.

"Why not eight really big eyes?" Jennifer asked.

The spider stomped one of its many feet. "I'm waiting, dinner pals."

"I'm not hungry," I shouted. "Are you ready to eat, Jennifer?"

She responded in a loud voice, "No, not yet. Isn't it time for target practice with these high-powered M16 rifles?"

From the other tents came the sound of metal clicking metal as our friends locked and loaded without an order from Tony.

"Where's Tony?" I asked.

"Don't you worry about Tony. I still have the flamethrower in the backpack someplace, but I can't find it. But the grenade launcher should work." Tony crawled out of his tent dragging his big rifle thing with a revolver mechanism that allowed for rapid fire launch of multiple grenades.

"Come out for a chit-chat," said the spider to the people. "I so rarely meet humans of any intellectual capacity. Most of my human meals, burp, I mean friends, are zombies."

"We aren't very good conversationalists," said Gilbert.

"That's right," said CJ.

"Oh, you'll do fine," said the spider. "We'll keep the conversation brief anyway. I wouldn't want to keep you fine folks from my dinner."

A loud swoosh noise was followed by a second noisy swoosh. I gawped at the blackness above and noticed two thick white strands of web material float down upon our campsite. The spider was building a web with us trapped beneath.

After a few more loud swooshes, the crisscross pattern emerged. Snpgrdxz stretched out his arm to snag a strand that landed in front of his pup tent.

"Don't touch it," yelled Third Jennifer, but she was too late.

Snpgrdxz was stuck in the giant spider's web.

CHAPTER 15

SPIDER ATTACK

"Stop the web or we'll open fire," screeched Tony.

"You meat chunks don't have a shell to protect you, so how do you expect to hurt me." The spider laughed.

Tony fired his grenade launcher. The grenade stuck in the monster's "forehead," the space above his twelve eyes.

"That smarts," said the spider.

"...three... two... one..." said Tony.

"Boom!" said the grenade.

Have you ever seen a cross-eyed, twelve-eyed giant spider with a hole the size of a baby's wading pool in its forehead?

The spider screamed with a force that knocked Tony to the ground. The rest of us already were flat.

The scream was the spider's big mistake because wounded spiders attract hungry spiders in search of an easy snack. Three monster spiders attacked the one with the grenade headache who sounded a lot like Turpelator when he spoke. He had Turpelator's face, too, if you can imagine a bootlegger physics teacher with twelve eyes and a big hole where his forehead used to be.

While the spiders fought amongst themselves, Tony ordered us to beat feet into the desert. He insisted we pack our gear first or we would risk frying when the sun came up.

"Let's keep Snpgrdxz also," said Tony.

Snpgrdxz freed himself from his sticky situation caught in the spider web material by shape shifting his stuck places into little needle projections. It was a simple matter of yanking off the needle points one at a time. It sounded like the noise Velcro makes when you separate the two strips.

The three new spiders were smaller than the first one so they had difficulty standing up to it. As we raced into the desert, the rising suns illuminated the battle of four spiders for us. The clash was still on when we lost sight of the spiders late in the morning.

We hurried along until mid-afternoon when we stopped for siesta. We slept in our tents until the suns set and the air cooled. When Jennifer and I woke up, we pulled on our blue jeans and t-shirts. You have to stay cool in the desert heat.

And yes, we were good. You have to stop wondering about that. We were just teens after all. Jennifer was fifteen or sixteen depending on how you counted the time which we lost track of in this weird world.

Imagine what Principal Hawkins, her dad, would do to me if he found out his precious Jennifer and I slept together. Of course, we napped together during siesta time so that was not the same as spending the night, was it?

Tony prepared Army MREs for us. I chose a meatloaf with gravy packet while my Jennifer selected the vegie ration.

With everyone eating in a circle, Frank opened our conversation by asking Snpgrdxz how old he was.

"I'm a teenager like the other kids here," Snpgrdxz said.

"Yeah. You're like the oldest teenager on the planet" I said.

"I'm sort of equal in maturity to an earther teenager."

"But how old are you in actual years?" Tony asked.

"In earth equivalent years, I'm three hundred sixty-seven."

"I told you he was the world's oldest teen," I said. Jennifer punched me.

"You're three hundred sixty-seven years old?" Gilbert shouted.

"Yeah."

Paul R. Lloyd

"How's that make you a teenager?" my Jennifer asked.

"Puberty kicked in, both sexes in my case, and I have another one hundred forty-seven earth-equivalent years before reaching my majority under our laws."

"Wait. Wait. Did you say both sexes?" CJ asked.

"Yeah. You get the idea aliens are different, right?" Snpgrdxz bit into his chicken MRE.

"But both sexes?" Gilbert asked.

"Humans! Some species have three or four sexes." Snpgrdxz shook his head.

"On your planet?" I asked.

Snpgrdxz rubbed his chin. "No, we have the same two as earthers except we have them rolled up into one individual. One person, two sexes. Makes reproduction easier if you find yourself marooned on a strange planet by yourself."

My Jennifer scratched her head. "So how does it work? I mean, do you have to do yourself?"

Snpgrdxz's eyes popped wide open. "Do myself? You mean... Oh, I understand. Yeah, I can have fun like any other teenager whose hormones run rampant. And yes, if I'm not careful, I could make myself pregnant."

"So your hormones are like running wild right now?" Tony asked.

"Yeah, for the past one hundred nineteen years I've overflowed with too much female hormones in my system counterbalanced by too many male hormones. I should settle into a normal hormone flow in, let's see, about another one hundred fifty earth-equivalent years."

"Your people are stuck in high school for about 300 years?" Tony asked.

"More like two-fifty, two-seventy-five. Depends," Snpgrdxz said.

"Can you make it with other individuals of your species?" Gilbert asked.

"Naturally. We prefer to mate with others."

"But you don't have to?" Third Jennifer asked.

90

"Like humans, we're made to live in community. You need more than one person to raise a child. Two parents work best for us."

"So how do you... I don't even know how to ask this next question." My Jennifer rubbed her chin.

"You want me to tell you how we decide who to ask out on a date?"

My Jennifer giggled and shrugged. "Yeah. If you're like both sexes, how do you, you know... decide?"

Snpgrdxz laughed. "Very carefully. Usually an individual member of our race will develop a preference for one sex over the other. Most times, they appear in their female form or male form. Persons in the male form are attracted to persons in the female form and vice-versa. But remember, in our natural state, you can't tell the difference anyway. We don't look much like you earthers. You people enjoy showing off your sexuality. We enjoy showing off our brains which explains why our heads evolved to such a large size. Or our heads evolved first and we enjoy showing them off. I'm not sure which. It's like your chicken and egg controversy."

"What about gay, lesbian and whatever people?" Gilbert asked.

"It's complicated. Some couples like to switch back and forth and some have a preference for remaining together as the same sex. Depends. We recognize many forms of joining."

"Can you mate with other species, like humans?" Tony asked.

"What do you think?" Snpgrdxz grinned. I should say "Daniel" here because, like most days on our journey, Snpgrdxz stayed in his Daniel Brickmaster form during this conversation. Gawking at Daniel while he spoke made the answer to his rhetorical question obvious and humorous enough to elicit a giggle or two.

"You were pretty frisky with me the night you climbed through my bedroom window and pretended to be Jennifer Hawkins," I said.

"So you want to have fun now?" Snpgrdxz asked.

Jennifer slapped Snpgrdxz on the face.

I fell off my rock. "No! Never. Don't do that to me. I mean really."

"Humans are so uptight about mating rituals," said Snpgrdxz.

"Mind if I interrupt, chums?" asked the giant spider with the hole in his head.

CHAPTER 16

HIGHER EVOLVED FOOD ITEMS

"What happened to your spider friends?" Tony leaned a foot on a rock while resting his rifle butt on the ground.

"Tasty treats for me. Postponed destruction for you," The spider with the hole in the head wiped his mouth with a front leg.

"How very kind of you," CJ said.

"Not at all, my dear. I'm full from having devoured three rebellious spiders. Let's talk. I seldom meet up with a group of higher evolved food items in this world." The spider went through an instant evolution from giant spider to modern human being, including a white suit suitable for a desert visit in say nineteen forty-six. The particular human form happened to be Turpelator.

"That's a change, Mr. Turpelator. Pardon my inquisitiveness, but didn't we bury you a short while ago, back in nineteen twenty-three?" asked CJ.

"Oh, yes, about that. You can't exterminate someone on a permanent basis when they travel in a time loop. But then, you knew about that, didn't you, my dear?" Turpelator smiled.

"So you're stuck in a time loop like me?" asked CJ.

"And me?" asked Third Jennifer.

"Am I stuck in a time loop?" my Jennifer asked.

"Not yet," said Tony.

"To answer your question, dear CJ, yes, when I die, I wake up in my default time. A time loop makes one indestructible, old girl. You'd be amazed how eternal life facilitates evolution." Turpelator's smile was wicked. And I mean "wicked" in its original wicked definition.

"You're devolving instead of evolving, *old boy*," said Tony.

Turpelator paced. "Oh, you mean the spider? Let me explain. You see, you will die here in this desert on a strange world for one simple reason. You refuse to embrace the world as it is. For example, you fight the zombies, instead of embracing them. You fight the spiders, instead of becoming spiders and joining in their evening rumps through the desert. Spiders are docile creatures. They merely wish to dine when they are hungry, like you. And they appreciate leadership because they have none. They roam the desert at night like a runaway mob. By embracing them, they have accepted me as their leader and follow where I go."

"I guess we're not as highly evolved or devolved as you," Frank said. "I can't turn myself into a giant spider."

"You're not as highly evolved as I am. I am beyond human, you know. I've raised myself into a daemon."

"Did you say 'demon?'" Gilbert asked.

"No. A demon is an evil spirit, a fallen angel. I'm a human who has evolved into a god. It's what you do when you pass through the monster process. First I became a vampire. Next, a werewolf. After that, a warlock. Along the way, I perfected shapeshifting. Now, I'm a god with the power of Thor." Turpelator shot a bolt of lightning from his palm. It struck in the midst of our gathering circle. I blacked out.

When I came to, the others were rubbing their heads like they just woke up so I assume the bolt knocked them loopy as well. We couldn't have been out long because Daemon Turpelator hadn't eaten us yet.

"Becoming a daemon is an honor we'll pass on, if you don't mind." Tony yanked his grenade launcher out of his tent.

"Too bad, old boy. I did mention that the horde of stampeding spiders follow me wherever I travel in the desert night, didn't I?"

In the darkness, we couldn't see anything. But the thundering roar of giant spider feet in the distance was unmistakable.

***

Daniel Brickmaster stood. "Do you ladies mind if I strip naked?"

"Yes," said my Jennifer.

"Then close your eyes, please. It's necessary to save you." Daniel stripped off his clothes in the dark so no one saw anything worth mentioning. Once naked, he morphed into a giant mountain troll which we could clearly see despite the darkness. Size trumps dark apparently. He picked up Turpelator and threw him about a hundred feet from camp.

In midflight, Turpelator devolved into a giant spider again.

Daniel, as Snpgrdxz, shape-shifted into a giant flesh dome that covered the entire camp. He shape shifted again into stone.

Tony said, "I get it. He turned himself into a hollow rock with us inside. The giant spider horde will pass us by, if his trick works."

"Put out the gas fire," said Frank. "The heat might burn Snpgrdxz's underside."

Tony turned off his gas stove.

Our stone cover shook and wobbled in the blackness of our hollow rock. Something, most likely Turpelator, tried to overturn our stone of Snpgrdxz. The wobbles stopped when the murderous thundering herd reached us.

My Jennifer jumped onto my lap. "We're about to die."

A thunderstorm of spiders passed over Snpgrdxz Rock. To our amazement and joy, Snpgrdxz did not collapse under the might of the monster black spiders, although his rock developed a long crack off to one side that ran about fifteen feet. Twenty minutes of the pounding noise kept us huddled together until the dark silence.

I patted my Jennifer on the butt so she'd lift off my lap. She didn't seem to mind. I drifted around our little hideaway, my biggest mistake to date.

Daemon Turpelator, the giant spider, grabbed me with a foot he poked up through the desert sand where he must have dug his way toward us while the horde of spiders passed over Snpgrdxz Rock. The spider horde must have been a diversion. He yanked me under the sand before I could shout for help. A pinprick to my butt made me groggy immediately. Within seconds my mind faded to black.

***

I woke up as from a long sleep. After a few minutes of wiggling, I realized Turpelator had encased me inside a cocoon of spider web material. My left butt cheek throbbed. Numbness radiated from my butt throughout my body. My head spun and my brain weighed about fifty pounds.

My face stuck out of the cocoon. I opened my eyes to a black world. I wiggled some more but couldn't shake free of the cocoon. With the drug Turpelator had injected into my butt, I couldn't tell if the cocoon was real or a result of my stupor.

The drug was venom from Turpelator, the spider, I was certain. I couldn't move. He would eat me the next time he desired a snack. Or being a spider, would he suck all the juice out of me?

I fell asleep expecting never to wake up in this lifetime.

But I did wake up. I had no idea how much time had passed, whether a few minutes or many days. My throat was dry. I was hungry and thirsty. My head buzzed.

Footsteps echoed off the rocks in the distance. Those sounds may have woken me. I couldn't perceive anything in the blackness so I didn't know if my friends had arrived in time to rescue me or if Turpelator stomped my way in need of a quick snack. Did I hear the eight feet of one giant spider or the many feet of my companions?

A light bounced around in the distance. Then another light appeared and another. Either my friends were searching for me with their lamps in a giant cave, or Turpelator had headlights where his eyes should be. I voted for my friends.

"Help!" I shrieked.

"Bryan!" my Jennifer screamed. I heard her run towards me, but couldn't see her. Then one of the lights became larger and brighter. The lights picked up speed.

"Wait up, Wild Thing," Tony bellowed. "It could be a trap."

"It may be Bryan. Oh, God, please, it must be Bryan. He's alive. I know he is." My Jennifer's desperate, emotional tone brought tears to my eyes, but I couldn't move my hands to wipe them.

My whole body bounced as though I was attached to a trampoline mounted to a wall. I moved back and forth like the trampoline was behind me rather than under my feet.

"Oh, shit," Jennifer shouted. "I'm stuck."

Frank roared, "Stop. It's a giant spider web."

"Too late," shouted Snpgrdxz.

The gang pulled and yanked to remove Jennifer from the web. Tony pulled a small gas tank out of Gilbert's backpack. He lit it and used the flame to burn the web away from Jennifer. As soon as she was free, the web began to vibrate from far above.

CJ shined a flashlight up to the top of the cave. "Here comes Turpelator."

The gang opened fire. I had never heard a spider scream until Turpelator leaped on top of my friends.

CHAPTER 17

SPEARING A SPIDER

My friends fired round after round from their M16s as Turpelator dropped to the cave floor. Third Jennifer killed him with a deep thrust with her silver spear. Turpelator impaled himself when he failed to spot it on his way down from the ceiling to the floor where he no doubt had in mind to eat us.

Tony cut me out of my spider cocoon with his bowie knife.

"This is like cutting wire," Tony said.

Snpgrdxz and Gilbert half-carried me by holding my arms and dragging me along the route back out of the cave while I waggled my feet to pretend to walk.

We were in a hurry to leave because the spiders behind us in the cave ran toward us at a fast trot that suggested they were on their way to dinner. Turpelator's spider web made an effective blockade to keep them from us, but we had no idea how long it might last.

The mouth of the cave opened onto the desert floor. Once out, we couldn't see the entrance because bushes and scrub brush hid it. I asked how the gang had found it in the first place and Tony explained they had followed Turpelator. One glance at the sky told me the time was early morning. Gilbert informed me I had been in the cave for three days.

My friends continued to half drag my dizzy self as I ate a cold MRE and drank plenty of water.

"I need to rest," I said.

"You'll rest at siesta time," Tony said. "We have to get as far away from the spiders as possible by then."

In the distance behind us, a giant spider eyeballed us from a hilltop covered with cactus. I wasn't sure if the spider planned to attack us or was simply out for a morning stroll. I passed out.

I woke up with Snpgrdxz and Gilbert dragging me across the dunes. Based on the position of the two suns, it was mid-morning. I gawked around but spotted no spiders. By noon, our feet sunk up to our ankles in the deep, dry sand. Each step was like lumping along with iron shoes. Well, iron shoes for me. Gilbert and Snpgrdxz continued to drag me while my Jennifer tugged on my elbow. As a result, we lagged behind the others.

One high dune blocked our way, but cast a shadow on the side away from the two suns.

"Let's siesta here in the dune's shadow until nightfall," Tony announced.

As the shadow spread during the afternoon, the air cooled down to about one hundred degrees. Our water supply was low so we were on strict rations, but Tony scrounged enough water from his backpack for all of us. I got extra because Tony said I needed to flush the poison out of my system.

To minimize the dryness, Jennifer and I shared whatever moisture we could conjure up while playing tonsil hockey. I ate a granola bar Tony scrounged from one of the backpacks. I needed to sleep and not just nap either.

I blinked for what seemed like two seconds and then opened my eyes to spy the two suns settle into the west. I'd been out for hours. Tony roused us to break camp.

We trudged around the big dune to find Turpelator the spider waiting for us.

***

"Greetings, old chums. I've decided to eat you tonight. Except CJ. I may want to play with her for a while. I may show you how to become a spider, my dear, and we can make spider love together."

"Over my dead body." Frank brandished his M16.

"Technically, you don't have to be dead when I suck out your juices, old boy."

"You're not about to kill anyone." I'm not sure where I conjured up the courage to say anything to a giant spider.

"And why is that, young Ganarski, the runaway snack?" Turpelator the spider giant asked.

My Jennifer shouted, "Because the snake slithering behind you has hungry eyes."

"Yes. Nice try, little Miss Skin-and-bones," said Turpelator, but he couldn't resist turning around when the giant snake shook its two rattles. "Oh, I see. It's your friend Snpgrdxz."

Snpgrdxz stepped to the front of our group. "I'm down here, oh majestic king of the spiders and feeder of split-tail rattlers."

"Yes, I um see I... I may have to eat you nice folks later. Fatten yourselves while I'm away, will you please?" Turpelator ran off into the darkening desert.

The split-tail rattle snake struck at the spider but missed. It chased after Turpelator while we headed into the night with a vague sense of moving in the right direction but anxious it may be the wrong way. How could you be sure of anything in this strange world where the dead refuse to stay dead, and the monsters of our imaginations are as real as the next horrific attack?

***

"We're going around in circles, aren't we?" asked Third Jennifer. "Now you know why I didn't make any progress in the three years before you came along."

Paul R. Lloyd

As we trudged through the sand the next day, with our feet on fire, we doubted Tony's compass. Uncertainty and fear combined for a depressing mix in the heat of two suns.

We trudged forward in pairs with Tony and Third Jennifer in the lead. Behind him were Frank and CJ followed by Snpgrdxz in his Daniel Brickmaster form and Gilbert. My Jennifer and I lagged behind.

"What's that?" Jennifer asked.

"What?" I asked.

"That whoosh, pop noise."

I heard it as soon as she said it. I didn't see anything, but the popcorn sound increased in frequency and number.

Jennifer turned about and squealed, "Oh, how cute."

I turned and spotted the little noise makers. Hundreds of yellow flowers popped out of the sand of the desert. Each plant had a single, large yellow flower made of thin petals that formed a globe or head above the green leafy shoulders and body. They bloomed as quickly as they popped out of the ground.

"I bet we can eat them," my Jennifer said.

The others gathered around.

Frank said, "You have to be careful with flowers, Ganarski Girl. Many aren't edible."

"Come away from those plant things," said Tony.

"Why, what's wrong?" asked CJ.

The flowers rose out of the ground in mass revealing root systems that formed powerful woven basket feet. One of the plants squealed in a high pitched tone.

"Run," Tony yelled. It was becoming his favorite word.

CHAPTER 18

FLOWERS ON THE WAR PATH

The flowers pulled their feet out of the ground and sauntered forward. We took off at a full gallop across the sand.

People may run faster than flowers, but after a time, we poop out. I bent over to catch my breath and checked back to see if the flower creatures followed us. A dust cloud in the distance showed their slow paced advance in our direction. Tiny versions of the flowers led their army. This vanguard was about a hundred yards away.

"Keep moving," Tony said.

We marched on across the desert in hopes of discovering no more surprise flower patches. Later as the two suns set, Third Jennifer said, "There are hills in the distance. We can climb them and camp out for the night without the flowers climbing them."

"They look like sheer cliffs from here, Third Jennifer. How will we climb them?" Gilbert asked.

"I don't think those are rock cliffs," said Tony.

We hurried toward the safety of the shelter whether cliffs or something else.

"They're buildings," said Frank as we came closer.

"You're right," said CJ.

"How come they're so dark?" asked my Jennifer.

"It could be a blackout in case of an air raid," Gilbert suggested.

Tony said, "You may have noticed that we are within a mile or two of a desert city but we haven't seen one person or hobgoblin or troll or even a giant spider around. And you may also have noticed that we haven't spotted a single highway. It's as if the city rose out of the sand complete, but where are the people and monsters?"

We continued in silence for the rest of the journey into the black, deserted desert city. We saw no houses or low buildings. Only tall skyscrapers. Once inside the city, the flowers stopped following us.

"This city has been empty for a long time," said Tony. "The streets long ago gave way to the sand. Now there are only the tall buildings."

"Are we even on the first floor level or has the sand piled up over the centuries to hide several floors of these old structures?" Snpgrdxz asked.

"Let's make our way into this building here and see if we can climb about ten stories up for safety," Third Jennifer said.

Tony said, "First let's find one that still has windows. It would be great to escape the windblown sand for one night."

After two more blocks of hiking, we spotted a building with the glass intact. We circled it in search of an entrance but found none.

"Daniel is right," I said. "We're not on the first floor. The desert has taken over."

"This pane is cracked," said Third Jennifer. "Let's break our way in."

"We might go to jail," Gilbert laughed.

My Jennifer snagged her M16 and shot out the glass. "Anyone want to explore an old building?"

We stepped through the window opening into a dark office. The room we entered contained wooden desks in an open work area. Wood file cabinets lined the interior walls. Typewriters sat on the desk tops along with old-fashioned electric desk lamps and desk sets, including a blotter pad, letter trays and pencil cups. Most of the desks had file folders and papers on them. The paper was not our standard letter size but more like nine by thirteen.

"Did they go home from work one day and simply not return?" Third Jennifer asked.

"This office appears right out of the mid twentieth century," Tony said.

"I'll bet it's much older, right?" Gilbert asked.

"Much older," Tony said. "We may have found Atlantis or another ancient city."

"How can you tell?" I asked.

"I doubt the desert would have eaten this much of the city in only a few decades," said Tony. "And within a few hundred years, there would be some stragglers still living here and maybe even a guard force to protect the city from vandals. There's no one around. I'll bet a little carbon dating of that wood would tell us the city is ancient."

Gilbert waved his hand to indicate a no. "You're forgetting the joys of time travel, Tony. We have no idea what troll world year we are in. For all we know, this city could be mid-twentieth century by our world's reckoning, but we may be here hundreds or thousands of years after the twentieth century."

"You're right, of course, Gilbert. The troll-zombies were another indication we may have landed much farther in the future than we thought.

"Let's find the stairs and climb to safety," said Third Jennifer.

A doorway opened on a dark hallway. It was the neatest, cleanest cave we travelled through on our journey so far, except this cave formed a perfect rectangle and there were doors on both sides. The cave floor and walls were marble. The ceiling was decorated metal, like the copper ceilings in old buildings in our world. The doors had markings on them, but they weren't English. No surprise there. A sign in the middle of the long hallway hung from the ceiling.

"I'll bet that's an exit sign," said Third Jennifer. She led us to it.

The sign was positioned above a junction of two hallways. The new hallway was short and opened onto an elevator bank. My Jennifer pushed a button with an up arrow. Nothing happened.

"You expected the elevator to come after a thousand years without power?" CJ asked.

"There's a door," Gilbert said. A heavy metal door stood next to the elevator bank. Gilbert pulled it open. It resisted at first, but then squealed on its hinges.

Gilbert stuck his head in the space opened by the door. "It's the stair well."

We trudged ten stories up without reaching the top. The door to the floor we stopped on took a lot of pushing before it opened. The floor was identical to the first floor we climbed in. My Jennifer pushed the elevator up button and it flashed on. She screamed. Lights came on in the ceiling lamps. A fan began blowing warm air through the building's ventilation system.

"Let's hide," said Gilbert.

"There's no one here," said CJ. "The building generator turned on. The people probably set a timer in motion thousands of years ago."

"Where does the generator obtain power and fuel if no one is around?" Gilbert asked.

The elevator clanged to a stop and the doors opened. We ducked behind the stairwell door. Tony and I peeked with the door open a crack. The folks out of the elevator wore conservative business attire that would have worked well in the mid-twentieth century, except for the tattered and torn places. The people walked in silence to the main hallway where they disappeared. I assumed they were headed for their respective offices.

"What do you see?" Third Jennifer whispered.

I said, "Zombies."

***

A tall male zombie stepped into our already crowded elevator on the eighth floor.

"Argrumf." The zombie flashed a grin, turned and faced front. Even zombies didn't like to take the stairs.

The elevator continued making stops on the way down. A female zombie boarded on the fifth floor. She and the tall male became chummy while exchanging sweet nothings.

"Urgumf."

"Murgromp."

"Bingflaughter?"

"Glumph."

Laughter by both zombies. Female zombie glanced over her shoulder at us behind her. She turned back to the tall guy zombie. "Miggleslumps."

"Harbooky."

More laughter.

Girl zombie looked back at us again. "Alplopf." It sounded like an apology. She shrugged and faced front.

The zombie pair exited in front of us on the third floor, the one we came in on.

While the zombie couple meandered off in one direction, we headed the opposite way towards the broken window and our exit. Thirty zombies approached from down the hall as fast as their zombie legs could motivate. They hissed at us.

"They probably think we're in sales," Frank said.

Rather than work our way through a herd of zombies for our broken window exit, Tony shot out the glass in a window where we stood. The zombies continued in our direction as we made our way to the street outside.

Zombies filled the street like Michigan Avenue at noon. We trudged along close to the buildings. The actual street was probably a hundred feet or more below the sand.

A nineteen forty-six Dodge taxi scurried down the street and pulled up next to us.

"Jump in." The taxi driver wore a white hat, shirt and slacks. His bowtie was black. His face was pale, but not zombified.

"Let's vamoose," said Tony.

We squeezed the seven of us into the taxi. A horde of zombies followed us, but the taxi was too fast for the slow poke crowd. Within a few blocks, we lost the zombie mob. The streets were still filled with other zombies bustling about, but they ignored us.

"Keep the windows up," said the driver. "We don't want them to get a whiff of fresh meat."

"Who are you?" Third Jennifer asked.

My name's Jimmy. At your service, Miss."

"What happened to the city?" CJ asked.

"You mean you don't know?"

"Would I ask if I did?" CJ asked.

"You missed the apocalypse. Zombies took over the world and there's no going back."

"How did you avoid the zombies?" Snpgrdxz asked.

"I hid at home for weeks."

"Yes, but why aren't they chasing you now?"

"They only chase the living."

We sat in silence the rest of the way. No one wanted to comment on the taxi driver's claim to be not counted among the living or to ask why.

After ten minutes, Tony asked, "What manner of creature are you, exactly?"

"You know. Here's your stop." The driver pulled over to the curb.

"How much do we owe you?" my Jennifer asked.

"No charge. I'm happy to have made your acquaintance."

"What city is this?" I asked.

"You know, El Dorado."

We climbed out of the car. I was last. The old Dodge became transparent by the time I made my exit. When I joined the others on the side of the sand road, the Dodge and its driver had vanished.

"Now what?" I asked.

"We walk," said Tony.

As it turned out we were only a few blocks from the edge of the city. We ambled into the black of night, keeping to our own thoughts. My Jennifer held my hand.

Several hours passed before we stopped for breakfast and to watch the suns rise over the sand. El Dorado, the golden city of zombies, had vanished over the horizon. After breakfast we trekked on across the sand dunes.

Our water supply, already low, disappeared by midday, except for a few emergency bottles Tony found in his backpack and shared with us. We couldn't find shade so everyone took a pass on siesta time after we left the dunes for a sandy beach. The beach led to the horizon with no sign of an ocean to splash in. We called it a beach as a sick joke, but by the time the two suns settled along the horizon, we smelled the water in the distance.

The aroma combined wet mud, rotten fish and damp fur, but we loved it. We found the river a short time later and ran toward it. With so much open land around us, I had no idea where Turpelator the spider came from unless he jumped out of the ground or dropped from the sky, but there he was in front of us spitting flame.

***

"Do you have time to play with me on the beach, friends? We could build a sand castle and fill it with bones," said Turpelator the spider.

Tony fired a grenade. It exploded in Turpelator's head in the same spot as his first grenade days ago. This time the grenade penetrated deeper because the critter stood so close to us.

Turpelator appeared ill as his twelve eyes rolled upwards toward the giant crater in his skull. He wobbled on eight legs. "Oh, my," he said.

Turpelator the spider rolled over on his back with his legs pointed to the sky.

We charged the river bank in hopes of a way to cross.

"That's the second time we killed Turpelator the spider. What is this place?" Frank asked.

CHAPTER 19

DRAGON'S BREATH

The boatman wore a ragged hoody draped to his ankles. His feet were bare and skeletal. His face, what we could see of it, featured a long nose and thick lips. He opened his mouth to reveal bleeding gums but no teeth. Where his eyes should be, we stared into the dark depths of nothing.

"Will you take us across?" asked Tony.

"He better take us across," said Gilbert. "Or else we're stuck here."

"He'll take us," said Frank.

"How do you know?" asked CJ.

"The name of his little boat is Hope," Frank pointed.

My Jennifer pulled a fish net away from the side of the boat. "It says 'Abandon All Hope.' What a funny name for a ship."

Tony squatted to make a closer inspection of the side of the boat. He rubbed off a layer of green slime. "Rather than the name of a boat, it's a message, 'Abandon All Hope Ye Who Enter Here.'"

"Sounds familiar," CJ said.

"In Dante's Inferno, the message appeared over the gates of Hell," said Tony.

"We just left Hell. How bad can it be up ahead if there's water?" Gilbert asked.

The boatman stretched out his left arm to point across the river to the bank on the other side. He held his right hand palm up towards our little group.

"How much?" Gilbert asked.

The boatman imitated a marble statue.

"Give him the gold coin I told you to save," said Tony.

"All of us?" Gilbert asked.

"Only those of you who want to cross the River Styx."

"Sticks?" my Jennifer asked.

"S-T-Y-X, children. You are about to embark on the Stygian Sea."

***

The others handed their ten-dollar gold coins over to the boatman while I gaped. I paid last, climbed into the boat, dropped my backpack and fell overboard.

My darling Jennifer snagged me by my t-shirt and pulled it off in an attempt to rescue me. Her actions allowed me to grab hold of the side of the boat. Snpgrdxz and Gilbert tried to yank me back onboard, but my belt caught on the side and my pants slipped off taking my undies with them. I dropped back in the water butt naked except for my shoes. I tossed my shoes and socks aboard. "Anyone have soap?"

Tony, bless his heart, snagged a blanket out of his backpack and held it up while Frank and Gilbert yanked me into the boat. At best, the ladies only got a quick peek at my equipment.

The boat was small with a mast and sail in the center. We took seats on the benches, with me still wrapped in a blanket and my clothes laid out to dry as best they could in this creepy, overcast and misty world. The boatman worked the tiller to steer us across the river.

"You know what this means, don't you, Bryan?" Tony asked.

"What does what mean?" I asked.

"Falling into the River Styx." Tony patted me on the shoulder.

"I'm wet and covered in river muck?" I asked.

"I know," Gilbert raised his hand up like we were back in high school.

"Yes?" asked Tony.

"He's like Achilles. We studied him in English class last year, except Homer was written in ancient Greek," said Gilbert.

"You're right. You can't be killed, Bryan. You're like a god." My Jennifer kissed me. "Yuck, you are covered in muck."

Tony laughed. "Not a god exactly, but invulnerable. More like Superman without the other powers but in a world without kryptonite.

"You believe that crap?" Frank asked.

"I'm all wet," I said. "I feel baptized, except my real baptism in Jesus is what gives me eternal life."

"Good for you," said Gilbert.

The dragon rose from the deep murky waters about a hundred feet from our little boat. It breathed fire in our direction.

***

How we ended up in a swamp with a dragon on our tail we couldn't tell. When we boarded the little boat, we could see the other side of the river in the distance. But a fog rolled in about half way across. When it cleared up, we noticed the swamp. It reminded me of the pictures I've seen of the Bayou in Louisiana except no mosquitos. The boat navigated among Cypress trees that rose a hundred feet above the green, murky water.

"What should we do?" CJ asked.

"Nothing," said Tony. "Leave it to the boatman. We paid our fare so we're protected until we reach our destination."

A flock of Pterosaurs flew overhead. Three of them broke formation to dive bomb us. They passed within a few feet of our heads. Tiny feathery filaments covered the creatures like a bat's black fur.

We entered another fog bank which blinded us with a white haze. The boatman relied on his own internal radar or sixth sense to maneuver us around structures hidden by the fog. I guessed the structures were trees, but I had no way to know for certain. We were in the fog about two hours when we smelled sulfur. The aroma grew stronger until we crashed into land.

A large flame shot out of a two-foot wide hole in the ground on shore where the boat landed.

***

The zombies attacked within a few minutes of landfall. We disembarked on a field of natural exploding and burning gas outlets that we had to dodge. The smoke of fiery sulfur replaced the fog with a less dense cloudiness. We made our way through the field of burning gas with the light of the flames as our guide.

The zombies sang their "zom... zom... zom" song as they stumbled toward us. They were in a herd of twenty or so. They didn't have the business-like rag suits of El Dorado zombies. Instead, they wore rags indicative of left over Saturday night revelers.

"They look like lost souls in Hell," Gilbert said.

"They are, and we're in Hell with them," said Frank.

"Smells like Hell." CJ said.

"When did we die?" I asked.

"Where's the devil hiding?" Tony asked.

A vague form came into view in the cloudy distance. "Hot dogs, old chums?"

Daemon Turpelator held a hotdog on a stick over one of the gas fires. A picnic table held a stack of cooked hotdogs and fresh buns. He also had condiments available.

Turpelator appeared in a dog body with three non-dog heads. One head was a spider, another our physics teacher from high school, and the third Turpelator the rumrunner from nineteen twenty-three.

"We'll pass," said Frank.

"Too bad," said Turpelator the rumrunner. I expected you for some time. I suppose I'll feed my other meat loving friends." The zombies zombed over to the picnic table and snagged hotdogs, not bothering with the buns or mustard.

We quickened our pace but kept an eye on Turpelator.

"Why didn't the zombies attack us?" CJ asked.

"We may still be under the protection of the boatman," Snpgrdxz said.

"Or Turpelator doesn't want his precious zombies blown away with head shots from our M16s. There weren't a lot of zombies," Gilbert said.

"He may be waiting for the rest of the zombie nation to show up," Tony said. "The faster we reach the other when portal, the better."

We hiked our way out of the smoke and sulfur into a meadow. The narrow field led to a forest. We followed a path for several hours in the hope it would lead to a when portal, but all we found were the trees.

We made camp in a small clearing near the outlet of a spring. While a group of us gathered wood for a fire, a small deer passed through the clearing. Frank shot it.

"Frank!" my Jennifer cried.

"Dinner," said Gilbert.

"I'm hungry," said my Jennifer. I hugged her while she cried on my shoulder for the sacrificial deer.

Later, we sat in a circle around the fire to chew our venison and drink fresh spring water.

"I hadn't realized how dehydrated we were from the desert," said Third Jennifer.

"I've been drinking water nonstop since we arrived in the clearing and I still don't have to pee," said CJ.

"Thanks for sharing," said Snpgrdxz.

Tony and Gilbert took the first watch while the rest of us rested in our tents.

I woke up to gunfire and screams.

***

The vampires attacked before first light. Frank shot at the creatures with the bow and arrow he carried in his backpack. Third Jennifer stabbed the vampires with her silver spear. The spear managed to push the creatures away from her, but did little damage to them.

Snpgrdxz saved the day, or rather the night, when he snagged a burning stick from the campfire and set the vampires on fire. With three of them in flames, the others vanished into the trees. The fiery vampires flapped around setting trees and bushes ablaze until Tony pulled a rope from his backpack and lassoed each of them. While he yanked a flaming vampire to the ground, Snpgrdxz jumped on top and pounded a wood stake into its heart. When the three vampires had been vanquished in this way, we gathered around the fire and held hands. Tony led us in a prayer of thanksgiving.

Bats flapped their wings in the trees near our camp, but they vanished when the two suns broke the horizon.

The daylight protected us from more vampire attacks so we crawled back into our tents to sleep. Darling Jennifer and I took time to strip down to our undies which proved to be a mistake. Don't get me wrong. We didn't do the deed. We hugged and fell asleep in each other's arms. The problem came later when we woke up. Jennifer pulled away from my arms and screamed like I was a total stranger.

CHAPTER 20

NOBODY HOME

Gilbert stared off into space when I joined him by the remnants of our campfire. I dressed while attempting to engage him in conversation.

"Waiting for the coffee?" I asked.

Gilbert didn't respond.

I waved my hand in front of his face to see if he was conscious. "You awake?"

Gilbert ignored me.

My Jennifer came out of our little pup tent to join us by the ashes of our campfire. She stared in the same cold, dead way of Gilbert. I couldn't engage her in a conversation. I tried to hold her hand but she yanked it away with a fearful glance.

CJ screamed. Frank backed out of their pup tent carrying his clothes. He was butt naked so I suspect he and CJ had gone a bit farther than I did with my Jennifer. But they were older, not that age made it okay, but what can you do? And as far as age goes, CJ was a one-hundred-fifty-year-old virgin. Well, she was a virgin before she met Frank.

I think.

Frank dressed by the campfire. Watching him was weird. He put his underwear on backwards, then took it off and tried again never mind that my Jennifer stared off into space in his direction. My Jennifer didn't seem to notice his nakedness.

Me she screamed at when I was in my underwear. Him she ignored when he was naked right in front of her. As I considered what this meant, I realized my Jennifer had reacted to my touch, not to the way I was dressed or undressed.

Frank put his pants on backwards.

"Umm, Frank, you might want to try the other way," I said.

Frank tried again with the pants the right way. He put his tee shirt on backwards. He put his shirt on backwards, took it off and dressed the right way. He fumbled with the buttons like they served a purpose, but whatever it was, he couldn't grasp it. Frank joined our little circle around the fire.

Snpgrdxz climbed out of his tent. "Morning everyone."

"Good morning," I said.

"We're a quiet bunch," Snpgrdxz said.

I hadn't thought much about the silence until then. Snpgrdxz was right of course. The Jennifers were talkers and none of us guys was the silent type.

"Something's wrong, Daniel," I said.

"Nothing wrong with quiet."

"There is this morning."

As if to prove me right, Third Jennifer crawled out of her tent. She was still dressed from the night because everything was on the way it should be. She strolled over to our little group and sat down without a word.

"Morning, Third Jennifer," Snpgrdxz said. Third Jennifer stared ahead like Snpgrdxz had spoken to someone else.

CJ emerged from the tent she had shared with Frank. She had dressed herself okay from the waist down, but from the waist up we had a problem or two. The concept of a bra had eluded her as she didn't have one on. The other issue was her inability to figure out how to button a blouse.

Snpgrdxz was a gentleman as he stepped up to place himself between her open shirt and our little circle, not that anyone seemed to notice her situation except me and Snpgrdxz.

I was glad Snpgrdxz didn't ask me to perform the shirt-buttoning service. There was no way I wanted to see parts of CJ she had not chosen to show me.

When Snpgrdxz finished buttoning CJ's blouse, she wiped morning snot across her face. Snpgrdxz pulled a handkerchief from his back pocket to wipe CJ's nose and cheeks for her. CJ joined the rest of our silent party around the campfire.

"Do you think Tony has turned into a zombie?" Snpgrdxz asked.

"They're not zombies."

"They're like zombies. What did you feed them for dinner last night?" Snpgrdxz asked.

"We ate deer meat, and we're okay."

"It could have to do with the vampires," Snpgrdxz suggested.

We turned toward Tony's tent at a rustling sound followed by Tony singing Morning Has Broken, a hymn we sang at church.

"Morning everyone. Sorry I slept so late. You ready for break... Oh, shit. I forgot about this phenomenon. Let's run, everyone. We've got to get out of this place pronto."

"You noticed?" Snpgrdxz asked.

"You have your memory?" Tony asked.

"Yes," said Snpgrdxz. "Why wouldn't I?"

"Anyone else?"

"Yeah, me," I said.

"What about the rest of them?"

"Zombie heads," said Snpgrdxz.

"Let's see. Snpgrdxz Daniel, you're an alien so you must be immune. Bryan makes sense because he fell into the River Styx so he's invulnerable. Everyone else is regular human and likely to forget."

"What do you mean I'm invulnerable?" I asked.

"You fell into the River Styx, dude. We talked about this on the boat. Don't you remember? Makes you invulnerable like Achilles."

It took half a minute to remember Achilles was one of the guys in the Illiad. He gets killed when somebody shoots him in the heel. That's why we all have an Achilles heel. "What about my heel?"

"Achilles's mom held him by the heel. You soaked in water top to bottom, dude. You're invulnerable."

"What about kryptonite?" I asked.

Tony glared in my direction.

"Why didn't you forget?" asked Snpgrdxz.

"I'm the Timekeeper. Now, let's tie them together like kindergarten students on a field trip." Tony dug a rope out of his backpack.

Before leaving, Snpgrdxz and I loaded our stuff into the backpacks and managed to help each of our friends shoulder their packs.

Our forgetful associates proved compliant as we lined them up in a row and tied their wrists to a length of rope. Tony led the way through the forest as I considered how being a timekeeper at basketball games protected Tony from whatever caused our friends to lose their memories. I made the mistake of taking a gander at my Jennifer. When I noticed her blank zombie stare, I cried.

***

Tony spotted the mouth of a cave in the rock wall in front of us, so close we could almost touch it. We had been hiking for three hours when the forest opened onto a small field, no more than twenty or thirty feet from the edge of the bottom of a cliff that rose above us about two thousand feet. I would have run up and hugged the cave except for the rope full of friends we tugged along and the giant mountain troll sleeping across the mouth of the cave.

"Let's go." Tony headed across the clearing.

I yanked his arm. "What about the troll giant?"

"We'll climb over him. Let's hurry before he wakes up." Tony yanked us towards the cave and the sleeping troll.

"How come he's so big when the trolls back at the Wheaton When Portal are so small?" Snpgrdxz asked.

Tony rubbed his chin. "He's a different breed. Has but one eye. Some people call it a troll while others call it a Cyclops. Either way, this monster is a big, mean killer. Now, let's move out before he wakes up."

Snpgrdxz and I must have been too tired from fighting vampires because we followed Tony up to the troll, who picked that moment to pass gas. Sorry if you find it amusing or inconvenient, but you never know when a giant troll will cut loose.

We had to cross a soft mountain of blubber filled with the wrong kind of gas while we held our breath. We pulled and prodded our little charges to climb with us.

We descended the Cyclops into the cave while we were connected so we could cross the when portal to the same when and where. This of course assumed the cave led to a when portal.

I brought up the rear. The rear of our party, not the troll's rear, which at the moment was parked against the cave. The troll roared when I jammed Third Jennifer's spear into his cheek by accident. His butt cheek. He roared from both ends, releasing a huge aromatic green gas cloud. The sound and smell must have scared my Jennifer because she picked this moment to slip down the back of the troll toward the cave entrance while tugging the rest of us along.

The troll jerked up which knocked us into the cave.

***

My Jennifer hit the cave floor right below me as I plopped on top of her. She screamed as I rolled off. The others landed around us. Memory or no memory, my Jennifer did not appreciate my touch.

"Run!" Tony yelled.

The troll or Cyclops reached into the cave with a giant fist. We avoided him by dragging our zombie-head companions deeper than his arm could reach. He expressed his frustration by roaring at us.

"So, where's the time portal?" Tony asked.

Snpgrdxz responded, "How should we know?"

"We better find one because we can't go back the way we came," I said.

Snpgrdxz led the rope of friends deeper into the cave. "Follow me. And grab hands everyone."

I laughed at Snpgrdxz's command while I held fast to my Jennifer. No way would I lose her. "Stop," I said. "We need to have everyone join hands."

Our friends resisted holding hands so we retied them at the wrist but tighter than before. Now, everyone touched someone else. We had our line of people to go through the portal together, if we found a when portal in this troll cave.

Tony said, "This is good. Let's bow our heads before we go deeper."

Snpgrdxz surprised me again as he bowed his head with us.

Tony prayed, "Lord, we don't know when or where we're headed, but you do. Lead us where you want us to go and bring us home safely. Amen."

Tony taped a flashlight to his M16 and led us into the depths of the cave. I carried Third Jennifer's silver spear because you never can tell what you'll run into in the dark. Snpgrdxz took charge of the rope as we moved forward.

"I didn't know aliens prayed," I said.

"Why wouldn't we?" Snpgrdxz replied.

Before I could answer, Tony passed through the portal. We were about a hundred paces into the darkness.

Fortunately, the rope trick worked as we headed into the light.

CHAPTER 21

A NEW WHEN

Tony splashed and screamed in the water of our new when place. "It's freaking cold."

"Where are we?" I asked.

"Under London Bridge," Tony said.

"How can you tell?" Snpgrdxz asked.

"Been to Lake Havasu City, Arizona. This is it." Tony climbed out of the water and patted the stone arch we stood under.

"This doesn't look like Arizona," I said. "Too much smog. How about Los Angeles?"

"It ain't." Tony gazed around at the bridge. "And how did we get here?"

"We must have come through the stone arch, but where's the opening on this side?" I asked.

"It's a one-way portal," said Snpgrdxz.

"So we have no way back?" I asked.

"Not through this portal." Tony pounded on the stone support for the bridge above us.

"I'm cold and we're stuck in the wrong time forever." I became weepy again so I hugged my blank Jennifer. We were both shivering. My Jennifer pushed me away.

"At least you're not in nineteen eighteen," Tony said.

"We're together even if our friends have forgotten us," Snpgrdxz said.

"And none of the Jennifers showed up in nineteen eighteen Wheaton, but where are we?" I asked.

"Earth," said Snpgrdxz.

Tony said, "We're in a city. It must be London if this is London Bridge. Let's go up to street level and find a hotel. We can use a hot bath and a hot meal. Along the way, we can figure out how to restore everyone's memories. Then we'll shop for proper attire consistent with this time period, whenever we are."

"What about money?" I asked.

"How about that solid silver spear you're carrying. And we have our gold rings." Snpgrdxz jiggled his pocket.

"Let's find out when we are before worrying about where we will stay," said Tony.

"Let's snag a hotel room and clean up so we can catch a flight home. If we don't have enough money, we can always use plastic. I have a card Mom gave me for emergencies," I said.

We were under the first arch of the bridge and climbed up the river embankment to the street level. The smog curled along the cobblestones and mud used for streets. The aroma of molten iron, burning coal, raw sewage, rotting vegetables and dead meat combined into one awful smell. We were in a loud neighborhood where horses clopped, wagons squeaked, and people hustled along as they shouted to each other. They wore clothes appropriate for a Dickens novel costume party.

"Don't think your plastic will work here, Bryan" said Snpgrdxz.

"What can we use for money in Dickens's day?" I asked. "I mean this spear and our gold rings will take us so far, right?"

Tony glared at me like I was crazy and my IQ had dropped about twenty points. "So, Bryan, what do you think the solid silver spear in your hand is worth?"

With the smog, all three Jennifers wheezed and sneezed by the time we crossed the street. Tony inquired of a portly gentleman for a silversmith in his best imitation English accent.

"Oh, Americans is it? And whores to boot? And with a Negro slave in tow? Yes, of course. Silversmiths you say? Go down this street straight as it parallels the Thames. Turn left at the first corner there by the pub. You can't see it at the moment what with the foul air about, but it's the Bull and Crapper. Don't ask why. Not a crapper in the place. Everyone uses the alley or the river. Once you've had your pint at the corner pub, turn left, as I said, then you go straight one more block and turn left again. Yes, that should do it. Oh and on the next corner, turn left. Silversmiths is the second shop from the corner."

"Let's see, three lefts, you say?" I asked.

"Yes, that's it. Start here. To the Bull and Crapper, have a pint, then two more lefts. Second shop from the corner. Did I mention stopping at the Bull and Crapper for a pint?"

"Or we could skip the pint and go up the street here about three quarters of a block," said Snpgrdxz in his best Daniel Brickmaster form.

"No, no, you would miss the pub. The Bull and Crapper. Very important place. Friendly to visitors. We allow a few of you ladies of the evening if you don't mind my saying so. Leave the spear outside, I'm afraid. Don't like weapons unless you're in uniform. And the Negro slave won't do at all."

Tony backed the man up against the wall of the nearest building. "Good of you to notice our weapon, but bad form to call our women whores. And you're not to call the King of Ethiopia here a slave. He's liable to slit your throat."

The Englishman belched. His breath made us turn away to gag, including our brainless friends. His teeth, what there were of them, were green with rot. "Yes, I calls them as I sees them, don't I? And I says I sees whores and a slave boy. No way of telling you're not whores. Why aren't you? You dress them as men or worse. What are those strange things you're wearing?"

Snpgrdxz said, "The clothes are from America. We're off the boat from our African safari."

The Englishman smiled. "Safari, you say? What's that?"

Tony chimed in. "We hunted elephants in Niger and lions in Ethiop."

"Yes, lions and elephants are good, but for now I'm off to the Bull and Crapper. Good day to you." The man smiled at us like a used car salesman lost in a Dickens story and strode off in the direction he had indicated for the Bull and Crapper.

"This way," Tony said and headed in the direction opposite the way the Englishman had suggested.

Over his shoulder the Englishman called, "Yes, you could go that way, if you wish. It works. But you'll miss the pub as I said."

"Important to you, Mister pub owner," I said.

The portly gentleman stopped a man dressed in what appeared to be a police officer's uniform, but it was difficult to say for certain. The two of them engaged in an animated conversation as the pub owner's arms flailed about and pointed often in our direction. The cop's uniform had a nineteenth century flair to it. But he also wore a tall silk hat which confused me.

We could hear their voices rumble but couldn't make out what they said until the cop shouted, "Whores is it? We shall see to that, we shall."

As the police officer headed in our direction, he shouted, "Hey, you there."

CHAPTER 22

A TINY JENNIFER HAWKINS

"Bug-ger." The little girl picked herself up and shook dust off her rags. About five years old, she shivered and rubbed her upper arms.

"Sorry," I said. "I didn't mean to knock you down. We're in a hurry to the silversmiths."

"Silversmiths, sir? Follows me. I'll show the way for but a ha'penny." The little girl held out a tiny, frail upturned palm.

"But it's right there," said Tony.

I picked the frail child up. "A ha'penny for the little girl, says I. She needs it more than we do. And we've not time to argue." I carried the girl as we tugged the rope of friends to the silversmiths.

Along the way, the little tyke stared at Third Jennifer. "Mommy?"

Despite the gray, sooty fog, we found the shop under the sign of J.R. Pierpont, Silversmiths. Lost in the fog behind us, we could hear the footsteps of the cop as he approached. We followed Tony into the store, roped friends in tow.

A gray-haired man dressed in a beige vest decorated with violet maple leaves approached. He wore a fine silk waist coat and pinstriped cotton trousers with alternating dark blue and white stripes. The stripes were about one-quarter of an inch wide. I didn't see a belt, but lots and lots of buttons lined his clothes from neck to feet. His shoes were black leather polished to a high shine. Laces held his shoes in place not unlike shoes in our day.

As the man approached, he waved us towards the exit. "Hey, you, no beggars allowed. This is a decent shop. What would the neighbors think? Off with you before I send a clark for the constable."

"You look like my mommy," the child said to Third Jennifer.

Third Jennifer did not respond.

Snpgrdxz said, "We're newly arrived from foreign lands, sir. We're not beggars, but we are short of funds, except for a bit of gold and this spear of solid silver given to us by the King of Ethiopia himself. Perhaps you'd like to examine the thing with an eye toward purchasing it for the value of the metal. It's heavy and I have been given to understand it is of the highest purity. You may make an offer, if you wish or we may remove our business to another purveyor of silver."

"Little Jenny there in that one's arms, the one with the fleas hopping about her head to keep her lice company, is the local sort. Out w'her. She's nothin' but trouble since her ma passed."

I lowered the girl to the floor. "She's with us now, but we'll need to bathe."

Snpgrdxz stepped in front of us. "About the spear, sir?"

"Solid silver, you say? Please allow me to examine it." The silversmith held his hand out.

"How come she looks like mommy? And that one, too. And that one. Three mommies but not my mommy." The little one sat on the floor and cried.

I handed over our fortune to the silversmith.

A bell over the shop door jangled as the cop in the tall silk hat entered. "There you are. Come along now. Don't give us any trouble. Whores and slaves and their ruffians to boot. And brandishing a weapon is it? And what's this, Little Jenny 'awkins to boot? I'll take the belt to her, I will, or my name isn't Officer Barnaby." Officer Barnaby turned to the silversmith. "Hope these rapscallions haven't been a bother to you, sir?"

"No bother, officer. Quite interesting. How in blazes did the King of Ethiop end up with a troll spear? See here, officer, we haven't seen a silver troll spear in the neighborhood since the new bridge opened back in 'thirty-two. It appears to be authentic, but why a silver troll spear, may I ask?" The silversmith held the spear to his mouth and took a bite.

The policeman grabbed for the silver spear, but the silversmith stepped back.

The officer's face turned red. "Now, now, we can't have any of that. I'll take the spear for evidence, I will. Hand it over."

"But, officer," said the silversmith, "These aren't the scamps you suppose them to be. Why, they're distinguished visitors from America on a world tour. They've run short of capital upon arrival in London and seek to exchange their most treasured possession for the funds necessary for their return trip home and to replace their garments lost at sea. Isn't that correct, your majesty?"

Snpgrdxz stepped in front of Gilbert. "His majesty agrees, my good man."

"Your majesty? I'll be tarred if this bloke's a majesty," the officer harrumphed.

"Why he is no less than the King of all the Ethiops landed upon our shores," said the shopkeeper. "You'll be lucky to escort him to Buckingham Palace, I'm sure."

"I suppose if you vouch for them, I have no need to arrest them, but careful now. They may yet turn out to be thieves and liars, what with Little Jenny amongst them. King of Ethiop my donkey's bottom." The officer huffed through the door as the bell tinkled above.

***

130

"You'll have to leave it for a few days." The silversmith leaned our spear against the oak-paneled wall behind him.

Snpgrdxz said, "That ain't about to happen."

"What's the problem?" the silversmith asked.

Tony reverted to the sixties hippie language which sounds a lot like English except for the part where you don't understand most of the words spoken. "Dude, the spear belongs to us. We don't be needing to leave it with nobody what then don't never heard of us when we come back in a few days, like you say."

The silversmith scratched his head. He checked with a glance to Little Jenny as though she may have understood. Giving up hope for help in her direction, what with Jenny's face buried in my shirt, he turned back to Tony. "I say, you are from America are you not? Can any of you tell me what the gentleman said in his native Algonquin language?"

Snpgrdxz took a crack at responding, "He means if you mess with us, we'll have to kill you."

"Yes, I see. Here in London, of course, the word of J Rutledge Pierpont is good upon any arrangement. But in your wilderness country with so many natives with tomahawks and chopping one's scalp off, yes, you must need everything in writing as your business associate may at any moment lose his mind and not recall the details, so everything is written upon velum, never mind the goose or his sacrifice of a tail feather. I'm certain you Americans must insist on everything witnessed and attested to by a bailiff. As that is your custom, then J Rutledge Pierpont will accommodate your wishes, my friends."

"Say what?" I fixed my eyes on the silversmith.

Little Jenny took a gander up from my waist. "Says I, you receives his paper for your silver, says he. Legal and right proper to boot, says he."

"He agreed to give us a receipt for the spear," Snpgrdxz said.

"Yes," said Tony.

"Here's what I suggest," said J Rutledge Pierpont. "First, may I introduce myself?"

We waited.

He waited.

Little Jenny kicked me in the shins as I caught onto the culture. Words here meant exactly what they meant. He asked for our permission before he introduced himself. I figured I could handle the task and broke the silence. "Yes, of course you may."

"I am J Rutledge Pierpont, proprietor of Pierpont Silversmiths, your humble servant. May I inquire of you as well?"

We introduced ourselves, but stuck with the unlikely story that we were a band of American adventurers, newly arrived from Ethiopia. Little Jenny introduced herself as "Little Jenny 'awkins, says I, orphan to the world, in search of vittles and a warm bed."

"Why are your silent friends tied together at the wrist?" asked J Rutledge Pierpont.

"All the better to keep them from wandering off," I said. "They're under a spell."

"Spells is it?" asked J Rutledge Pierpont. "Appears to me your friends passed through the underworld. More like to see vampires and zombies come out of the underworld then Ethiops. Least in these parts. That's why we walled it up so as to keep the villains out and us in London."

"Believe what you wish, Mr. Pierpont. We deny nothing," I said.

"Where there are spells, there are counter spells, gentlemen. I'll send my spells remover to you. For a fee she'll soon restore your friends," said J Rutledge Pierpont.

"We pay upon results," said Snpgrdxz.

"Then results ye shall have or my name's not J Rutledge Pierpont. And you'll want clothing appropriate to London and a place to stay, I suspect." J Rutledge Pierpont tapped his nose with a forefinger.

"And we'll need to eat," said Tony.

"What say I advance you a small sum to tide you over until I can have the value of your spear ascertained? Would, say, fifty pounds serve your needs?"

"Having no knowledge of the value of an English pound sterling in, what year did you say it was?" Snpgrdxz asked.

"My word, one suspects the same year it is in your America and Africa." J Rutledge Pierpont lifted a monocle from his vest pocket and squished his right eye upon it. "But never you mind, sir. J Rutledge Pierpont understands your predicament in not knowing the when of your when. You're not the first to pass through the London Bridge When Portal and I suspect you'll not be the last despite our poor attempts to block it off with a new bridge.

"And this year would be?" Snpgrdxz asked.

Little Jenny pointed a tiny index finger to the ceiling. "Says I, I says, you have arrived in the year of Our Lord one thousand eight hundred and thirty eight."

Paul R. Lloyd

CHAPTER 23

SETTLING IN LONDON

"Let's see, a twenty pound solid silver spear would be worth about three hundred fifty pounds sterling, and fifty pounds sterling should see to our immediate needs for some time. In fact, it should serve us." Tony held out his hand.

"Bug-ger," said Little Jenny.

J Rutledge Pierpont ignored Tony's hand. Instead, he disappeared into a back room. He called behind him, "Won't take long. Patience please."

I grabbed the spear and took up a battle stance.

Snpgrdxz asked, "You don't trust him?"

"Trust will get you killed faster than caution." Tony stared into the back room. He yanked his M16 from his backpack and held it at the ready.

A knock on a distant door from above followed a set of footsteps on a stairway. Muffled voices sounded, one male and one female. Feet pounded in the reverse direction on the steps. A daintier foot patter came next. A general knocking about of things in the back room brought the sounds closer. There was a call of "blasted key!" from a male voice that I took to be J Rutledge Pierpont. An elderly feminine voice cackled. Metal squeaked upon metal. A sack of coins or screws or other small metal objects rustled. The metal squeaked again, followed by the clanging of keys.

J Rutledge Pierpont returned to the front room. A gray-haired, wrinkled woman in a torn and tattered old gown

134

followed him. The black dress with its many patches covered her from neck top to toes. The woman stood with hands folded over a large carpet bag. She wore a toothless grin.

J Rutledge Pierpont held out a small carpet bag to Snpgrdxz. "I've thrown in a purse for you to keep your funds. You'll find both silver coins and paper currency. Sorry for the inconvenience of paper, but most shops will accept it in these modern times. If not, the paper is good to exchange for silver or gold at any bank."

I took the purse. "Count it, Daniel."

Snpgrdxz rifled through the bag. "The numbers add up to fifty."

Tony grabbed the sack and stuck his nose into it. He lifted his face out. "It's here. Give the man the spear."

"What about our gold rings and coins?" Snpgrdxz asked.

Tony stuffed his M16 into his backpack. "Let's hold onto them. We have enough in our purse for now."

"And if need arises, we still have gold rings and coins. Good thinking," said Snpgrdxz.

The old lady appraised raggedly Little Jenny. "What's the likes of 'er doing 'ere?"

I handed our silver spear to J Rutledge Pierpont.

The elderly lady continued to glare at Little Jenny.

J Rutledge Pierpont sniffed the spear as though he hadn't tried to take a bite out of it earlier. He positioned it next to his body like a warrior at the ready. "Now as to your garments, victuals and other essentials, Miss Merklebun will be glad to assist. She lives upstairs in rooms rented from me. If you like, you may also rent rooms above or choose an inn in the city to your own pleasure. And if you are of a mind to restore your friends, she'll know who to send for to mix the potions and say the spells sure to work wonders for you."

Miss Merklebun bowed. "I'm pleased to accommodate such distinguished guests as you might be. You'll soon have your rooms above and clothing and victuals to boot once I takes out this bit of garbage as followed you in."

"She's with us," Tony said.

"What, 'er?'" Miss Merklebun cried. "She has the devil in her, she has. Best to drag her to the river and drops her in weighted to a stone."

Tony's face reddened as he pointed a bony finger at Miss Merklebun. "I said the tiny Wild Thing is with us. She's related, a long lost member of our extended clan."

Miss Merklebun backed away from Tony. She glanced at his finger and then to J Rutledge Pierpont. "She do resemble your women."

J Rutledge Pierpont shrugged.

"As you wish, then. Not my doings. Not upon my 'ead is she? Come along then." Miss Merklebun headed for the shop's front door.

"Wait," said Snpgrdxz. "What will this cost us?"

After a discussion among ourselves and Tony's assurance the price was within reason, if a tad inflated due to us being strangers and imposing the "likes of the wee flea-bitten bit of 'ell upon the 'ouse," we accepted the offer.

***

"Don't mind the darkness nor the cold, my dears, as these upper rooms have not been let in these many months since the last tenant, God rest her poor soul, met with an untimely, as they say, departure. And the lack of renters is not because of the resulting ghost, I'm sure." Miss Murklebun opened the entrance door with an old-fashion iron key.

The door to the "upstairs rooms" opened on a common room with a fireplace big enough for heating and cooking. A worn wooden table and chairs provided a space for eating. Wooden shelves covered the wall next to the chimney to complete our little kitchen. China plates, bowls and cups lined the shelves.

"If the rooms have not been let in months, how come you have a fire burning?" Tony asked.

Miss Murklebun started to answer, but froze with her hand partially raised and her toothless mouth wide open. She raised a finger as if to speak, but stopped. She paced in front of the fireplace before poking at the fire with an iron rod she found leaning against the wall. "The mores I thinks on it, the mores I thinks there's no telling in ways you will believe."

"Try us," I said.

The old lady glanced about the room. "I feeds the fire to keep the ghost warm. There, I said it. The poor dear as departed these premises spent many a cold night in here, I can tell you. Now as she's gone to a better place, I'm hoping a warm spirit darsen't haunt them as warms them so I keeps a fire in 'ere, I do, and you'll have no midnight visits from ghosts nor ghouls."

Not spying any "ghosts nor ghouls," nor worrying about how her former tenant could be in a better place and still haunt the premises, I looked for the silverware, but didn't find any. A bench under the shelves appeared as though the seat opened, however.

The common room included several oak chairs upholstered in a red, green and yellow plaid. They were more like large dining room seats than living room furniture. Carvings of angels and gargoyles decorated the straight back and curved legs. They didn't appear comfortable, and when I lowered myself into one, it wasn't.

Miss Merklebun pulled a large teapot from one of the shelves and set it on the table. She snagged an iron pot from the hearth and placed it on the fire. "Now whilst the water simmers on the fire, I'll run along to find my friend Rosie. She performs the memory restorations. I won't be long for she has let the second floor parlor, she has."

Miss Merklebun vanished out the door and down the stairs.

***

We heard her loud knock upon a door on the second floor.

"Rosie, I've customers for you. Are you about, my dear?" Miss Merklebun banged on the door again.

We heard the squeal of door hinges, "What-a-yer want, Miss Merklebun? You know I sleeps when I sleeps and works when I works which isn't your timing but mine."

Miss Merklebun said, "Come see the new tenants upstairs, Rosie. They've troubles only you can fix for a many of them has lost their memories."

"Ah-ha, travelers upon the Stygian sea as overstayed their welcome in the land of old Daemon Turpelator. I shall find what I needs in this here traveling bag and follow you and it up the stairs. They shall part with a pretty coin or two for old memory's sake or my name's not Rosie." She laughed.

Two sets of feet pounded up the staircase. Daniel held the door for them. Miss Merklebun entered carrying the satchel mentioned by Rosie below. Rosie appeared at the door dressed in a bright yellow dress with large flowers of every sort of color printed upon the fabric. The dress covered every inch of her head to toe, the same as Miss Merklebun's rags. Rosie's skin was as dark as Gilbert's. Her hair was raven black and curly with many hints of gray splashing about. Her accent, while suggesting a long time among Londoners nevertheless sported a Jamaican twist.

As she passed Daniel, Rosie patted his chest, "No needs to change this one, he changes himself." She laughed the rest of the way into our new accommodations.

"Gather them as needs their memory restored about the table 'ere. That's right. Sit down nice and cozy like. I've just the thing for them that forgets." Rosie withdrew a large glass jar filled with tiny dead plant leaves from her carpetbag. She handed it to Miss Merklebun.

"And before I forgets, tis a gold coin I'll be having for me troubles." Rosie held out her hand as Tony placed a gold ring on her palm. She rubbed the ring, gummed it, I supposed, more out of habit and to honor the memory of teeth than to test the quality of the metal. She held the ring in front of her eyes and then placed it on the ring finger of her right hand. "Pretty as you please, but so many of you, I'll be needing a coin or ring each."

Tony made no attempt to negotiate with Rosie. Instead, he paid the bill from coins he found in his backpack rather than our carpetbag.

Rosie glared at Tony as though he did something wrong in not negotiating the price. To Miss Merklebun, she said, "Will you be so kind as to lift the cork from me jar, my dear."

"What is that?" I asked.

Rosie crushed some of the weeds between her thumb and fingers before dumping it into the teapot. "Not your usual tea leaves, young man. What we have here is a powerful concoction of special herbs known only to meself."

"What do you call it?" Snpgrdxz asked.

"Weed. Now quiet yourselves and let me pour in the water uninterrupted." She filled the teapot from the hot iron vessel. She inhaled the steam before placing the lid on the teapot. "She'll brew up right fine as we set our minds on prayer for those that can't pray for themselves."

"You will restore their memories with prayer?" Snpgrdxz asked.

Tony slapped Daniel on the shoulder. "Never underestimate the power of a Christian prayer, especially when combined with medical use, young man."

"Now let's pray for the strengthening of your faith for it is by faith we are healed or so says the good book." Rosie bowed her head and recited a most poetic entreaty that praised God and begged for healing of the memories of our friends. After a few minutes, I noticed she had moved into preacher mode and from there to ranting about the evils of this world and how it is well with our souls to ask God to forgive and forget the evil of our ways "as far as the east is from the west."

She finished with a petition for the eternal rest of "the ghost of our dearly departed Millie as still walks these halls unencumbered by the distractions of neither life nor limb, despite her being dead and buried at St. Edmunds, Staffordshire, these past many months, the poor dear." She also asked for "the conversion of us heathen visitors from foreign shores who know not the ways of the Bible." She closed with an Amen that we all repeated.

"Let's pour a cup for them as needs it. And add a spoon of honey if you mind the flavor." Rosie yanked a jar of honey and a teaspoon from her carpetbag. She poured the brew for each of our mindless friends. The amazing thing was they knew to drink their concoction. Their forgetfulness did not take away their understanding of English or their ability to drink when ordered.

CJ was the last one to take a sip but the first to come around. Within a few minutes everyone's memory awakened. They each asked the same question: How did I get here?

Except my Jennifer. As tears streamed down my face, I begged her to come around, but she didn't respond to the tea despite her two other selves popping right out of it.

We gathered in a circle and prayed again. With the aroma of the odd tea wafting about the room, our tiny new friend prayed a beautiful little prayer for her new auntie to come around.

My Jennifer woke up at the end of Little Jenny's prayer. She gazed about with a confused, frightened face. "I want my mommy."

"Shh, no worries, darling." I hugged my Jennifer.

She glared at me and pulled away. "Who are you?"

"I'm Bryan. You know me." My stomach flopped over.

"I do? I know Tony and Gilbert and Daniel and my other selves, CJ and Third Jennifer. I know me. But I don't know you or this little girl or these women. And where are we? Aren't we still in Wheaton?"

Gilbert said, "Don't you recognize Bryan? You two have loved each other since kindergarten and first grade."

"We know each other?" my Jennifer asked.

Tony stood up. "Let's give Wild Thing time. She'll come around. Meanwhile, let's figure out the sleeping arrangements and find dinner. I don't know about the rest of you, but I'm starved."

Three bedrooms opened off the common room. The three Jennifers took one room. Fireman Frank and Tony took the one in the middle. Gilbert, Snpgrdxz and I took the third.

"Where do I sleep?" Little Jenny asked.

"You'll crash with me, missy," said Third Jennifer. At some point, Little Jenny had wandered into Third Jennifer's arms.

"Ah, bedfellows well met," snorted Miss Merklebun.

"Where's the bathroom?" asked Third Jennifer.

"Yeah, the bedfellows want to bathe together," laughed Tony.

"Bathroom?" gummed Miss Merklebun. "A room for bathing? Your America must be rich indeed if your houses have a room set aside to clean yourself. Best I cans do is offer a bowl and pitcher of water once a week. Cost you extra, it will."

"How about every day?" CJ asked.

Rosie laughed. "Every day is it? What with your falls at Niagara I'm sure you have more water in America than all England combined, but here we don't always sees fresh water unless you goes yourself to the river to fetch it, never mind the sewage."

Fireman Frank had a look on his face that my English teacher, Miss Throngbottom, would have described as bemused. He said, "We'll need a bowl and pitcher for each of us, Miss Merklebun. You may run and fetch them for us. We'll pay you a reasonable price and no more. I don't know much of your currency as yet, but I suspect it shouldn't do to pay you more than a shilling for your effort."

"A shilling is it? You'll pay the shilling and shares the bowl and pitcher I brings you. The very idea of a house with eight bowls and pitchers or do you not mean to bathe your African?" Miss Merklebun asked.

"We need to wash up, Miss Merklebun. And we'll need clean water that you have boiled for at least ten minutes," said Frank.

Rosie busted out laughing again. "Ten minutes a bubbling on the fire? Eight bowls full? Carried up here?" She laughed her way out and closed the door. We heard her laughter with each footfall on the steps down to the second floor.

Miss Merklebun said, "I'm an old lady of forty-five, and I'll not kill meself for the likes of American strangers. The very idea. You'll pays me a shilling each time you wants a pot of boiled water. You can wash yourself in the pot for all I care. I may flavor the soup with your leavings. And I'll have a boy bring it to you. Fresh water, cooked. Next you'll want meat in your victuals."

Miss Merklebun bowed her head and retraced her steps to the door where she turned, smiled and held out her hand. "I'll take the shilling in advance and because you've but big coins in your purse from Mr. Pierpont, you can give us a pound and I'll hold it on account. Covers room, rent and food, too. Can't get a better deal this side of the Thames."

"Who bathes first," Gilbert asked.

I gazed at my friend Gilbert like he had lost a few brain cells back in troll land. "Third Jennifer and Little Jenny."

Everyone else had the same idea because they named Third Jennifer at the same time.

"Three years in troll land works up a bouquet, I'm sure. I'm used to the foul perfume of troll and have no complaints of the rest of you, so for the sake of your noses, I'll take the first bath and the tiny sister here will join me. "

The tiny sister scratched and made no protest. "What's a bath?" she asked.

CHAPTER 24

LEARNING THE BASICS

"Where do we pee?" my Jennifer stood with legs crossed.

Miss Merklebun smacked a young boy about the head while he carried a large pitcher of water to the table in our open room. "Peas is it? Why in summer vegetable season I suspects you would find your peas and carrots to boot." Miss Merklebun laughed.

CJ said, "Follow me."

"Oh, the privy pails are under the beds. Just dumps it out the back winder. You'd think you lacked for privy pails in your America." The old lady sat in one of the stuffed chairs and laughed so hard she had to grasp hold of her sides.

"What's a privy pail?" I asked.

My Jennifer followed CJ into her bedroom. She slammed the door behind her. She knew what to do with a privy pail and was in a hurry to do so.

Snpgrdxz and Miss Merklebun led a shopping expedition that returned an outfit for each of us, except for shoes, socks and underthings.

"You'll want to purchase them unmentionables and shoes to fit. Not proper for an old woman to guess about a man's personals," said Miss Merklebun.

Third Jennifer prepared our evening "victuals." Little Jenny ate like she had never seen a supper before. The rest of us had hardy appetites for the lamb stew as well. The stew was a meager mix of lamb, potatoes and onion in a thin broth. Third Jennifer served us bread Tony picked up from a local bakery.

"Now that Little Jenny is presentable, I agree she could be another Jennifer," said Gilbert.

I had noticed this also. I've known Jennifer Hawkins since kindergarten and Little Jenny reminded me of those ancient days.

"Who's your mother?" Third Jennifer asked.

Little Jenny bowed her head to supervise herself as she twiddled her thumbs. "Jennifer 'awkins, Miss, of this 'ere parish where they kep' us 'til the orphan man come for me and I rans away and you founds me."

CJ burst into tears. "Another me trapped in the time loop. Broke through the troll world same as us and came out in London. Married, had a child and died."

"Me mother never married," said Little Jenny. "Never a daddy for the likes of me. I'm no good they say."

"She has the Hawkins name," said Tony. "She has the Jennifer Hawkins aspect. And she is a mini Wild Thing. I say she's family and so she is." Tears dripped from Tony's eyes as he hugged Little Jenny.

Third Jennifer snagged Little Jenny and hugged her close. "You're with family now, sweetheart. And you are good as gold and among your aunts for we're sisters here gathered and we're all named Jennifer Hawkins, same as you, except it was your mother who was our sister, and you're sure enough our niece. Our long lost niece we didn't know was missing 'til now."

Little Jenny sat upon Third Jennifer's lap. She popped a pointer finger into the air. "Then I'm as happy as one little girl can be, new Aunt Third Jennifer. Will you be my new mommy, because I like you best? You're the most like my mommy."

"How's that, dear, as we're three twin sisters of different ages?" asked Third Jennifer.

The rest of us stared at Third Jennifer as if she didn't realize how different she was from her two younger Jennifer sisters.

"Three years among the trolls toughens a person, Third Jennifer," I suggested. "In the same way, a life in old London will toughen a street urchin, especially if she arrived penniless from the land of the trolls. I suspect Little Jenny sees her mother's toughness in you in a way CJ and my Jennifer can't have because they didn't undergo the same long trials."

"Where can we learn more about you and your mother, Little Jenny?" Snpgrdxz asked.

"Until the orphan man came, Reverend and Mrs. Turpelator cared for the likes of me and Ma. Please don't make me go back." Little Jenny ran into the bedroom and slid under a bed.

Fireman Frank poked his noggin under the bed. "You may stay here with us, little darling, where you are so loved. We'll not permit any harm to come to the likes of you."

Little Jenny, full of sniffles and boogers, crawled into Frank's waiting arms where she hugged him about the neck and wiped snot upon his shoulders.

"But we'll need to visit this Reverend Turpelator," Tony said. "He may have certain items that belonged to Jenny's mother. We'll need them for another time."

***

"I'm the girl's aunt from America. I've come for Little Jenny's things," said Third Jennifer. Snpgrdxz and I sat on either side of her on the couch in the manse where Reverend Turpelator lived with his wife.

The reverend was a tall, husky man who didn't look like our other Turpelators, from nineteen twenty-three, the troll world, or our twenty-first century home time. This Turpelator wore a heavy gold chain around his neck with a six-inch long cross attached. The cross came to a point at the bottom. He had an ugly, cruel complexion. He had more scars than skin on his gray face. I guessed he was in his fifties, but you can never be sure in eighteen thirty-eight. Everyone appears much older than they are. And if our Turpelator can morph into a giant, blood-sucking spider, he can morph into an ugly old pastor.

Mrs. Turpelator, on the other hand, had that submissive appearance people have when they cover up bruises and sore ribs. Her face was red, except for a black eye and scabs around her lips.

A third person was in the parlor with us. He wasn't introduced, but he seemed familiar. He had dark hair that reached almost to his shoulders and pork chop sideburns. A snarl appeared on his lips whenever he spoke, but overall the man appeared nice enough. He was younger than the reverend, maybe in his mid-forties. He didn't say much from his stuffed chair in the corner between a large window and the fireplace. He dressed in a nice suit with a funny checkered vest. He also wore heavy boots. They were more like the kind you'd expect a modern Texan to wear than an Englishman from Dickens' Day. The surprise was his bright and perfect set of teeth, something that didn't exist in nineteen twenty-three on forty-something aged adults and certainly didn't exist in middle aged adults in the eighteen thirties.

The room smelled of perfume and old cooking odors. To be honest, the house would benefit if aired out, but people didn't open their windows in January in this culture.

"What things?" Reverend Turpelator asked. A sly, thin grin crept across the full width of his face in the same way our other Turpelators smiled, so I was on my guard.

Third Jennifer glared hard at the reverend. "She and her mother lived with you for a time. We found Little Jenny on the street, no thanks to you. I want any possessions that belonged to her or her late mother. They are important to me and have no value to you."

"A thing has value in proportion to its desirability. And the child and her mother lived in my home at my expense for a period of years. A small remuneration for my services on the girl's behalf would be appropriate, don't you think?" Reverend Turpelator leaned back in his chair and played with the large cross he wore around his neck. The smile remained as though painted on his face. "I wouldn't bring this up, but you understand how difficult finances are for a man of the cloth."

"Very noble of you, Reverend, I'm sure. Downright Christian in fact. But I'll have her things now, and we can discuss who the child's father is when you return them." Third Jennifer scowled at Reverend Turpelator.

Reverend Turprlator changed his smile from Christian to agnostic and cynical by the mere pressing of his lips tighter. "But my dear woman, we have nothing to return. What few articles the mother owned were given me upon her death to fetch what little I could for the charity I gave her for many years."

"We can discuss the child's father and any rights you may have in regard to the child after you give us the things we expect returned. For now, I need my dear departed sister's possessions. You wouldn't deny a woman a few mementoes of her departed sister, would you?" Third Jennifer stood.

Reverend Turpelator stood up. "As her property is no more, I suggest you return home now and tend to the child's needs. Will we see you at services on Sunday?" He smiled his best imitation believer's smile.

Snpgrdxz rose off the couch. "Let's go. Reverend Turpelator is right. We should return to Little Jenny."

"But I won't leave until I've seen what we came to see." Third Jennifer insisted.

"Daniel is right," I said.

"Why?" Third Jennifer asked.

"We've done all we can do here today," Snpgrdxz said.

Third Jennifer glowered at me. "Okay."

"Okay?" Reverened Turpelator turned the word over in his mouth. "What a queer way you Americans speak."

"I'll walk out with you," said the quiet gentleman.

CHAPTER 25

ANOTHER TIME TRAVELER

"Mayhaps I can assist you?" the quiet man said out on the street in front of Reverend Turpelator's manse.

"You can drop the imitation Dickens speak, Time Traveler," I said.

"Time traveler? How does one travel across time? The very idea is absurd." The quiet man rolled his eyes.

"As absurd as perfect teeth in the mouth of a mid-forties man in eighteen thirty-eight?"

The quiet man rubbed his teeth with a forefinger. "I thought my teeth would give me away eventually, but you're the first to say anything. Your teeth appear as though they've been cleaned by a dentist and well-preserved by fluoride toothpaste. Am I right?"

"You don't meet a fellow time traveler every day, do you?" Snpgrdxz asked.

"You're my first, friends," said the quiet man.

"You look familiar. Do we know you?" I asked.

"I don't think so. I'm an ol' hound dog from the Heartbreak Hotel." The man swung his hips about.

"Something about you is familiar," said Third Jennifer. "What's your name?"

"You may call me Tommy King, at your service, ma'am."

"And how might you help us?" Snpgrdxz asked.

"I share your concern for Little Jenny. I would have helped her myself, but she disappeared and I couldn't find her. Reverend Turpelator had turned her over to the workhouse, and she disappeared a short time after her arrival. They don't worry much about their orphaned young in this culture."

"We found her on the streets by London Bridge when we first arrived in the city. It took all of five minutes to find her, and we weren't searching for her. We didn't know she existed until we bumped into her." Third Jennifer glared at Tommy King.

"I thought you were her aunt?" Tommy asked.

"In a manner of speaking." Third Jennifer flashed a knowing smile at Tommy.

"Then you're not related?"

"We're more than related, Mr. King. Let us say she is an extremely close relative."

"In any case, I believe I can help if you'll permit me." Tommy made a little bow.

"Because you have such a lovely Tennessee accent, Mr. King, I will," said Third Jennifer.

**

My Jennifer refused to go out with me when I asked her, but with the persuasion of Gilbert and Tony, she acquiesced with a hesitant, fearful reply.

CJ offered to go with us. My Jennifer relaxed. She grinned. She said, "Thank you."

CJ replied, "But I won't. You have to face the love of your life alone. You may break up with Bryan if you wish, but you'll live to regret that, my dear sister. Just go out with him once and have fun. He doesn't bite. When you get to know him, you'll soon realize that you are the gutsy one, but he has his own charming ways."

My Jennifer faced me. "Once, okay?"

"Thank you," I said.

In the foul air of London, Jennifer and I meandered around the block without holding hands to the Bull and Crapper pub where we sat at opposite ends of a small table rather than side-by-side. I ordered tea for both of us.

I poured cream into my cup but it curdled. "I'm sorry you don't remember me, but we were in love. It saddens me to lose you."

Jennifer picked up the cream pitcher and took a whiff. Her face curdled. "Aren't you the boy in the tent? I was so embarrassed. But if you think about it, you didn't see anything you wouldn't have seen on a girl in a bikini at the Michigan Dunes. Still, it was embarrassing what with you in your underwear in a tent. You scared me. I may have screamed."

I stirred my tea, but the curdles refused to dissolve. "You did. And not to worry. You didn't see anything of me you wouldn't have seen at the beach."

"That's not funny. I thought you attacked me, but now that I think about it, were we lovers?"

I scooped sour stuff from my tea, but it appeared just as curdled. "We're both still virgins, but we cared deeply for each other. Dare I hope you will remember our love even if you can't remember me?"

"I don't think so, but I respect you for recognizing that I am a good girl. You frightened me, Bryan Ganarski, and I'm still afraid of you. I'm sorry." Jennifer dumped a heaping teaspoon of sugar into her tea.

"At least you remembered my last name."

"I did?" Jennifer dropped another scoop of sugar into her tea.

"You just said it."

Jennifer stirred her tea. "I did, didn't I? Where did that come from? I feel as though you're a nice person so my first impression was wrong about you." Jennifer's face reddened, "But why would you strip me naked in a tent if you weren't about to rape me?" She lowered her face to examine an interesting appearing fleck of black muck on the table.

I piled sugar into my tea, but it didn't help the spoilage. "You took your own clothes off so we could snuggle and stay cool."

"I undressed in front of a boy? I don't think so." Jennifer peeked at me once before returning to her biological study of the table dirt.

Stirring my tea caused an interesting design to form out of the dead cream curdles floating at the top of my tea. I may have invented a new art form for Tony's club back at Lincoln High. "Think again. Please. What might you do in front of the boy you love? "

Jennifer peeked again. "I wouldn't strip to my underwear, that's for sure. Not until we were married. Oh shit, are we married?"

"I would never hurt you. I don't have the guts to fight."

"You can say that again."

"I love you."

"No, the part about not having any guts. That I remember." Jennifer moved her tea cup to within a fraction of an inch of her lips.

"Well, I'm becoming braver, ain't I?"

Jennifer placed her teacup back on its saucer. "Are you? You must because you scare me. Oh, I don't know. I feel as though you're special, so I must remember things about you, or my body remembers you, or I don't know what to say without embarrassing myself. If you give me time, maybe I'll remember more and perhaps I won't be so afraid."

"We're not in a hurry, Jennifer. We'll have plenty of time to get to re-know each other before we return home."

"I miss mommy so much, but don't change the subject just yet. You didn't answer my question."

"No."

"You remembered my question?"

"You asked if we were married. The answer is no. We weren't engaged yet either. But we were in love with each other. Everyone knows we're a couple except you."

"I wish I could remember."

"Can we go out together in the meantime? We'll start over with a new first date."

Jennifer gazed into my eyes. "No."

"You said no the first time I asked you out so we're making progress." I stared into her soft, delicious green eyes.

"You have to know my mom and dad won't let me date until I'm sixteen." Jennifer shrugged.

"You are sixteen, Jennifer."

"Fifteen."

"We've been on the road for more than a year so you're closer to seventeen than to sixteen." I lifted my teacup. How bad could tea taste with curdled milk?

"Has it been that long?"

"Yes. More than six months in nineteen twenty-three. Who counted the months in the underworld of troll land and beyond? And now we're stuck in eighteen thirty-eight."

"Bryan, I've known Gilbert Armstrong since forever. He's too good of a friend to be dating material. Daniel is the new kid Snpgrdxz. I don't think I want to date an alien shape shifter from outer space. That leaves you as the other teenager in our group, but we just met, or so it seems to me. You appear to be a nice enough person once I get past the idea of you trying to rape me back in that tent."

"So you'll go out with me?" I spit a mouthful of tea back into my teacup.

"I'll think about it, okay? No promises. You have to make me not so scared of you."

I reached across the table to take her hand, but she pulled back as soon as I touched her.

CHAPTER 26

THE WEREWOLF OF LONDON

The full moon splashed ethereal light in my eyes when I opened them at what sounded like a madman attacking one of the Jennifers. Or the woman moaned from an insidious infection of this dark age we found ourselves in without benefit of antibiotics, although the mold on our bread looked promising. And you never knew what Tony would drag out of one of our backpacks. He found penicillin for my gunshot wound in nineteen twenty-three. Cholera was rampant in our neighborhood, and he found a sufficient amount of vaccine to inject us, not to mention the throwaway needles that he couldn't throw away as they were out of time. He returned them to his backpack never to be seen by the rest of us again.

I hurried into the common room and stumbled about until I found a curtain and opened it to allow the full moon's light in. I noticed a pile of ripped and torn rags in the middle of the room. Upon closer inspection, I identified these as a woman's shredded nightgown.

A scuffling noise came from below the floor. A woman screamed and a dog howled.

With my fears for Rosie below and that one of the Jennifers had been attacked and dragged off, I knocked upon the ladies' chamber.

I pounded on the door and waited.

I pounded again.

A groggy Third Jennifer cracked the door open. "What?"

155

"I heard noises. There are clothes torn and ripped. Someone may have been attacked. And I heard the most awful groans and grunts as when an animal is in peril." Don't you love the way I learned how to speak Victorian? Or pre-Victorian.

"In your dreams." Third Jennifer slammed the door.

I prepared to knock again but before I could, Third Jennifer opened the door.

"CJ isn't here," she said.

I woke the guys. After a brief discussion, we agreed Snpgrdxz and I would search the neighborhood for CJ. Frank and Tony would check on Rosie and Miss Merklebun in their separate flats. Third Jennifer and My Jennifer would stay behind to protect Little Jenny. We put Little Jenny in charge of sleeping until morning. We took her silence as a sign of consent.

While Tony pulled several pistols from his backpack, Snpgrdxz morphed into a striking imitation of my Jennifer. He borrowed women's clothes from the ladies and dressed over his male clothes.

"Why does he have to look like me?" my Jennifer asked.

"All the better to seduce your boyfriend, my dear." Snpgrdxz used his best big bad wolf imitation grandmother voice.

"I'll give you both a couple of clips loaded with silver bullets. Use them when you find CJ." Tony handed us a Glock and two magazines.

***

My feelings toward Jennifer popped up as Snpgrdxz and I wandered the late night streets of London. Thick smog and gloom filled the air, but with a companion who looked like Jennifer beside me, my thoughts turned to her. Did I feel affection for a male buddy who imitated Jennifer? "Hey, you promised never to shape shift into Jennifer again?"

156

"That was a long time ago in the future so I haven't promised yet, have I?"

"You look too much like her. Can't you morph into someone else? I mean, you make my blood boil."

"I didn't think. How's this?" Snpgrdxz's hair turned blonde as he reshaped his head to look like that movie star, the one who was always in trouble in Hollywood with publicity stunts to keep her in the news. You know the one. She was a great child actress, but now she couldn't handle an adult role. Yeah, that one.

"That's better. You look good, Daniel. I'm sorry, but when you are that attractive, you... you're..."

"Sexy?"

"Yeah."

"Want to kiss me?"

"NO!"

"You can if you want to. It's what friends are for."

"Not."

"You'll miss out on a great friend benefit."

I changed the subject. "How are we supposed to find CJ anyway?"

"Let's wander the streets until we hear screams."

"What screams?"

"Ahhhhhhhhh!"

"Those screams." Snpgrdxz took off but fell face first into the muddy street. I helped him up, and we charged towards a park across the way.

A woman ran out of the grounds. "Run for your lives!"

I stopped her. She bent over to catch her breath. "Big. Really big."

"Big what?" asked Snpgrdxz.

"Monster." The woman pointed to a large, furry creature running along the stone wall that separated the park from the street. It stopped and faced us. The woman screamed and ran away.

The roar of the beast frightened me. "What is it?"

157

"CJ." Snpgrdxz snapped his clip of silver bullets into his Glock and fired.

CJ, the huge werewolf, bared her six-inch fangs when she roared at us. Snpgrdxz's shot missed her by a good foot and a half.

"Aim," I screamed. "What am I saying? This is CJ you're about to shoot."

Snpgrdxz fired again. "I'm trying to miss her. We can corner her until the moon goes down."

CJ roared again before she executed a perfect furry backflip into the park. We gave chase, but she moved faster than my mom's Chevy.

"We have to catch her before she hurts someone," said Snpgrdxz.

"I'm open to ideas."

"I'll duck behind these bushes." The shrubberies in question were on the inside of the park up against the stone wall.

I couldn't see Snpgrdxz, but his clothes flew over the bushes in my direction. I gathered up the dress and his guy stuff. His shoes came over.

"Okay, catch the gun and my spare clip." The pistol bounced off my head, flew about ten feet away and landed on a rock where it kick-fired into a tree. I retrieved the Glock and the spare clip. I now had the extra clothes, two pistols, four clips loaded with silver bullets, and a roaring headache. I was ready for anything.

Anything except Snpgrdxz as he trotted out from behind the bushes as a pony. He wasn't big, but I was able to mount him. Snpgrdxz whinnied.

"Okay, I get it. My job is to hold on for dear life." I stuffed the guns in my belt and the clips in my pockets. I placed the clothes on the horse's back and climbed aboard.

Snpgrdxz whinnied again and took off at a gallop in the direction of CJ, the werewolf.

Three blocks later, Snpgrdxz stopped.

"What is it?" I asked.

His whinny sounded angry.

"Oh, you want me to shut up and listen." I dismounted and scoured the sky which was almost useless through the pea soup fog. A faint but large glow appeared above the house tops to the west. It was the moon. What else would be up in the sky in eighteen thirty-eight? But with time travel anything was possible.

For example, I don't think Snpgrdxz expected the roar to be so close to him or so loud. CJ, the werewolf of London, pounced on his horse back. Snpgrdxz crumpled into a huge ball of silly putty and rolled away.

Werewolf Jennifer gave chase like a dog after a ball, but gave up at about the same time I dropped the clothes and aimed my Glock.

Werewolf Jennifer roared once and rushed at me.

I shouldn't have closed my eyes before I fired.

CHAPTER 27

CJ THE WEREWOLF ATTACKS

I opened my eyes to find CJ, still the werewolf, charging at me. She roared her head off. Well, her head was still attached, but she had a bald streak off center of the top of her head.

She was a target headed in my direction so I aimed between where I thought her eyes were. Despite being a monster, she seemed to understand the intent of a pistol aimed her way because when I fired, her eyes weren't where they should be. But I caught her in a mid-leap and spin maneuver such that a patch of fur vanished from her butt to be replaced by a red streak as she bounded over the park wall while yelping in pain.

Snpgrdxz showed up as a butt naked version of my Jennifer. "Thought I'd entertain you."

In the distance, the beast howled, but the scary part was when the second beast hollered much closer to us.

Daniel Brickmaster (aka Snpgrdxz) dressed in his guy stuff but carried the girl clothes. We searched the park for CJ, but she had vanished.

"How does a werewolf disappear?" I asked.

"Two werewolves vanished. When the sun comes up, like now, for example, you can forget about spotting a werewolf."

"So she's CJ again?"

"She's naked so she may be hiding in the bushes."

She was. We whisked past a wiggling bush where a female voice whispered, "Bryan."

"I'm here," I said. "Where are you?"

"Here."

"I can't see you," I said.

"That's the idea," she said.

In the movies, a naked girl could hide in a bush and not become scratched. And in the movies, you wouldn't be able to penetrate the thick foliage to see her bare butt. The real world was not the same as the movies. I tapped CJ on her bare shoulder.

She jumped up so Daniel and I received a full frontal peak before she arranged her hands for her privacy. She ran around to the other side of the bush for more concealment. Her move provided us with a great rearview for half a second. So much for my worries concerning the concealment of Jennifer's private body parts until my Jennifer was ready to show them to me. I wasn't sure it made any difference anyway because my Jennifer no longer considered herself a "Ganarski woman."

Snpgrdxz handed the dress to CJ.

"Turn around, you jerks." CJ pulled the dress on over her head. Her breath reminded me of sardines, onions and old dead fish. This was not what I expected from a werewolf's mouth.

I complied with CJ's request to turn around. Daniel morphed into a Danielle but CJ didn't buy it.

"I said turnaround," she shrieked. "And please explain how I ended up naked in a park?"

***

"You guys didn't do it. You're too nice. Was it Frank?" CJ was dressed as she stepped out from behind the bush.

Snpgrdxz took a gander my way that made me feel like it was my job to tell her.

"You realize what happened to you last night, right?" I asked.

CJ raised her eyeballs like she was lost in thought as she attempted to find the answer to a math equation in Miss Gunderson's Algebra class. "I went to bed around tennish and woke up buck naked in a park in front of you boys. Hope you enjoyed the show. And by the way, my butt is frozen out here. Can we go home now?"

I checked out a few trees, made sure the grass was green even though it was February, and noticed a few plants sending up shoots around the edges of the greenery. London's climate was warmer than Chicago's. "You have no idea how you ended up here, dressed or undressed?"

"How much did I drink? It couldn't have been much. Did one of you boys slip me a Mickey Finn?"

"Mickey Finn?" I asked.

"Yeah, you know, knockout drops in my drink. Oh, I guess it's more of a nineteen twenties term than twenty-first century kid talk. Anyway, I drank wine with dinner."

I checked out what Snpgrdxz was up to. He waved his hand at me to indicate I should tell her. "Jennifer, I can't think of any easier way to say this, but you are a werewolf."

CJ landed butt first on the ground. She laughed so hard she was about to split her dress open. She wore the kind that's tight around the waist.

CJ slowed down to a few chuckles. "No, really. How did I end up butt naked in the park with you guys?"

Snpgrdxz offered a hand to help her up. "Bryan is correct."

"He is?" CJ planted her feet on the grass.

"I am," I said.

"How do you figure?" she asked.

I took CJ's hand in both of mine. "The full moon came out and you turned into a rip snorting werewolf. Ripped your things off and took off naked out for a night of dining on the town. Of course, you grew a fur coat for the occasion, but it vanished when the moon set."

"I went dining on the town dressed as a werewolf?" CJ asked.

"In a manner of speaking, of course," said Snpgrdxz. "What Bryan means is you set out to eat the people here in London, but you are not a capable hunter."

CJ slipped into a fit of coughing until she hacked out a fur ball.

I stroked CJ's hand. "Okay, so you caught a few squirrels or rats or cats or the occasional dog, but you had no such luck chasing down people."

CJ picked up her fur ball. "You're telling the truth then, aren't you?"

"Yes," said Snpgrdxz.

"You wore your fur coat." I patted her hand. "And we shot you with our silver bullets."

"You shot me? Good thing you missed."

"I didn't exactly miss," I said.

"You shot me? But Bryan, you're in love with me. How could you?"

"I'm in love with my Jennifer, not you."

"Same difference," she said. "Why didn't the silver bullets kill me?"

"I grazed you. You should have a scar along the left side of your scalp." I ran my fingers around her thick hair in search the scar and found it. "Your hair grew back while you changed to a regular person. And your wound healed right away, but the silver caused you to have a permanent scar."

"Let me feel." CJ fingered the scar. "This is new."

"You want to tell her about the other scar?" Snpgrdxz asked.

"She'll find out on her own," I said.

"What other scar?" CJ ran her hands around the front of her body. She patted down her boobs.

"Check your butt and you may find an extra crack." I took three steps back, but not fast enough to avoid the slap.

"You shot me in the butt with a silver bullet?"

"I grazed your ass. You may have a lovely scar to make your butt unique among Victorian ladies." I fell down as soon as her fist hit my jaw. When I came to, I laughed.

CJ cried. "You have to shoot me, don't you? I mean you can't let me stay alive come the next full moon, can you?"

"There has to be another way," I said.

"I prefer you shoot me, Bryan. You were my first love. You'll either shoot me or I'll shoot myself."

CHAPTER 28

DEATH OF A ROSE

CJ, Snpgrdxz and I pushed through a group of about ten people gathered at the entrance to our building.

"Officer says old Rosie's murdered," cackled a toothless old hag.

"She of the dark arts? Terrible plague upon us, I'm sure when she joins Old Scratch in his fiery furnace." A second neighborhood housewife laughed.

"Rosie weren't no heathen. A Christian she were and one as prayed for me manys the time, since the rhematiz invaded my knee." A third woman bent over to rub her knee.

Officer Miller blocked the way to our front door. "No one up or down, mates. Been bad business hereabouts or have you not heard?"

"Officer Miller, you know us. We're the Americans with the silver spear. We live here now."

"That do make a nevermind, I suppose. I'm thinking you are part them that stole Little Jenny off the streets and promised her a home better'n the workhouse."

"She's upstairs now fit as a fiddle," Snpgrdxz said.

"Then you best be up there but no stopping on the second floor where there's murder about."

We climbed to the second floor to find Tony in conversation with a uniform police officer and a plain clothes detective at the entrance to Rosie's parlor room.

Tony spotted us "Go on in. You three need to see this."

The police allowed us to enter. No one had bothered to cover poor Rosie so we gasped to see the huge bite taken out of her neck and the scratches on her body.

CJ fainted.

Daniel and I carried her up to our apartment.

CJ recovered in her own bed with Miss Merklebun and our ladies gathered around her. Tony, Frank, Daniel, Gilbert and I waited in the kitchen area eating lunch with Little Jenny. CJ's wailing and crying made us sad until she quieted down to sniffles and nose blowing. CJ entered the kitchen area assisted by my Jennifer and TJ, as we began referring to our Third Jennifer, on either side to support her.

CJ glanced at me like she needed a hug, but she reached out to Frank. "I killed her, Frank. I murdered that poor old lady."

"No you didn't." Frank patted CJ's head.

CJ sniffled. "What do you mean? I'm a werewolf. I ripped her throat out and scratched her body."

"No you didn't. You can't do that sort of thing. You're not wicked." Frank hugged her tighter.

"But I must have. I'm the only werewolf here."

Snpgrdxz Daniel said, "Technically, that's not true, CJ. Bryan and I heard a second werewolf while we chased after you."

"See, my dear. You're innocent of this madness," said Frank.

"Madness is right. I killed her. I must have. She lives just downstairs. Even if there was another werewolf, I would have gotten to her first."

I washed down a bite of sandwich with a glass of Miss Merklebun's well-boiled water. "If it's any consolation, I don't think you did it either, CJ. You may have the werewolf curse, but you're not a killer."

"Hey, are you guys eating lunch while I'm contemplating killing myself as a murderess and worrying about being strung up by my skinny girl neck?" CJ knocked over a chair and placed her hands on her narrow feminine hips.

Tony spoke through a mouthful of food. "We were hungry."

A knock at the door silenced us. Gilbert answered the door. Police Detective Barnaby entered with Officer Miller behind him.

Officer Miller dangled a small watch. "We found this watch in poor old Rosie's hand."

Detective Barnaby snatched the watch from Officer Miller. "We opened the back and noticed a name engraved on it. Jennifer Hawkins it reads. Mayhaps it belongs to one of your Jennifers?"

CJ fainted.

Frank caught CJ in his arms. "Isn't that the watch great grandma gave to CJ?"

***

"I confess," said CJ from her position on the floor.

"You do?" asked Detective Barnaby? "You killed old Rosie?"

CJ sat up and leaned against Frank. "I confess you found my watch. It was a gift from my great grandmother."

"Where's this great grandmother now?" Detective Barnaby asked.

"Busy being conceived," said Daniel.

"What's that you said," asked Officer Miller.

"Nothing," said Snpgrdxz.

"Anyway, ma'am, you may have your watch back. You no more killed old Rosie than you murdered your great grandmother," said Detective Barnaby.

"Did you kill your great grandmother?" asked Officer Miller.

CJ glared at Officer Miller.

Officer Miller returned the glare. "Well, she could have done them both. She's a werewolf, Detective Barnaby, sure as I'm standing here. Look at her. She has big teeth as white as snow. Whoever heard of a grown woman with white teeth? It's proof she's a werewolf."

"It proves she cleans her teeth right proper like. Let's go, Officer Miller." Detective Barnaby turned for the door.

"But how do we know she isn't the one as killed old Rosie?" asked Officer Miller.

Detective Barnaby said, "Did you see the size of the bite taken out of her neck? A young girl like our Miss Hawkins here couldn't possibly open her mouth that wide. The victim was killed by a man with a big mouth or jagged knife, but a werewolf didn't do it."

"How can you say a werewolf isn't on the loose here in London, Detective?" asked Officer Miller.

"Because there's no such thing. Werewolves are old wives tales and rubbish. Our job is to find a mad dog killer which none of these Miss Hawkinses is." Detective Barnaby stepped into the hallway.

"How do you explain the watch?" asked Officer Miller.

Detective Barnaby sighed. "Officer Miller, do you see a wild animal or mad killer here? Or smell such a thing?"

"This Miss Hawkins could a done it by faking the teeth marks," said Officer Miller.

"How?" Detective Barnaby asked.

"I don't know how, but she done it sure. Old Rosie nipped the watch off her dress when she were kilt."

"Okay, add Miss Hawkins to the suspect list, Officer Miller." Detective Barnaby pointed at CJ. "Miss Hawkins, you are now a suspect in the investigation of the murder of old Rosie downstairs. Don't leave the city as you may be needed for further questioning, and you may be subject to arrest should we find any evidence of your guilt."

CHAPTER 29

CJ GOES MISSING

To cheer CJ and make amends for shooting her twice during the night, Snpgrdxz and I invited her to The Bull and Crapper pub to celebrate the end of the full moon cycle. The others had eaten breakfast while waiting for us to return from our overnight werewolf hunt. They opted to stay behind to assist Miss Merklebun in cleaning up Rosie's rooms.

We found Tommy King nursing a cup of coffee in a corner. The walls were lined with oak boards darker than the early Middle Ages. A lone candle attempted to make light of Tommy's table.

"Need company?" CJ asked.

Tommy lifted his head from his coffee. "I'm not much company, I'm afraid. You see, I'm lonesome and I'm lovesick."

"We had a tough night, too," CJ said. "My boys here shot my ass."

Tommy tilted his head to the side. "Why'd they shoot your donkey?"

"Not my donkey, my ass. And they shot me in the head."

Tommy took on a thoughtful pose. "I see two fellas and a beautiful girl. That alone is enough to explain why one fella shot the other fella, but why would they shoot you? Oh, you cheated, you lied, and you broke their poor hearts, didn't you?"

"No, the moon was full and I turned into a werewolf," CJ moaned.

Tommy said, "Sit down and let's eat breakfast. Unless you already ate?"

"I'll stand if you don't mind," said CJ.

Snpgrdxz and I sat. CJ sat down gingerly. She glowered my way to remind me that it was my silver bullet that double-cracked her butt.

Half way through a plate of fried eggs, sausage and biscuits, Tommy said, "You folks will have to excuse me. I have someplace I need to be this morning. I forgot about it till now."

As Tommy disappeared out the front door of the pub, CJ headed for the ladies room, aka the alley behind the pub. CJ's scream was loud enough for us to hear in the pub. Snpgrdxz and I charged out to the back alley, but by the time we arrived, we saw no sign of CJ.

Snpgrdxz turned into a hound dog and stepped out of his man clothes. I picked up the clothes while Snpgrdxz nosed around. He changed his face back into a human shape and said, "This way."

I followed as Snpgrdxz tracked CJ.

Snpgrdxz lost CJ's scent in the middle of the block on Manfred Street by St. Ambrose's parish where Reverend Turpelator pastored.

Snpgrdxz morphed back into Daniel Brickmaster and dressed.

"Hey, what are you two up to?" screamed a voice from a window on the second floor of the house across the street.

"We're searching for a friend," I called back.

"No wonder your friend's gone missing, what with you boys parading about in the all together as it were."

"We weren't naked. Just my friend here." I pointed a finger at Snpgrdxz.

"Keep your shirts on in me neighborhood. We're descent folk here. You see the church you're in front of, don't you?"

"Will do," I said.

Snpgrdxz finished dressing. "It's like she vanished into thin air."

"Could her kidnappers have picked her up and thrown her into a wagon?" I suggested.

"Hey, mister, did you see a young woman thrown into a wagon and hauled off against her will?" Snpgrdxz shouted.

The man in the window rubbed his chin. "Indeed not unless…"

"You must have seen something," I called.

The man leaned far out his window. "I said indeed not and I means indeed not unless you means did I see a young lass taken by force into a wagon by her husband who has a right to abscond with a wayward whore of a wife, if you don't mind my using that word by the church."

"The man wasn't her husband. He kidnapped her."

"That may explain her resistance. Why would a lass resist her own family or isn't a man master of his own home no more?"

"Which way did they go?" I asked.

"The way you're pointed. And I have a bit of advice for you, lads, if you don't mind. Never interfere in a man's affairs, young men, especially if his affairs involve a resistant young woman."

"Thank you, sir." Snpgrdxz called.

"My pleasure, lads. Say, what have you boys done with the dog as led you up the street before?"

***

A conspiracy of friends set up the next situation where my former Jennifer and I found ourselves alone in the common room of our Dickens day digs.

"Hi," I said.

"We need to talk," my former Jennifer said.

"So the empty apartment, except for us, was a scheme of the heart?"

"CJ came up with the idea before she turned into the werewolf of London and disappeared. I had nothing to do with it and didn't want them to do it, but they believed we needed to talk, and they were right. They are our friends. And they're CJ's, too, which explains why they're off searching for her while we discuss us."

I poured tea for both of us.

Jennifer took my hand, the first time she reached out to me since she lost her memory. "Bryan, CJ and Third Jennifer both love you so much. They took me aside and said I needed to know about you. You were their first love and mine too. I don't remember you, but they do. They explained how you and I met when I was in kindergarten and you were in first grade. They talked about how we grew up together in the same schools and the same church. And they tried to instill their memories of you in me. They told me about the first time you asked me out with a kiss out of nowhere in front of the whole school at my locker. That took a lot of courage, Bryan, and they told me it meant a lot to me before I forgot everything. I still don't remember you, but I admire you for the fond memories CJ and TJ have of you. TJ and CJ are both too old for you and they've moved on. CJ likes Frank, by the way."

"I enjoy seeing them together."

"CJ and Third Jennifer said they used to enjoy watching us together. They said they felt like a version of themselves finally hooked up with the boy they loved. And it worked out for me in a way that it hadn't for them. They both felt robbed of your love by the insanity of time travel so they were sad to see my memory loss rob me of your love, also. Wow, I can't believe I said that."

"I don't mind, Jennifer. I love you so much."

"I know. I can see the sparkles in your eyes every time you gaze my way. I don't share your feelings, Bryan, but my other selves inform me that I used to. They've asked me to give you a chance. They said to forget my fear about the time I woke up with you in your tent. They thought I should be okay with it because you and I had spent a lot of time together. They said we were a cute puppy love couple who didn't mess around too much or go all the way, if you know what I mean."

"We agreed to wait until marriage, but I always figured if we didn't, it'd be okay because I can't imagine not spending the rest of my life with you no matter what time we have or what time we live."

"I like you, Bryan Ganarski. And I shouldn't say this, but I'm attracted to you in a physical way. It's more about lust than love at this point. Don't get me wrong. I don't want to sleep with you in my underwear like the morning I woke up and didn't know who I was let alone who you were or why we were together. I've been told I lost someone very important to me that morning so I will let the undies incident slide to give you a dating chance. Dating may be good for both of us, but you have to promise me one thing first."

"Anything." And did she say she wanted to slide her undies? Things may be on the upswing.

"Stop gazing at me with those lost puppy eyes. I like you, but that's it. If you like me, than look at me like you like me. I'm not your long lost lover. I'm a girl who happens to find you attractive. You have to promise to treat me the same way."

"I promise." Of course there was no way to keep my promise. She was my long lost lover or not all that long but certainly lost. I was hopelessly and forever in love with my Jennifer Hawkins.

"Then the answer to your invitation to go out with you is yes."

CHAPTER 30

BREAK-IN

On Sunday morning Snpgrdxz and I snuck into the parsonage through the back door, while Reverend Turpelator sermonized and collected funds from his congregation. Snpgrdxz appeared in the form of Mrs. Turpelator in one of Third Jennifer's new dresses.

We climbed the winding oak stairway to the second level where we explored three bedrooms, a sitting room and an office or den with a big desk. But we didn't find any sign of our vanished fourth Jennifer, Little Jenny's mother. Or anything out of time. And we didn't find any sign of CJ.

But we discovered a window with the glass broken out. Tufts of fur stuck to the edges of the broken glass. Under an old-fashioned roll top desk we noticed a pair of men's shoes covered in blood. We spotted a broken gold chain similar to the kind you might place around your neck to wear jewelry. The chain was heavy gold with large links.

"Isn't this the chain Reverend Turpelator wears with his cross?" I asked.

"Could be," said Daniel. "But where is the cross?"

"Where's the evidence of the murder of Little Jenny's mother?"

***

Creaking steps, a narrow dark stairway and creepy noises like nails scraping metal set my heart fluttering as we climbed. We found the stairway behind a door we thought led to a closet. The sole source of light derived from a lonesome ray of sunshine that passed through a small round window at one end of the large, open attic.

Near the top of the steps, we found an oil lamp attached to a dowel on an oak post. I fetched a kitchen match called a "Lucifer" from downstairs.

The attic was empty, except for an iron-framed bed covered with a sheet of canvas. I pulled the dust cover off to reveal a thin mattress. Chains were attached to each of the four corners of the bed. Old brown stains covered the mattress. The marks could have been blood a long time ago but were now rusty discoloration.

Snpgrdxz waved the lamp about the walls, but we found nothing else in the attic.

"We came up empty," I said. "Want to search the basement?"

"Something is wrong here. See how this wall is slanted and the studs are covered with wood planks of roofing."

"How can you tell," I asked.

"See the little nails popped through from the other side of the roof boards?"

Upon closer inspection I could see the square ends of old-fashioned nail metal stick out of the boards.

"Those nails hold the wood shingles in place on the other side," said Snpgrdxz.

"What's it prove?"

"No hiding places along this side of the house. Now take a gander at the other wall."

I snatched the oil lamp from Snpgrdxz and waved it about the wall on the other side of the attic. "What should I see?"

"The wall is straight, not slanted. The roof is slanted. No nail pops. This is a false wall. Feel around for a loose board."

I knocked with my fist on boards. "Nothing loose here."

Snpgrdxz stepped back and stared at the wall from the other side of the attic. "Aha." He stepped forward and yanked on one of the studs that made up the vertical wall supports. It pulled away and a hidden door swung open.

***

The patter of footsteps below us about stopped my heart. Snpgrdxz smiled which relaxed me. We both stared at the trunk in the closet. It had a round top. The whole thing was covered in leather.

"Can we open it?" I whispered.

Snpgrdxz inserted his old-fashioned skeleton key finger into the lock and fiddled with it. He withdrew his finger without opening the lock.

"Transform into a hacksaw," I suggested.

"Had to fix the key to fit the lock. This should work." Snpgrdxz stuck his finger-key back into the lock and popped it open.

Inside we found our Jennifer's twenty-first century clothes, gold coins from the nineteen twenties, a broken wooden spear, and an automatic pistol. Under her clothes we found a set of iron chains like the ones you see in old movies about the slave trade. The iron was rusty and crusted with blood. There also was a nightgown covered in blood stains and sheets that had been soaked in what could have been blood.

"He murdered her," I said.

"He chained her to the bed up here and abused her. Eventually he killed her."

I wept. I couldn't help it. She was my Jennifer. That I had three other Jennifers didn't matter. This was my Jennifer's blood I was staring at.

My blood boiled. I hadn't realized my heart went so deep as a scream arose from its depths. The thing bubbled up like vomit. As I opened my mouth, Snpgrdxz covered it with a large hand. A key dangled from the place where you would expect to find his index finger.

Snpgrdxz placed a finger over his lips. I forced the scream down where it pounded into my stomach like a rock the size of a Michigan apple. We stared into each other's eyes until the sound of footsteps wafted from below to break the silence.

"This is what we came for," Snpgrdxz whispered.

"We need to call the police."

"This stuff is out of time. How would we explain it?"

"We don't need the bloody bits. They're current."

"We'll leave the evidence, but we're out of here with the stuff from our time."

"How will we sneak it out?"

CHAPTER 31

INVESTIGATING TURPELATOR

"Turpelator's behind this," Snpgrdxz lifted a cup of tea to his lips in our apartment kitchen area.

"Let's pay Reverend Turpelator a little visit," Third Jennifer said.

My Jennifer said, "I'll go."

"And I'll escort you," said Tony.

"I'm in," I said.

"Why don't you and Snpgrdxz visit the police," my Jennifer said.

While Tony and my Jennifer visited Reverend Turpelator, Snpgrdxz, aka Daniel Brickmaster, and I called upon the police. Gilbert joined us.

"First off, you want to accuse a reverend. He's not like to travel about and murder people when his job is to save us body and soul, is he?" Detective Barnaby chortled.

We brought the current age stuff with us that we had taken from Reverend Turpelator's attic when we snuck out after midnight.

"What about these things from the attic," I asked.

Detective Barnaby shook his head. "As for your bloody rags and chains and such, I see no reason to suspect more than a cut upon someone's wrist or toe as needed attention. As for them chains, mayhap they once kept a slave or two in the old manse back when slavery was legal like. It's not as if you found an actual slave in them chains, is it? You'd know all about the slave trade, wouldn't you, Mr. Armstrong? No crime in having old chains about, is there?"

"But what about Little Jenny's mother?" Gilbert pleaded.

"What about 'er?" Detective Barnaby asked. "Dead past year, isn't she? Dead of natural causes as told us by Reverend Turpelator himself and his missus too. Not a sign of foul play. She took ill is all and died. Folks are prone to die once they catch the grippe bad or the unending craps if you don't mind my mention of such a distasteful disease."

"So there's nothing for you to do in this case?" Daniel asked.

"As you've brought the thing up, I'll visit with Reverend Turpelator and ask him about the attic and if he has any suspicions of foul play or unlawful entry or any other such thing."

"But he's the one we suspect," I said.

Detective Barnaby snickered. "If you folks appreciated how devoted Reverend Turpelator was to his congregation, you would laugh, too. Reverend Turpelator a cold-blooded killer? You've made my day, if you don't mind my saying so."

"What about finding CJ?" I asked.

"Oh, we'll find the missing Miss Hawkins, don't you worry none about that. We've decided to charge Jennifer Hawkins, alias CJ, with the murder of Rosie so her disappearing like this is more than suspicious. Could she have sailed off to your America?"

"CJ is innocent. You said so yourself, Detective Barnaby," said Gilbert.

"That was before she disappeared. And you have to admit that finding Miss Hawkins's watch in Rosie's dead hand raises concern. Combine that with her running off like that —"

"She didn't run off," said Gilbert. "She was kidnapped. Why won't you believe us?"

"Has anyone asked for ransom? Do you have a note from her kidnappers?" Detective Barnaby asked.

"Not yet," I said.

"She's run off making herself look mighty guilty if you don't mind my saying so." Detective Barnaby lit a pipe while leaning back against his chair.

"What about the cross?" Snpgrdxz asked.

"How'd you know about the cross?" Detective Barnaby asked.

Snpgrdxz sat on the edge of Detective Barnaby's desk. "It belongs to Reverend Turpelator. You can tell because it's a good six inches from top to bottom and it comes to a point at the bottom."

"Indeed it does," said Inspector Barnaby. "We found it in Rosie's other hand, but I was keeping it secret. Since you know about it, I suspect it belonged to your CJ, and you're covering for her."

"Have you checked the blood on Reverend Turpelator's shoes?" asked Gilbert.

"Bloody shoes, is it?" Detective Barnaby asked.

"They're under his desk in his upstairs den, the same room with the broken window with the fur stuck to the glass," I said.

"How do you know this?" Detective Barnaby's face scrunched into a glare.

"Just check it out," said Snpgrdxz.

"And so you believe Reverend Turpelator is somehow mixed up in Rosie's death and CJ's disappearance?"

"Yes, we do," Gilbert said.

"Well, I don't," said Detective Baranaby.

"So you don't plan to talk to Reverend Turpelator?" Gilbert asked.

"I didn't say that. The best place to begin the search for your missing Miss Hawkins is a visit to Reverend Turpelator because you believe he was involved. We need to eliminate him as a suspect or count him as one. To my way of thinking, he won't be a suspect longer than one conversation. I knows him as a right religious gentleman," said Detective Barnaby.

***

Daniel and I strode to Reverend Turpelator's manse with Detective Barnaby. When we arrived, Mrs. Turpelator answered and invited us to "join the others."

Mrs. Turpelator led us into the drawing room. I sat on the couch while Daniel took a seat on a stuffed arm chair.

"I'll inform them you're here," said Mrs. Turpelator. "And I'll bring the tea."

Reverend Turpelator entered followed by my Jennifer and Tony. Tony took a seat on one of the stuffed arm chairs while my Jennifer sat next to me. She squeezed my hand with her beautiful teenage hand. Bouncing from the nineteen twenties across a continent in the underworld to eighteen thirty-eight with the werewolf of London in our little group, made keeping track of time difficult so I guessed the hand I held was sixteen or maybe even seventeen by now.

We had no way to return home except across the Atlantic Ocean and then we had to travel west to old Chicago and the Wheaton When Portal. And that trip assumed we could access the portal in eighteen thirty-eight. Maybe it wouldn't be open yet. The things you think about while dealing with a Turpelator.

"She's not here." My Jennifer yanked a handkerchief from the sleeve of her dress and blew.

"Reverend Turpelator was kind enough to escort us around the entire manse from attic to basement," said Tony.

"I call it the grand tour, old boy," said Reverend Turpelator.

"I do hope your young friend finds her way back to you. Imagine a girl lost in London." Mrs. Turpelator served tea.

"She was kidnapped," I said. "We heard her scream behind The Bull and Crapper."

"What's kidnapped?" Mrs. Turpelator asked.

"She was stolen away by someone," Tony said.

"I doubt we'll learn much here and we've taken the time of a busy reverend and his wife. I suggest we return to the search for the missing Miss Hawkins." Detective Barnaby stood up.

"Aren't you going to search Reverend Turpelator's upstairs den?" Gilbert asked.

"Your friends have said they searched the house. If there was something in the den surely they would have said something," said Detective Barnaby.

"You're welcome to visit the den," said Reverend Turpelator.

"For the formality of the investigation only, Reverend. You are most kind to show us your private room." Detective Barnaby followed Reverend Turpelator up the stairs. Gilbert and I went with them.

Turpelator had the window fixed and no shoes, bloody or otherwise, covered the floor under the desk.

The chain remained on the desk top.

"What about this broken chain?" asked Gilbert.

"What about it, Reverend Turpelator?" Detective Barnaby asked.

"I used to have a cross attached to it. As you can see, someone broke the chain and stole the cross."

"Did you report the theft to the police?"

"I believe one of the young people in my congregation to be guilty. I thought to interrogate the lad at the first opportunity with the hope of demonstrating the error of his ways, as they say. No need for police and jail for the lad if I can persuade him to repent." Reverend Turpelator folded his hands as in prayer.

"No need to arrest the lad. I leave him in your tender mercies, Reverend, but remind him that jail is certain if he repeats his crime. However, I will need to speak with the boy since he was the last in possession of the cross." Detective Barnaby yanked his pipe from his jacket pocket.

"I think it best if you don't," said Reverend Turpelator.

Detective Barnaby filled his pipe from a tobacco tin on Reverend Turpelator's desk. "Ordinarily I'd agree with you, Reverend, but not in this case. The cross was found at the scene of a crime. The vile act must be investigated and the lad interviewed. If he was involved, he may be in much deeper trouble than the purloining of a cross."

"And you believe one of the Hawkins ladies guilty of Rosie's murder?" asked Reverend Turpelator.

"She's our leading suspect. Until we find her, the case will be open." Detective Barnaby lit his pipe.

"If only we knew where she was hiding," said Reverend Turpelator.

"She was kidnapped," Gilbert said.

"There's one more place we should check, now that we're finished here," said Detective Barnaby. "The Bull and Crapper is a notorious hangout for thieves who sell their victims to shorthanded ships about to leave port. And Miss Hawkins has reason to want to escape to foreign shores away from the scrutiny of a murder investigation. But it's unlikely thieves would steal a woman for a sailor. Women are bad luck aboard ship."

"I hate to say this, old boy, but she may have been taken by a local house of ill repute," said Reverend Turpelator.

CHAPTER 32

FIRST DATE AGAIN

My Jennifer and I went on the first date of our "second season." We spent the evening at the Bull and Crapper followed by a stroll along the river in search of CJ.

"Thanks for tonight," I said as we traversed the bank of River Thames.

"You're welcome, Bryan. Thanks for not trying to be too affectionate."

"I want to go at your pace. I can be patient."

"I like that about you. You consider my needs and not just your own. Not every boy thinks the way you do."

"I know you can't remember any of our years growing up together so I wanted tonight to be like we just met for the first time, and this is our first date."

"Smart. The other thing, Bryan, is I'm not fifteen anymore and you're not sixteen, are you?"

"No. I'm almost eighteen and you're like seventeen or close to it."

"So let's not pretend we're innocent little teeny boppers. I may not remember you, but I remember everything else about this journey. We've been to hell and we're not done yet. War and carnage changes a person. We've seen people die. I killed people, not to mention several zombies, a few vampires and a werewolf or two. And I miss my mommy. But it feels more like combat fatigue than homesickness. I mean I miss Mom, but why do I think and act as though I miss my mommy like a child?"

"Good question."

"And oh my goodness what will Mom say when I bring home Little Jenny? She's my daughter as much as the other Jennifers. She's like my flesh and blood. She is the daughter of a version of me. If I can't explain her to me, how will I ever explain her to Mom? And Dad. Daddy will flat out kill me. Bryan, you can bury my body behind the storage shed at your house."

The panic on my face dissipated within about three seconds at the mention of a dead Jennifer behind my storage shed. No way did I want to revisit that scene and no way did I want this Jennifer to know I was insane as a result. "Jennifer, let's cross the home bridge when we get there."

"Okay. I can wait, but I still miss them."

"Me too."

"You miss my parents?"

"I meant I miss my parents, too. And my little sister. We all miss our families so it's past time to go home."

We arrived back at our apartment building home with the silver shop on the first floor. "Thanks for a wonderful evening, Miss Hawkins."

"You're welcome, Mr. Ganarski."

I leaned in for a kiss. Jennifer didn't.

"Sorry," I said.

"Let's not spoil our first date. I'm not sure about you yet. But I like you. Will you call me?"

"As soon as Mr. Bell invents the telephone. In the meantime, I'll bump into you in the common room, and if you're available, would you like to go out with me again soon, say tomorrow evening?"

Jennifer Hawkins laughed for the first time in our new life together. "Yes, silly. Were you always this much fun?"

"Once I worked up the gumption to kiss you, we enjoyed each other."

"Save your gumption for down the road, okay? I want to get used to us first."

***

My Jennifer and I held hands on our second date the next night before the big fight. The Bull and Crapper crowd cheered for our new friend Tommy King who played guitar and sang ballads like Barbara Allen in his southern twang. We drank pub beer with ham sandwiches. The server cut the ham from a giant hunk on a table. He topped it with cheddar cheese cut from a wheel. Brown spicy mustard covered the cheese. He sliced the bread thick and slathered on a generous amount of butter.

"Imagine a drink of beer back home," Jennifer said.

"My parents would ground me for a month," I said.

"Remember the time my parents grounded me because I snuck into the boys side of the campsite when the youth group went to northern Minnesota?"

"Yeah, the guys thought you were awesome to visit us."

"You shared your last chocolate bar with me, remember?"

Before I could respond, a local person who could have been the stunt double for Long John Silver, complete with a peg leg and parrot on his shoulder, placed a grubby hand on Jennifer's shoulder. "You'll do, missy. Let's be off with you."

"Leave her alone," I said. "You don't know who you're about to mess with."

"She's but a scamp of a girl and a wild thing, too. Money's to be made with her so avast shipmate. I'll be taking her from here." Was this guy out of central casting or what? He yanked my Jennifer from her seat.

I'd had enough. I stood up and punched the rapscallion in the jaw with sufficient force to knock him head over keister. "Rapscallion" is one of those Dickens era words I learned to use.

The villain rose off the floor with a flintlock pistol in his hand. He fired pointblank at my face. The flash and smoke filled my view. A lead ball smashed into the space between my eyes. I fell back but caught myself before I hit the floor.

I already held enough anger at this pirate to want to destroy him, but a new, deeper anger rose within me. The evil of this journey, the insanity of events, pushed forward in my mind to boil my blood. I knocked my enemy down again with a single punch to the jaw. I threw it so fast he had no way to block me. He hit the floor so hard I had no question in my mind that I had killed him. He didn't move.

Before I could take in the craziness of what I had done, six of the pirate's friends jumped me from behind.

Twenty-first century Americans were bigger and huskier than most folks from the first decades of the nineteenth century. We ate better, took our vitamins and benefited from tae kwon do lessons. And with our time travels, this was not my first fight.

Two of the scoundrels slugged me hard enough to land me on the floor before I worked up the gumption to knock their blocks off. The good news was Jennifer took them out when she smashed a beer mug over their heads. When I swung around to take on the other four, I discovered that Tommy King had come to my rescue.

Tommy was no stranger to fist fights. He had two of the four others knocked out before Jennifer clunked another crook on the noggin with a double dose of beer mugs.

The remaining pirate thrust a bowie knife into the center of my back but he didn't thrust hard enough. I could feel the point but it didn't break my skin. Anger roared into my mind. This wasn't an evil anger, but a righteous one. I was the angel of retribution about to smite my enemy. I spun around fast and he swung at me but I backed out of range so that I caught the breeze as his fist passed by my jaw. Jennifer smashed the pirate with a haymaker that knocked his jaw loose from his skull. He collapsed to the floor.

"We've got to get out of this place," Tommy said. "They'll be coming on strong when they wake up."

I saw no reason to disagree with Tommy so I took Jennifer by the hand and led the way out of the pub. Tommy left a fist full of pound notes on the table for the cleanup and to cover our beer.

Tommy accompanied us. "How'd you do it, son?"

"You mean how did I avoid their punches? I was angry," I said.

Jennifer took my arm. "He means how did you take a bullet to the face and a giant knife in the back and not get hurt?"

"Yeah, how'd you do it, boy?" Tommy asked.

"I have no idea. The bullet crashed against my face between the eyes, but it bounced off. I can't explain how the knife didn't penetrate my skin, but there was no damage to me. I can't say the same for that sailor's cheap blade."

We ambled along in silence the rest of the way. Jennifer held onto my arm. I assumed she and Tommy were deep in thought about how I survived. It was a miracle, but why me? Add this evening's events to the list of crazy things that have happened since the long ago evening when Jennifer Hawkins took a shot at me.

"I'll leave you here so you can kiss your girl good night." Tommy patted me on the back, tipped his hat to Jennifer and strode off into the night. He didn't get far.

"What makes you think I'll let him kiss me?" Jennifer asked.

Tommy King gazed back at us over his shoulder. "Because I know a hunk, a hunk of burning love when I see one, Wild Thing. And two hunks are easier to spot. But if Bryan doesn't want you, remember you make my heart sing, girl." Tommy spun around in a circle, wiggled his hips and took off down the street.

Jennifer and I sat on the stoop at the entrance to our building. The door to the upstairs room was next to the silversmith shop door. Neither of us seemed in a hurry to go in.

"Let's go back to your memory, Jennifer. I thought you didn't remember me at all, but now you recall a certain bar of chocolate I gave to you."

"I don't have any memories of you except for that chocolate bar you handed to me. A girl never forgets chocolate. You said you gave it to me for my prize as most valuable player among the girls."

"You were always the MVP of my life, Jennifer Hawkins."

"That's what you said then, too. I remember. How come I can't remember other stuff about you?"

"It'll come with time." We didn't kiss, but she let me hug her.

We went upstairs and to my delight, Jennifer told everyone how I had defended her from vicious pirates, a whole pack of them. She told them their bullets bounced off me and a knife blade bent against my back. "It was like watching a superhero in action," she said.

Gilbert laughed. "You've got to be kidding, right? Our Bryan Ganarski found the guts to fight?"

Snpgrdxz said, "It could happen. Not! You're not a shape shifter, Bryan.

Tony said, "No surprise here, boys and girls. Bryan dunked himself into the River Styx. He is invulnerable like old Achilles. Knives and bullets can't hurt him."

I loved the way Jennifer's eyes lit up when she lied to everyone about our adventure, but this was a new bit of the insanity surrounding my life. "Jennifer did the heavy hitting."

CHAPTER 33

SEARCHING FOR CJ

Three weeks of searching turned up no sign of CJ. We checked everywhere we could think of. Detective Barnaby explored the red light district and the outbound ships for any sign of her.

We identified six houses of prostitution near The Bull and Crapper. Snpgrdxz morphed into a girl to seek employment with the various madams of the district. In her "she" mode, Snpgrdxz purchased dresses and changed "her" appearance so she was a new person at each of the bordellos.

Frank, Tony, TJ, Gilbert, Daniel, and my Jennifer sat around the kitchen table in our common room one afternoon at the end of the third week. Little Jenny played with her new doll on the floor by the fireplace. I sat next to her and played with splinters I yanked out of the wood floor.

Little Jenny had changed so much from a filthy street urchin dressed in rags and near collapse from starvation. Now she was a clean, well-dressed little girl who benefitted from an overabundance of love and food. To see her hollow cheeks fill out will forever be one of the great joys of my life.

"I had a blast," Snpgrdxz said. "Who knew you could have a night of pleasure with so many guys and get paid for it?"

"I don't want to know about it," said my Jennifer.

"You should try it," said Snpgrdxz. "You could make a fortune."

My Jennifer clasped her hands together. "I'll pray for your immortal alien soul."

"I'd prefer to slit a man's throat and rob the bastard then submit to sex for pay," said Third Jennifer. "And his throat wouldn't be the organ I'd slit."

Gilbert leaned back in his chair. "So can you imitate anybody?"

Snpgrdxz adjusted a wide leather belt left behind by a pirate at one of the bordellos. "Anybody. I can create my own look, too, like my Chinese girl character. Or the prostitute beauties I created. I don't have to be somebody's duplicate to make the johns happy."

"We have to get this on Facebook," Gilbert said.

Snpagrdxz threw his hands up while sending his belt flying. "No! They'll come after me and kill me and dissect me and turn me into frozen chopped liver and chopped hearts and chopped brains. If you tell, I'll have to leave the country and start over in South America or Siberia or some such place. Or stay here in eighteen thirty-eight."

I caught the pirate belt. "Who will come after you?"

Snpgrdxz buried his head in his arms. "The feds."

"The feds?" Tony asked.

"Yeah. Think about it. How did I arrive on earth?" Snpgrdxz raised his head.

"In a spaceship?" I asked.

"Ever hear of Roswell?" Snpgrdxz pulled a penknife out of his pocket.

"You were at Roswell?" Tony asked.

"I was a stowaway on the ship that crashed a year before Roswell. It was back in nineteen forty-six on your calendar. Gzpnxbx on ours. My fault the ship crashed. I was playing with... I mean... well, never mind."

"You were a stowaway space voyager?" my Jennifer asked.

"You can't tell anyone. They'll come for me. I'll have to hide." Snpgrdxz gestured like he was whittling wood. He whined like a teenager because he was one and has been one for about one hundred fifty years. His race moves slower than humans through puberty. You'd move slower if you had to deal with pubescence for both the female and the male sexes.

Tony handed Snpgrdxz one of his oak vampire stakes. "They can't still be interested in you after all this time, can they?"

"I haven't seen the men in black since oh-seven, but I've learned to be more careful. If you tell anyone, the feds will investigate. They always do. They say there's no such thing as flying saucers but they always investigate. You don't always see them, but they're around in their black suits with the narrow lapels and thin black ties." Snpgrdxz scraped wood shavings onto the table.

"So your ship crashed and you were the sole survivor?" Tony asked.

"We all survived."

"So where are your fellow space aliens, now?" TJ asked.

"How do you think I know so much about what the feds do to you when they find out you're a space alien?" Snpgrdxz focused on his whittling.

"They killed your crewmates?" my Jennifer asked.

"Dissected, bisected, chopped, flash frozen and stored." Snpgrdxz held up a vampire stick with a harpoon hook.

"They couldn't have killed all of you. One of the adults must have escaped." Tony could have scratched his whiskers, if he had any, which would make for a nice description here, but he scratched the other end of his anatomy.

Snpgrdxz stroked his bare chin. "We crashed in the middle of the last century. Well, the middle of the next century from when we are now, but many decades before our home time. If another shipmate survived the crash and evaded the feds, don't you think we would have found each other by now? Don't you realize how much I miss my father and how much I wish I could go home to my friends? I've already missed decades of high school on my home world."

"Decades? Of high school?" my Jennifer asked.

"Yeah, adolescence lasts a long time in our species. You have to think about how much we have to learn before we grow up. We're about three million years ahead of earth. That span has given us time to evolve. We stay young long enough to learn everything we need as adults."

"So you've been in high school here on earth since nineteen forty-six?" I yanked a floor splinter out of my thumb.

"I take time off once in a while." Snpgrdxz continued working with the knife.

"You must have gone to a lot of proms?" my Jennifer asked.

"Think about the detentions," said Gilbert.

"I'd prefer to think about your prom dates. Were they gorgeous?" Frank asked.

Snpgrdxz flashed a giant smile. "The girls were."

"Right. Forgot. So you've dated a lot of guys over the decades, too?" Third Jennifer asked.

"And I've driven a lot of different cars. Fifty-seven Chevy, sixty-five Mustang, seventy Bacaruda, seventy-eight Pinto. Even aliens make mistakes."

"Have you lived in the same place the whole time?" Tony asked.

Snpgrdxz carved the other end of the vampire stake, the one without the harpoon hook. "I move around. I join one class and continue at that school until graduation. While the other kids head off to college or work, I move away and join another class somewhere else."

"Don't you have to live with a family? Somebody has to sign your papers and stuff." TJ scratched the polite end of her anatomy.

"Did you forget I'm a shape shifter? I can morph into my own mom and dad. I appear as an only child. Siblings create complications like when you have to be at the same place at the same time." Snpgrdxz shaped a round wheel on one end of the oak stake.

My Jennifer pouted. "So you are alone in this world. What about your folks back home? Shouldn't they be searching for you?"

"Mom died when I was young. Dad was on the ship. He was the reason I stowed away. I didn't want to spend fifty of our years without him while he travelled around the galaxy. He explored backward planets as a producer for our equivalent of your reality TV shows."

Tony said, "Okay. Your secret is safe with us, right gang?"

While the others nodded agreement, I sat still.

"What about you, Bryan?" Tony asked.

I chuckled. "Who would we tell in eighteen thirty-eight? But I promise not to tell now or when we return home."

"You guys are the best," said Snpgrdxz, "And I can understand how time travel creeps you out. Creeps me out, too. As far as shape shifting into prostitutes, disease runs rampant among those houses. And that scares you delicate earthers. I'm immune to them. But I saw no sign of CJ in any of those houses."

"Fortunate for her," said TJ.

Gilbert said, "The good news is CJ is not a sex slave. The bad news is she is still missing, and we don't have a clue where she is."

"We'll find out next week," said Frank.

"I want Aunt CJ to come home." Little Jenny hugged me.

"How?" asked Gilbert.

"Full moon," said Frank.

"CJ will to destroy her kidnappers," said my Jennifer.

CHAPTER 34

BODY IN THE RIVER

We found the body in the Thames River on our next date.

"It's CJ," Jennifer shouted.

I descended the bank to the river's edge and dragged the body ashore. It had been in the water for a while. Despite its swelling, the face could match CJ or any of the Jennifers. I studied my Jennifer's face and then looked back at the body. "Is this one of her dresses?"

"I think so. Oh it must be." Jennifer sat on the street and cried.

I ran to a shop nearby. "Call the police," I yelled.

"Do what?" asked a young clerk.

"We've pulled a body from the river. We need the police," I said.

"What for? Sounds like you need the undertaker. Down the lane two blocks, end of the street but two shops," said the clerk.

I returned to where Jennifer sat with the body. "I'll find help. Do you want to wait here?"

"Cover her up," Jennifer bawled.

I removed my jacket and placed it over the dead woman's face. "I'll be back."

The undertaker dropped his fork and left his victuals to follow me to a fresh customer. Well, not too fresh.

The undertaker removed my jacket from the dead body's face. "She been in the water long enough as to give off the odor of death. We'll need to bury her quick like. I'll get the cart. Meanwhile, fetch an officer to make a report."

"Where do I find the police?" I asked.

"They're about. Officer Miller should be making his rounds soon enough."

I ran around the block in search of a police officer and returned without one. Officer Miller stood over the body on my return. My Jennifer stood next to him with a hanky to her face.

"Appears we've found the guilty party," said Officer Miller. "Case closed."

***

I collapsed by Officer Miller and my Jennifer. I had held up while busy searching for a cop and an undertaker but once I returned to my Jennifer, I lost it. The sight of the cop somehow brought home the reality that our beloved CJ was no more.

CJ was my Jennifer lost in time and caught in a time loop. As tears whisked down my cheeks, I felt the emotion of my loss for CJ because she was both a version of my girlfriend and a big sister to me. She gave me strength and advice. She advocated for my Jennifer to return to me. She helped to care for me when a Chicago gangster shot me in nineteen twenty-three. Okay, she was also a werewolf with no ability to resist her master Turpelator despite her love for Frank.

Jennifer and I informed the others after the undertaker took the body to his mortuary. Tony and TJ handled the arrangements despite their sorrow. Frank wept at the loss of his girlfriend. Gilbert cried because CJ was a classmate, a friend, a youth group companion and a fellow time traveler. Even Snpgrdxz shed tears for our CJ. Little Jenny cried for her lost Auntie.

We consoled each other with CJ stories. Despite the humor of the tales, we seldom laughed. My Jennifer slipped into a deep depression such that I worried about her. We had no medications in eighteen thirty-eight with the exception of the dried leaves in plastic bags that Tony carried in his backpack for "medical usage only."

For the funeral, Tony asked the undertaker to seal the body in heavy waxed paper and to seal that in wax.

When asked about this arrangement, Tony said, "We've little doubt that this is our beloved CJ, but we've no way to test. If we can preserve the body until we return to our own time, we can dig her up and have a DNA test performed. That way we'll know for sure."

"What good will it do?" I asked. "CJ will still be just as dead."

"We'll know for certain it was CJ," said Tony.

"Will we?" Frank asked. "What if the woman turns out to be another Jennifer lost in time and we abandon CJ in eighteen thirty-eight."

"If it was another Jennifer, then where is CJ? It had to be her. It looked like CJ."

Through her tears, my Jennifer asked, "CJ was a werewolf. How did Turpelator kill her?"

***

The funeral of CJ began with a service at a local Presbyterian Church. We chose it because we attended First Pres in Wheaton, Illinois, and none of us wanted Turpelator to conduct a funeral for one of our own. He was the enemy.

The pastor was a fiery-haired Scotsman with a thick accent which made the funeral interesting while providing a few chuckles as we tried to understand him. I'm certain Reverend Campbell meant to say CJ was a beautiful young girl, but with his accent, we heard "bountiful young girl."

We buried CJ in St. Mark's Cemetery. Tony ordered a large stone for her grave. "It's so we can find it easily in our time." I wept with my friends at the grave. My Jennifer jumped into the grave so Gilbert and I dropped down and yanked her out again. I sat on the grass and held my Jennifer to give her comfort. She must have forgotten that she didn't remember me or that she didn't love me. Allowing me to comfort her in this way suggested to me that she trusted me and must have some residual memory of our previous relationship despite having no conscious memory of it.

Detective Barnaby attended the funeral. "As far as I'm concerned old Rosie's murder case is closed. No sense pursuing justice where none is to be had in this life."

"What about Turpelator?" Gilbert asked.

"What about him?" Detective Barnaby asked.

"How can you close the case when you still have a living suspect?" Gilbert asked.

"He's not a suspect," Detective Barnaby said.

"He is if he turns into a werewolf and you weigh the evidence in that light," Gilbert said.

"If he's a werewolf, I'll buy you and your friends a beer at the Bull and Crapper, I will," said Detective Barnaby.

"We accept your bet," said Gilbert. "To prove he's a werewolf, join Bryan and me on a stakeout of Turpelator's manse tonight. It's the first night of the new full moon."

"What's a stakeout?" Detective Barnaby asked.

"Just meet us at the police station tonight before the moon rises," Gilbert said.

We trudged back to the apartment where Miss Merklebun had prepared a luncheon of sandwiches, tea and rum. As I looked around at our group, I couldn't help but notice the red, moist eyes and the exhaustion on all of us.

Little Jenny slept in TJ's lap.

My Jennifer held my arm while leaning close to me for comfort.

I placed my arm around Jennifer's shoulders. "Are you okay?"

"I'm going to jump in the river and drown myself. You should have left me in CJ's grave."

"Jennifer, you have so much. I wish I deserved you."

"I don't even know who I am anymore. I don't remember the boy everyone considers my boyfriend. He's so old. I look older than I feel. I miss my mommy so much. I just want to die."

CJ walked through the front door. "You people look like crap. What is this, a funeral? Hey, look, sandwiches. I'm starved."

CHAPTER 35

THE CAPTURE OF CJ

TJ slugged CJ.

CJ landed on the floor. She rubbed her jaw. "What?"

TJ assumed a classic boxer pose. "We buried you. You broke our hearts. Bryan's Jennifer jumped into your grave wanting to follow you to the Promised Land. Now she wants to off herself in the river. And poor Little Jenny has been beside herself with worry and tears for her dead auntie."

"I was around." CJ tried to stand but Third Jennifer knocked her down again.

CJ glared at us. "What's wrong with you people? Did you say you buried me? But I've been here all along. I never died yet on this time line. Who did you bury?"

"First off, no one saw you for weeks, CJ. The police have been looking for you for the murder of Rosie. How come she had your watch in her hand? You have a lot of explaining to do." Tony folded his arms and glared at CJ.

"Was I gone that long? I thought it was a few days."

"Who did we bury?" Snpgrdxz asked.

"Did we just bury another Jennifer?" Gilbert asked.

"She could have been a fourth, no make that a fifth Jennifer who passed through the London When Portal. How come the Jennifers keep landing in eighteen thirty-eight?" Frank asked.

"And how come I have no memory of landing in eighteen thirty eight, except for this one time around?" CJ asked.

"Maybe she was someone who looked like CJ," said my Jennifer.

"So either she was another Jennifer passing through this time alone who died or was murdered like Little Jenny's mom, our late fourth Jennifer, or she was a look-alike fake Jennifer," said Tony. "I'm glad we stored her in wax."

I knew we were all supposed to be angry with CJ, but I couldn't stand picking on her anymore. I left my Jennifer behind on her chair and assisted CJ to her feet. I hugged her. "I love you so much, CJ, and I'm glad you're alive."

My Jennifer joined in a group hug. "Me, too, big sister."

The rest of our crew gathered into the hug with expressions of love for CJ which led us into another round of tears, but happy tears this time.

"Okay, maybe I won't kill myself, but I still miss mommy," said my Jennifer.

***

Gilbert, Tony and I met Detective Barnaby at the police station at eight o'clock. Officer Miller joined us as we strolled to Turpelator's manse.

We used bushes for cover as we watched the window to Turpelator's second floor den. Shortly before midnight, Detective Barnaby said, "Looks like you fellows owe Officer Miller and I a pint or two."

"Wait," said Gilbert. "He'll change around midnight and fly through that window."

"I didn't know werewolves could fly," said Officer Miller.

Gilbert said, "I meant in a manner of speaking. He'll crash through the window and leap to the ground. He'll run off to the nearest park, which just happens to be where Daniel is waiting."

The moon appeared about a quarter of the way across the sky. The night was filled with stars. The roaring began at midnight. A werewolf reached out of the open window to Turpelator's study.

"Oh my goodness," said Detective Barnaby. "Perhaps I'm the one to pay for the pints."

The werewolf had animal ears and nose. It roared in our direction and chose me to attack. Before I could snag my Glock, the werewolf knocked me to the ground. It tried to bite my head off with the same type of bite that removed three-fourths of poor old Rosie's neck.

Turpelator the werewolf couldn't penetrate my skin. It felt like nothing, like I wore invisible steel armor and his teeth couldn't pass through the metal. I fired my Glock with the silver bullet clip. The werewolf must have smelled the silver in the bullets because it turned tail and headed for the park, but the silver penetrated the werewolf's tough hide. About fifty feet from us, Turpelator collapsed.

I followed the police and Gilbert and Tony to the werewolf. As we watched, the beast returned to the shape of Turpelator.

"You killed old Rosie, didn't you?" Detective Barnaby asked.

Turpelator shook his head.

"Yes, you did," said Gilbert. "You broke into our apartment house after CJ transformed into a werewolf and ran off into the night. You stole her watch off her torn dress on the floor. Bryan heard you but thought it was CJ. You turned into a werewolf on the steps outside of Rosie's apartment. You burst in and killed her. Then you left the building and enjoyed an evening of werewolfery. Your big mistake was not realizing that Rosie had ripped your cross off. She held it in one hand while you placed CJ's watch in her other hand. Being a daemon, you have the power to turn into a werewolf and back again at will, unlike CJ who is subject to the cycles of the moon. But you are subject to the moon cycle, too. Admit your guilt, Turpelator."

"He's beyond admitting anything, but your version sounds good enough for me," said Detective Barnaby.

"He's dead?" I asked.

"You killed a vicious beast, young man. Don't hold yourself guilty." Detective Barnaby checked Turpelator's body for a pulse.

"What about CJ?" Gilbert asked.

"She's free to go where she wants. We're finished with her. What do you say, Officer Miller?"

"Case closed," said Officer Miller, "excepting we owe these lads a pint a piece."

While the gang went off to the pub with the police officers, I headed to the park to catch up with Daniel.

***

Snpgrdxz and I spent the rest of the night in a failed attempt to corner CJ with our silver bullets while she howled at the moon in harmony with yet another werewolf several blocks away.

Once CJ reverted to her naked self when the sun rose, she explained how she disappeared from the pub. She was taken away by Reverend Turpelator, but she preferred spending time with him because he was the werewolf pack alpha. She was gone so long because she had lost track of time as she explained back at the apartment.

I was stunned. "You mean there are more werewolves?"

"Reverend Turpelator enjoys making converts." CJ flashed her biggest smile along with a plentiful display of skin. Snpgrdxz and I enjoyed the show unlike the last time when she became incensed that we dared peek at her through the bushes.

"Enjoyed, you mean," I said. "I killed him."

Snpgrdxz passed a set of female clothes to her. "Best you put these on, Jennifer, before Bryan has a conniption because his girlfriend ran around London au natural."

"If you insist, but I enjoy the freedom of movement." CJ dressed in front of us with no worries about remaining hidden in the bushes.

Instead of shooting CJ, we hauled her back to the apartment where Tony stuffed her full of the last of the aconitum.

"Are you sure about this stuff?" CJ muffled through a mouth full of the wolfsbane.

"Supposed to work," said Tony. "This junk is dried out, not fresh. I'm not sure how much you need. And maybe too much time has passed since the werewolf put the moves on you."

"So it either works or you shoot me?" CJ asked.

"Don't talk that way." Fireman Frank cuddled CJ in his arms.

"Okay, but you guys promise to shoot me if I turn."

"No promises, CJ. You're won't turn if we have a say in the matter." My Jennifer patted her older self on the arm, while she kept the universe from exploding due to the impossibility of one person being in two places at once. Or was it two versions of the same person in the same place at once? Either way the world should have imploded by now.

"If I do turn, I don't want to become known as the 'Werewolf of London.'"

"Too late even if you are prettier than Lon Chaney," Frank said.

"Lon Chaney, Junior," said Tony.

Snpgrdxz pointed a finger at the ceiling. "Henry Hull."

"Who's Henry Hull?" asked my Jennifer.

"The original Werewolf of London from the 1935 film. He played Wilfred Glendon, the man who turned into a wolf. Don't you people watch low budget TV?"

"What about Lon Chaney?" Tony asked.

"Lon Chaney, Junior, starred in the sequel, The Wolf Man," Snpgrdxz said.

"What's a see-kill?" Little Jenny asked.

"You are," said TJ. "You're the next version of us Jennifers. The sequel is the one that comes next. It's the same in a novel or movie so why not in a person?"

"What's a movie?" Little Jenny asked.

"So, where do we go from here?" TJ stared at the ceiling.

"Time to go home," I said.

Tony paced the room deep in thought. He turned to our little group. "Spring is upon us. I say we sail aboard the next boat home to America."

"But we need to go back to our own, you know," said my Jennifer.

"And we know where we can do that, don't we?" Tony asked.

"He's right," said TJ. "We have to sail to America so we can return to our home time."

"We're headed home," my Jennifer shouted. She grabbed my face and planted a major lip lock on me in front of everyone for the first kiss of our second season, after three weeks of almost daily dates. Come on, you knew I was patient with her. You have to wait for the girl to be ready for her special first kiss. And it's not like I had other girls to choose from. I was glad I waited. I loved my Jennifer with or without kisses.

When my Jennifer pulled back from our kiss, she smiled and hugged me. She took my hand and leaned against me. I didn't care who saw us and neither did she.

So far none of the others noticed.

"What about Maria Gonzalez?" asked Gilbert. "And what do we do about Reverend Turpelator?"

"Reverend Turpelator is dead for now. What more can we do. He's not our problem," said Tony.

"He was CJ's alpha werewolf so he was her problem," said TJ.

"The Turpelator in the troll world was CJ's alpha. We're not sure Reverend Turpelator was the same person. Best guess is he was. CJ saw him as her alpha so I suppose it's true. Either way, we're splitting. Isn't that good enough? It's not like he'll follow us buried in his grave." Tony scratched his head.

"What if he finds a way to pursue us?" CJ asked. "He always comes back to life, and I have no resistance to him. He can make me do whatever he wants. And I do mean whatever."

Tony patted CJ's shoulder. "Let's worry about Turpelator if and when he returns to the living and finds us. For now, we'll leave him dead and buried in eighteen thirty-eight London where he belongs. Meanwhile, we will make our way to America and then home to where we belong."

We said our goodbyes to Tommy King, J Rutledge Pierpont and Miss Merklebun.

"We could be home in a few weeks," I said.

CHAPTER 36

SEASICK
WITH A SIDE OF PIRATES

The gray sea swelled and shrank to the rhythm of my foul and useless stomach. Horizon to horizon, the world of eighteen thirty-eight remained gray like an old black and white movie.

The splash of the paddle wheels roared in my ears as I leaned over the ship rail as far as possible without falling overboard. I aimed for the sea to avoid the side of the good steamer Rapid. My Jennifer stood next to me, head over the railing. Next to her leaned CJ and Third Jennifer. Gilbert and Frank rested their heads over the rail down the line from the girls.

Tony, Snpgrdxz in Daniel mode, and Little Jenny ate cake and sipped tea in the steamer's drawing room. We were three days out of Portsmouth with about a baker's dozen days until we made our way into New York harbor.

I woke that morning and felt almost like myself again. When you're close to eighteen, depending on how you count the days, months and years when you time travel, your body adapts to the sea faster than old guys like Tony and Frank. Well, not Tony. Nothing fazed him. And I would have been okay if I hadn't tried to eat right away, but after three days, I needed the nutrition.

As for the girls, my Jennifer already told me her "friend" was in town, so it was safe to assume CJ and Third Jennifer entertained their out-of-town guests. That combined with seasickness, well, need I say more about their plights?

I joined the healthy members of our gang in the drawing room where I sipped warm tea and ate bread with peach jam. In my distressed state, I still appreciated how delicious food tasted in eighteen thirty-eight with none of the chemicals or mass produced food we were used to. Wholesome, farm fresh food. Homemade stuff.

Okay, the air quality in England left a lot to be desired, and the water in London was guaranteed to give you the shits, but the food tasted great despite the risk of lead poison from the canned goods.

"Uncle Bryan is back," said Little Jenny. Somewhere on the journey from London to the middle of the North Atlantic, the guys became "uncles" for Little Jenny. TJ was entrenched as "Mommy Two."

"Yes, I am," I replied.

"Are you well-enough for action?" Tony poured brandy into his tea.

"What's up?" I lifted a chunk of bread, but didn't bite into it.

"Nothing yet. Full moon will rise later."

"Didn't we cure CJ?" I closed my eyes and bit into peach jam on hard white bread.

Tony buttered his bread. "I love all three of our Wild Things…"

"All four wild things," Little Jenny said.

"Yeah, I love you, too, Tiny Wild Thinglette." Tony patted Little Jenny's head. "But we don't know if the aconitum we force fed to CJ worked. We need to be ready."

"You have the silver bullets in the guns?"

"Yeah."

"What are the silver bullets for, Uncle Tony?"

"Our protection, Little Jenny. Not for little heads to worry about."

"Okay." Little Jenny sipped her tea.

"We can talk about this later," I said. And we would have if the pirates hadn't burst into the drawing room.

***

Sixteen pirates with swords and flintlock pistols rounded up the one hundred fifty passengers and crew of the Rapid. They herded us into the cargo hold. These pirates boarded the ship back in Portsmouth as third-class passengers, except for their captain who reserved a private cabin in first class. Even pirates made a class distinction in eighteen thirty-eight. How they snuck their weapons onboard, I could only guess. It was not like they had airport security in eighteen thirty-eight. And no one checked our backpacks which were filled with twenty-first century military hardware.

Tony whispered in my ear, "If they find our cabin, they'll discover enough weapons to conquer New Jersey."

I glared at Tony before I realized the answer stood next to us. I turned to Daniel Brickmaster. "You have to keep them out of our cabin or hide our weapons."

Daniel was ahead of me. "What if I take these guys out with one of Tony's M16s?"

"You turn into one of them so you can sneak by them and make your way back to our cabin." I drew a map on my hand showing the way to our cabins.

Daniel raised his eyes as if to show how low my intelligence had shrunk since we arrived in Victorian England. "What should I do when I get the weapons? There will be one of me. If they get off a lucky flintlock shot, I'm dead unless I see it in time to reshape myself out of the bullet's flight pattern."

Tony whispered the solution. "Hunker down. Set up a defensive position with furniture and what-not. Then don't do anything unless they break into the cabin. And they will break in. They will have to enter one at a time so you can pop them off if they're dumb enough to go up against you."

It was a great plan. And it would have worked except for one minor detail. We were already too late.

The pirate leader, a mangy, toothless swashbuckler, sauntered down the ladder to the cargo hold carrying an M16. "Who belongs to this?" he shouted.

***

Daniel Brickmaster strode up to the pirate leader. "You have my rifle, captain."

The pirate leader backed up a notch, pointed the M16 at Daniel and yanked the trigger. "What's this? She don't bark none, do she, matey?"

"Give it here, captain. I can fix it." Daniel reached for the M16.

The pirate pulled the rifle back. "Say, do you think I'm stupid?"

Daniel stretched his arms to reach the rifle and pulled it out of the pirate's hand.

The pirate's jaw reached down to right above the knee area. "How'd you do that, matey?"

"Do what, captain?" Daniel released the lock on the rifle and fired a round. It missed the pirate's face but not by much.

Tony and Frank rushed the pirate, pulled his arms back and tied his hands behind him. They pushed the pirate down into a sitting position on the deck.

"Strip him," Daniel said. Tony and Frank complied.

Daniel changed into the pirate's clothes, fleas and all.

Captain Jenkins approached. "You can't fool the pirates in that get up. You don't look anything like this ruffian."

"It's close enough." Daniel climbed the ladder out of the cargo hold. No doubt he appeared to the pirates as their captain.

The pirate captain opened his mouth and screamed. Tony wacked him with his fist. Frank stuffed a rag into the pirate's mouth, and Tony tied a bandana around his head to prevent him from spitting out the cloth. The pirate shook his head and mumbled his favorite letter, "Arghhh!"

Captain Jenkins ordered several crewmen to set up a detention cell for the pirate captain by stacking boxes around him and standing guard. This kept the pirate out of sight in case his mates came back.

McNichols, the first mate, asked, "How'd your friend do that?"

"Do what?" I asked. People in the cargo hold witnessed Snpgrdxz stretch his arms out at least a foot beyond human capability. Someone would ask about the M16. How do you explain automatic weapons to a crowd of people in eighteen thirty-eight?

Paul R. Lloyd

CHAPTER 37

TRUE CONFESSIONS, SORT OF

"Our friend is an alien shape shifter and we're time travelers. The weapon is from the distant future." Tony flashed a broad grin with no worries about giving away our two big secrets. I wanted to kill him. Judging from the look on Gilbert's face, as well as the glares from the Jennifers and Frank, I sensed Tony was on his way overboard.

Captain Jenkins stared at our little group for a second or two longer than necessary before he said, "Naw. Really, how'd he move so fast? Is he a runner?"

"Yes!" I shouted. "He runs in races wherever we go."

"Hey, what about your fancy flintlock?" McNichols asked.

Gilbert picked up on the word "flintlock." From the way the people glanced around at each other, he must have figured they already reframed their image of the M16 into a Victorian reality. "It's a fancy military weapon for cavalry officers. Experimental."

"Is that so?" asked Captain Jenkins. "Why do you have it?"

Frank said, "I represent the company that invented it. I'm on the return leg from a trip across Europe to see if I could interest any of the armies of Europe to fund the research necessary to complete the design."

"What's wrong with the design?" asked McNichols.

Frank waved his hands about. "You observed how it misfired when the pirate attempted to shoot our friend Daniel. Then it fired when Daniel aimed at the pirate. The weapon is not reliable as yet. Our company needs to do more research and that costs money. We've exhausted our American sponsors. We hoped in vain for help from the Europeans."

"You say 'Europeans' like it's one country," said Captain Jenkins.

"Not at all. We visited France, Italy, Prussia, Russia. You name it, we've been there. We've heard the word "no" in most of the languages of the Western world."

"We?" asked McNichols.

"Me then," said Frank. "I used the editorial 'we.'"

"Can we go back to our cabins, now? I have to pee." Little Jenny's timing was perfect

"We have to wait until the pirates go away," said Captain Jenkins. "Why don't one of you ladies take this little girl behind some cargo boxes to do her duty."

TJ took Little Jenny by the hand and led her away. The rest of us sat down on the deck or on one of the wood crates scattered about the hold.

"When do we eat?" Gilbert asked.

Captain Jenkins tugged his pocket watch out for about the hundredth time. He was in the habit of not announcing the time, other than in terms of so many "bells," so I peered over his shoulder. I can't say I expected a digital readout, but I never paid a lot of attention in grade school when they taught us how to tell time the old-fashioned way. It was enough for me to know which way was clockwise and which was counter clockwise.

I could tell it was after eight because the little hand pointed at the eight. The big hand pointed between the three and four. I figured it must be about eight-oh-four. To be honest, I guessed. I wasn't too good at Roman numerals either. But VIII was eight.

We hadn't been fed all day. And we never heard from Daniel Brickmaster. We didn't know if he was still alive or what the status of our weapons might be. I trusted his abilities as Snpgrdxz, but the Jennifers looked worried.

"We're not concerned about Daniel." TJ read my mind.

"What are you worried about, then?" I asked.

"CJ. This is the first night of the full moon," TJ said barely above a whisper.

"What can we do if she changes? We don't have the silver bullets," I whispered in her ear.

"What did you guys whisper?" asked my Jennifer.

"CJ," TJ whispered. "What if she changes?"

As if to answer our concerns, two pirates barged down the ladder to the hold. One could have started for the Chicago Bears. So we weren't the sole group of big guys onboard. The other was tall enough to play shortstop on a Little League team so I was half right about how our team was taller and stronger.

The little pirate shrieked in a squeaky voice, "Which one calls herself CJ?"

I have to give CJ credit. She stepped right up to face the pirates rather than hide in the back of the crowd. You have to think about what pirates do to your women at a time like this.

"I'm CJ." She stood toe-to-toe with the big pirate, although the wee one was the speaker.

"We be having our fun with you now, Missy, if you darsn't mind, that is." The football player pirate grabbed CJ by the arm.

The shortstop grabbed her other arm, "Even if you minds, Missy, we be having our way with you. But Captain says, says he, 'I'm first. Bring 'er 'ere to me.' So 'ere we are a-bringin you to 'em for firsties."

The pirates dragged CJ up the ladder, big pirate first, CJ in the middle while the runt face brought up the rear. Before he reached the top, the shortstop faced us. "We'll return for the rest of you ladies, if'n you don't mind." He roared with laughter as he disappeared above. He didn't realize the girl he planned to ravage was riding the crimson tide on the night of the full moon.

Paul R. Lloyd

CHAPTER 38

SCREAMS AT MIDNIGHT

Screams arose around midnight followed by shots, but I couldn't tell if they were from the old flintlocks or our modern weapons. Tony said it was both. The passengers and crew with us in the cargo hold cried, expressed their fears, and prayed.

Some of the men broke into the cargo boxes in search of weapons or any cargo they could use to mount a defense.

The screams diminished around half-past twelve, but the roars and howls continued. In the distance feet scampered and large rats bustled about on the deck. By one in the morning, the cries had stopped, but not the other hideous sounds from above.

The roars came closer.

"There's two of them." Tony pointed to the deck above.

"Is Turpelator back?" TJ asked.

"Could be," said Tony.

Fireman Frank patted TJ on the shoulder. "What can we do?"

"Hope the cargo hold door stays locked." Tony moved to the bottom of the ladder. He climbed high enough to reach up and test the door. "The pirates latched it from the other side. No lock on this side."

"What about CJ and Snpgrdxz? Turpelator might kill them," said Gilbert.

Heavy footsteps approached the cargo door. Two somethings howled.

"CJ and Turpelator have joined forces," said Frank.

"Anyone have silver?" Tony screamed from the ladder.

Gilbert grabbed a hat from one of the passengers. "I can take a collection."

Tony climbed back down the ladder. "No time. We'll form a wall of people with coins held up. The werewolves will back away from silver. It's painful to them."

Gilbert and my Jennifer helped organize the people into a wall. Tony had the front row kneel to hold coins low in the wall. My Jennifer positioned the ladies in the second row to form the middle height of the wall. A group of the men stood behind the ladies to form the top of the wall.

Tony explained the battle plan. The front rows formed the defensive wall. Each person was to hold up three coins, one in each hand and one propped in their lips. This would at least slow down the werewolves. Tony told the people behind the wall to throw their coins at the werewolves as soon as they started down the ladder.

We held our position for what turned into several hours. Near dawn, the cargo hold door exploded in a cloud of splinters. Two werewolves dropped down the ladder and slammed onto the deck in front of our human defensive shield. The creatures wrestled like puppies. Within a short time, sunlight flooded the cargo hold.

One of the werewolves collapsed to the deck as soon as the light appeared. The other smiled at us. I'm not sure which was scarier, a roaring beast or a smiling werewolf. The smiling werewolf scampered up the ladder and out of sight.

A howl came from the deck above and then silence. I ran up the ladder with Captain Jenkins behind me.

"Where'd he go," I asked.

Captain Jenkins gazed over the sea off the side of the boat. "Werewolf, I mean man overboard!" The captain pointed in the distance.

Snpgrdxz the fake werewolf waved. He dove under. He didn't come back up.

I slid down the ladder and knocked over CJ. She wore Frank's shirt which was long enough to cover her bottom until she fell head over bare keister across the deck.

CJ belched. She smiled and waved at the people still in the hold. "I feel great."

"Man overboard," I screamed. The crew took off up the ladder.

CJ giggled. She belched again and covered her mouth.

"She's high." Frank placed his arm around CJ's shoulders.

"Thanks, Frankie, for covering my assets. It is cool down here. Let's go upstairs." CJ headed for the ladder.

"No!" Frank shouted. "You'll expose your bottom again."

"Oh my, I forgot." CJ giggled some more before she let out another large belch.

Frank asked, "Are there any clothes in those containers?"

My Jennifer ran to the ladder. "I'll get some from the cabin. That is, if it's safe to go on deck."

"It's safe," I said. "The pirates are gone."

"What about Turpelator?" my Jennifer asked.

"It wasn't him. It was a fake werewolf."

"He looked real enough to me," said First Mate McNichols.

"No need to worry about him, he's gone overboard." I followed my Jennifer up the ladder. Near the top I turned around. "Any ideas about where the pirates went?"

CJ belched. Her eyes twinkled as she positioned her long, lanky legs like a New York model. She shrugged. "I ate them."

***

Crewmen in two rowboats searched for hours, but they couldn't find the werewolf.

"Do werewolves swim?" asked Tony.

Daniel Brickmaster arrived on deck. He wore a hat, but his hair was wet where it stuck out beneath.

I sidled up to him. "Sweet move."

Captain Jenkins called off the search toward sundown. With the blood and miscellaneous body parts washed off the deck by the crew, and the pirate captain locked away in chains, the ship made its way into the sunset towards New York.

The sun sank below the western horizon when Captain Jenkins ordered CJ locked in iron chains in an iron cage in the cargo hold.

Frank protested, "You can't do that to her. She's an American citizen."

"It's okay, my dear. I'm not very hungry at the moment." CJ kissed Frank full on the lips before two of the sailors clapped irons on her wrists and led her away.

"We better keep an eye on her," Tony said.

TJ placed her arms around little Jenny. "I'll stay with this one tonight."

My Jennifer sighed. She put her arm through mine and snuggled close. "We'll keep an eye on CJ."

"Take the first watch then. I'll join you at midnight," Tony said.

"I'll stay the night with CJ. You can sleep in your cabins." I snuggled against my darling Jennifer. This was as warm and affectionate as my Jennifer had been in our second season.

"We'll take turns," said Gilbert.

Daniel moved to Frank's side. "I'll keep Frank company."

On the way to the cargo hold, my Jennifer and I stopped by Tony's cabin for a ration of silver bullets and Glocks. The others loaded up with silver bullets.

On the way out of Tony's cabin, my Jennifer clunked her clunker, knocked her noggin and restored her memory of me.

Paul R. Lloyd

CHAPTER 39

ABOUT TIME FOR LOVE

Jennifer, my beloved Jennifer, bent over in pain and cried a single "Ouch" followed by a string of profanities that reminded me that her days as an innocent fifteen-year-old were long past. She held her hands to her head in the spot above her forehead and past her hairline where the lump formed.

"The girl cusses like a sailor," Frank said.

"She is a sailor," said Tony. "She's sailing anyway. I suppose she can cuss like a passenger on a paddlewheel."

Jennifer gazed around the cabin at us. Tears fell from her eyes. Her face reddened. She took a deep breath and sighed. Her pained expression turned joyful. She smiled. She placed a hand on my chest and then she kissed me with all the passion of a lover as she slid her arms around my neck.

"It's about time," shouted Frank.

Tony said, "I agree, dude and dudette Wild Thing."

When Jennifer broke off the kiss and I opened my eyes, I noticed the whole gang hugged each other and cried. They clapped their hands. I hadn't realized what a soap opera my love life had become to them.

"I remember you," Jennifer said. "Oh, I am a Ganarski girl. Bryan, can you forgive me for forgetting?" A fearful shadow crossed Jennifer's face.

"It's not your fault, Jennifer. It was never your fault." Now I cried.

Jennifer and I hugged for a long while. The others left the cabin to give us alone time. Tony closed the door behind him.

"How's your head?" I asked.

"Sore." She touched her head. "Ouch."

I kissed her head.

"Ouch."

"Sorry."

"I know why I forgot you, Bryan."

"Why."

"I became afraid for us. I loved you and you loved me back. The thought of us together forever scared me. I know that now. I didn't before. I regained my memory, and now I have a whole new perspective."

"That's a lot to take in all at once."

"No, it's great, Bryan. You've been so good to me with my memory of you gone. You've been so patient with me. I couldn't ask for a better boyfriend. Oh, Bryan, I'm so happy."

My Jennifer didn't burst into song or dance across the ship deck, although I did receive a brief image of her running through a mountain meadow in the opening scene of The Sound of Music. Instead of singing, she grabbed a couple of Glocks off Tony's bunk and bolted from the cabin. I'm not sure I could duplicate her jumping-while-running motion, but she looked happy from the front and the back as she disappeared up the ladder to go on deck.

I stayed in the cabin for a few more minutes before I gathered my weapons. If my darling was so excited about her restored memory, why did she forget me in the cabin?

***

Our second night in the cargo hold was darker, colder and damper than the first. Fewer people around brought out the rats. I was so happy to be with my Jennifer and our friends. She continued to jump up and down as she stood next to me.

"I remember. I remember," she sang. Now she sang.

The crew had placed CJ in chains inside an iron cage. They placed the cage inside a large wooden crate.

At about eleven-thirty, Daniel asked, "Where are the rats?"

"They desert sinking ships," Frank said.

"Are we sinking?" CJ's muffled voice had a nervous twinge.

Frank placed a hand on the crate. "No. We were concerned about the rats. They've retired for the night."

"They know what will happen." CJ sniffled.

"Do you think you'll change again tonight?" Gilbert asked.

"Certain of it. My blood itches." CJ's voice cracked.

"Does her voice sound a bit lower than usual?" Daniel asked.

"We better get ready to shoot," I said.

"Over my dead body," Frank said.

Gilbert laughed. "No problem, Frank. You stand close to that big old box and the rest of us will wait back here. We can hold our fire until after CJ eats your ass. Wait, that didn't sound right."

I gave Gilbert a high-five. My Jennifer elbowed me in the ribs and giggled.

Footsteps drummed above and half a dozen crewmen came down the ladder. Tony followed them. Someone locked the cargo hold door from above.

"This could be a long night," Tony said. He held an M16 under his coat.

"I won't take long," CJ said. "I'll be out in a jiffy as soon as I change."

My Jennifer laughed and I snickered. The rest of them stared at us.

"She's about to change," my Jennifer said.

One of the sailors nudged a buddy. "Change. Get it, matey?"

"Aye," said the other. "There be no funny business in 'er changes, be there?"

"If you boys are nervous, I'll wait in…" CJ let out a growl in mid-sentence.

We backed away from the cargo container as a group.

"Think the chains will hold?" Gilbert asked.

At midnight the howls of a trapped and enraged animal began. The crate shook and bounced across the floor. The chains rattled. At about five past the hour, we heard heavy metal cracking.

The crate flipped over on its side with a yelp from the animal trapped inside.

"That must have hurt," said Tony.

The crate shook and rattled for hours. Based on the cracking noises, CJ had no difficulty with the chains, but the iron cage was sterner stuff. What frightened us more than a werewolf in a cage inside a wooden crate was a pissed off werewolf in a cage inside of a wooden crate. CJ, if it's okay to call an animal by that name, howled, clawed, scratched, yanked, and shook her cage.

Around two in the morning, we settled down. There was a common, unspoken consensus that CJ couldn't go anywhere despite her protestations.

The evening wasn't only about fear and angst. For my Jennifer and me, the night was about love and angst. Here we were, my Jennifer all of fifteen. Me sixteen. Or were we sixteen and seventeen? Or seventeen and eighteen?

Our ages depended on how you counted the months. It was spring. We left in August, arrived in July, stayed until January, crossed the underworld without a written record of our time, but we travelled weeks on end. We arrived in January of eighteen thirty-eight. So much in life depended on coming of age or growing up or reaching the age of majority. No matter how you described it, a kid had to know when he or she reached there. It was about freedom, dating and driving privileges. Were Jennifer and I old enough for an adult relationship?

Jennifer and I spent the night together down in the cargo hold. This was not our first overnighter because we spent our nights together back in troll land, and Jennifer served as my night nurse while I recovered from a gunshot wound in nineteen twenty-three. But it was better than a goodnight smile followed by a night apart, like we did back in our Dickens Day apartment.

Our make-out session began around two-thirty to the tune of CJ's cage bouncing on the deck. The trick was to scooch our butts into a dark corner behind a quiet crate large enough to hide behind while avoiding Little Jenny's pee spot from the night before. With privacy, we relaxed and enjoyed the moment. Sometime after four o'clock my Jennifer snored while she rested her head in the crook of my arm. I remember someone said we had an hour or so until sunup. The next time I opened my eyes, the sun shone through the hold.

"I love you," my Jennifer whispered and nuzzled my ear.

I tried to catch my breath and wake up at the same time. When I did, I said, "I love you, too."

I turned to face her. She smiled. I kissed her, despite her morning breath. Then we both turned away.

"Sorry about that," my Jennifer said.

"Me too." I stood up and buckled my pants. When had they become undone? And how far did we go? And what were we up to while we slept? And how was this sexier than sleeping together in our undies back in the troll world desert?

My Jennifer stood up. She straightened her skirts and petticoats or whatever you call those Victorian layers. She stepped close to me, placed her arms around my neck and hugged me.

"Thanks for last night," I said.

"Many more to come." My Jennifer blushed on the word "come" and pulled back from the hug. She shrugged and smiled.

The crate rattled. "Will somebody please let me out of here?" CJ sounded annoyed but human.

Tony and two of the sailors pried the wood crate open. They had nailed it together with extra-long spikes, so it took a good pull on a crowbar to yank one out.

CJ was dressed by the time they had the crate open. Tony unlocked the cage. The chains were in pieces on the floor like someone had broken them apart link-by-link.

CJ stepped out of the cage. "When do we eat, boys?"

No one came down to the cargo hold during the day, except my Jennifer and me. We chose it as our make out spot for the week after the last of CJ's full moon antics. In the evenings we hung out on deck with Frank and CJ who had their own thing in action.

The seas stayed calm as we made our way towards New York.

Three days out from New York City, I proposed to my beloved Jennifer Hawkins.

CHAPTER 40

THE LADY OF THE RING

Jennifer, my darling Jennifer, kissed me, hugged me and held her left hand out like she expected an engagement ring.

"Oh yeah, the ring. Hadn't thought of that." I rooted around in my pockets hoping to find what I knew I didn't have.

"How can you propose to a girl without a ring?"

"I can give you one from nineteen twenty-three. It looks like a wedding ring. I'll get you an engagement ring as soon as we hit New York. If you still want to marry me, of course."

"The plain one looks like a wedding ring, so I'll receive my rings in reverse order."

"Then we're engaged?" I asked.

"Do ship's captains perform weddings?"

"I'm not sure."

Jennifer shook her head. "It was a rhetorical question, my love. Of course they do. Imagine a shipboard wedding and a honeymoon on an antique ocean steamer. The girls will be so jealous when we get home."

"If we get home."

"What do you mean? Of course, we'll return home. Where else would we go?"

"Once we're married, home is wherever we're together."

"And whenever we're together, my love."

"Yes, whenever. There's no guarantee the Wheaton When Portal will return us to our time." I kissed Jennifer on the cheek.

"We have no reason to believe it won't either. We don't have to return to the exact time. All we have to do is get close enough to be home with our families and friends. I still miss Mommy." Jennifer kissed my lips.

"We still have the issue of the Jennifer Time Loop."

"What problem?"

"At some point in our journey, you'll become separated from the rest of us and end up in Wheaton in nineteen-eighteen. Remember, that's how we got CJ, Third Jennifer and Little Jenny's late mother."

Jennifer took my hand. "I'll never let you go, young man. You're mine. Forever. Whenever or wherever we end up."

"And I'm yours forever, but if we marry now, how come CJ never mentioned it? For that matter, TJ would have told us."

"Honey, it's because they both know they are married to you, but you belong to me."

***

"You're way too young to marry, little sister," CJ said. "Why, I'm not old enough to marry Frank." We were gathered in Tony's cabin. Daniel leaned against an open closet door. Behind him in the closet, I could see the backpacks with the guns, ammo and other weapons Tony insisted we bring on our journey. CJ sat next to Frank on Tony's bottom bunk. They held hands. Tony was next on the bunk. He leaned back against the bulkhead.

Gilbert lay on the top bunk, where he normally slept. Third Jennifer sat on Tony's bulky wooden travel trunk, acquired in London. Little Jenny snuggled in her lap. Snpgrdxz sat on the cabin floor or was it a deck? I stood propped with my back against the closed cabin door with one arm around my Jennifer.

"Marry me?" Frank asked. "Wow, sweetheart. I wanted to wait until we returned home, but of course I'll marry you."

CJ kissed Frank on the lips. They hugged. CJ pulled back with a huge grin on her face. "Turns out I am old enough to marry Frank, but you, little sister, are too young. You're only fifteen."

Gilbert waved a hand in front of CJ and Frank from his perch on the top bunk. "Did we just witness a proposal and acceptance here?"

Frank leaned in and kissed CJ on the cheek. "Did they witness an acceptance, darling?"

CJ's face brightened as her smile broadened. "I proposed to you, and I heard you accept. You can't back out now, pal."

"Never, my love." Frank gazed about the room. "I have an announcement to make, team. CJ and I are engaged."

Gilbert rolled onto his back. "Still doesn't answer that Ganarski girl's question. How come CJ and TJ never mentioned your marriage? And how could Little Jenny's mother marry in London if she was already married to Bryan Ganarski? And, to muddy things a bit more, how can CJ marry Frank when she's already married to Bryan? But wait, there's more. How can Bryan become engaged to his Ganarski girl when he's already married to her, CJ, TJ and the late Mommy Jennifer and who knows how many other Jennifers?"

"Is Uncle Bryan my daddy?" Little Jennifer asked. She jumped off TJ's lap to run over and hug my legs.

While my jaw scratched my belly button, CJ came to my rescue and her own rescue and everybody else's rescue. She pointed a finger into the air. Yeah, the one in the middle. She flicked it at Gilbert. "First, Gilbert Armstrong, I never married Bryan Ganarski. Not that I wouldn't have said yes if he had asked me when we were young."

She pointed the same digit at my Jennifer and then me. "Your engagement is a new wrinkle in time here. I became separated from Bryan, Tony, and Gilbert when we first tried to make our way out of the troll world on the other side of the Wheaton When Portal. This stuff is as new to me as it is to you."

TJ yanked Little Jenny off her life lock around my legs and planted her back on her lap. "I'm with CJ. I mean I'm really with CJ. Her story is my story through your nineteen twenty-three episode, but when we re-entered the troll world, I became separated from you guys. I wandered about for three years until you found me.

"Remember, there have been lots of CJ's. Every time I enter the troll world, I'm sucked back into nineteen eighteen in a time loop. And I'm always returned to young Jennifer's age. The difference is I retain the memory of every adventure. I can recall fifteen trips through the time loop. CJ remembers twenty-eight, so I know where I'm headed. As for the rest of you, good luck."

"We will get married," my Jennifer hollered. I hugged her closer.

"I can explain everything," Tony said.

CHAPTER 41

BUT NOT NOW

I waved my free left hand in Tony's direction. "Before you explain, Tony, my Jennifer and I are headed to see the captain. He can perform the ceremony for us." My mistake here was not allowing Tony to explain. In the joy of the marriage moment and related disaster, Tony didn't bring up the subject again.

My Jennifer and I took off in the direction of the captain's cabin. I could hear the others scramble along behind us out of sight in the soupy mix of fog and rain, which made me happy because we wanted them to attend our wedding. They were our family in this time before any of our parents and siblings were born. Well, my sibling. Jennifer was an only child before all the duplicates of herself showed up.

Captain Jenkins gave up on the weather and gathered us on deck in the fog and light drizzle of the afternoon one day out of New York. "We are gathered together in this miserable mess to join one man and one woman in holy wedlock. If there be anyone among us who has reason for these two not to marry, let him now speak or forever hold his peace. And what is that awful smell?"

The word "him" struck me as odd because our group included both men and women, but I had learned in our London days that the word "man" included both men and women by definition in the nineteenth century. This made it easy for a speaker to not have to say "men and women" all the time, but I never became used to it.

The other word that snagged my attention was "smell." A faint aroma of dead meat wafted in with the fog. Were we close enough to land to smell the meat rotting on the wharves? We were supposed to be another day out.

Despite the wafting aroma, I smiled my best smile at my friends and shipmates. Jennifer beamed with me. We knew the Captain's call for impediments was simply a tradition to be honored.

But as I contemplated the saying of the vowels, TJ spoke up. "Captain Jenkins, these two are not man and woman. They are boy and girl. They are too young for marriage. He is but sixteen and she fifteen."

"My dear Miss Hawkins of the many Miss Hawkinses, we are under British flag. A woman may marry at the age of twelve and a man at age fourteen. Why, see they are both mature adults, if a tad wet behind the ears. Now, then, if there are no other impediments to mention, let us proceed before this aroma sends us all below decks. Who gives this woman to this man?"

Jennifer's dad should have been here. Of course if Principal Hawkins had been here, he would have thrown us both into detention and put an end to what he would have called "this nonsense."

My sweet Jennifer spoke up for us, "I give myself in marriage." She grabbed my arm and leaned in close. She peered into my eyes and back to Captain Jenkins. "For now and for all times."

Captain Jenkins smiled as he glanced over our little group. "No finer words have I heard spoken as to love so I ask you, Bryan Ganarski, citizen of the United States of America, and traveler from who knows where to who knows when but aboard the good ship Rapid at this time, do you take this woman, Jennifer Hawkins, also a citizen of the United States, to be your wife for now and for all times?"

"I do," I said.

Captain Jenkins smiled at Jennifer. "And do you, Jennifer Hawkins, citizen of the United States of America, and traveler from who knows where to who knows when but aboard the good ship Rapid at this time, take this man, Bryan Ganarski, to be your husband for now and for all times?"

"I do," Jennifer said.

"Then by the power vested in me by her majesty Queen Victoria – "

A musket shot rang out. Captain Jenkins collapsed to the deck as blood formed on his forehead.

"But he didn't say we were married yet," Jennifer cried.

***

The pirate captain shouted, "Avast ye swabs, I'm captain of this here vessel now. Anyone objects and they walks the plank."

Frank laughed.

Tony ducked down to attend to the captain.

A few of the passengers gasped, but most of them simply held their noses and stared.

The pirate captain raised another flint lock pistol and was about to fire at Tony when my beloved yanked up her wedding gown, revealed her pretty reverse map of Italy birthmark, snagged a Glock from her baby blue wedding garter, and blew the pirate away with a single shot that struck him between the eyes.

"Nobody messes with my wedding." Jennifer spit into the wind, dropped her skirt, winked at me, dropped the smoking Glock into her bridal purse and caught the spit ball in the palm of her hand as the wind blew it back to her.

Tony assisted Captain Jenkins to stand. CJ held a handkerchief to his forehead to staunch the bleeding. My Jennifer wiped the spitball on the handkerchief.

"Eww, what'd you do that for," said CJ.

"Had to wipe it somewhere and Bryan's blue jeans are clean." Jennifer nudged me.

"How bad is it?" Gilbert asked.

"There's boogers all over the top side. I'll only be able to use the bottom," said CJ.

"I meant how bad is the captain?" asked Gilbert.

"He has a graze wound, lighter than the time Bryan was hit back in nine... I mean Wheaton," said Tony. "It's not bad. He should be okay in a day or two."

"Day or two! What about our wedding?" my Jennifer shouted.

"You folks won't be around in a day or two," said Turpelator.

We gazed at the port side of our little boat where Turpelator's voice came from. In the confusion of the pirate captain disrupting our wedding, a ghost ship had sidled up to the Rapid.

The ghost ship, while every bit as ugly as you can imagine a rotting wood sailing vessel that hadn't seen port in decades, was worse than it looked for it carried with it the aroma that we'd been suffering with. I now identified it as the smell of death.

Turpelator's voice scared me, but my fright increased when I noticed two Turpelator's standing on the railing. James Turpelator, the dead bootlegger from nineteen twenty-three, stood next to Rev. Turpelator from our current time. Just when you think you are overcome with fear, something truly awful happens to crank up the scare-o-meter. As I gazed about the ghost ship, I saw the rigging filled with tall, green zombie pirates. When the zombie pirates noticed me glaring at them, they began rattling their sabers and shouting "zom" over and over.

The zombie pirates didn't go unnoticed by the crew and passengers who returned the zombie pirate song with a cheer of their own, a series of unrelated screams. With our stuff below deck, I knew we were doomed. I cowered while the rest of our little group charged below.

As a person who thinks of totally unrelated things at times of great distress, especially mind-boggling fear, I wasn't surprised to have Jennifer's wedding dress pop into my mind. Where did she find it? It's not like you can go shopping in the middle of the Atlantic, even if we were closer to New York's fashion district than to London. I remembered Jennifer telling me that Tony pulled it out of his backpack. He told her he was saving it for her. Makes you wonder what else that man keeps in there. And why did he pack a wedding dress for what was supposed to be an afternoon jaunt through the tunnels beneath Lincoln High School? He promised we'd be home in time for dinner.

The two Turpelator's were natural generals, meaning the zombie pirates had to do the work of killing me. The first zombie pirate, a short fellow who wore a pirate hat to bring himself up to five feet tall, swung his cutlass at my head. I ducked, but not fast enough. The cutlass banged off the top of my head without injury. I became enraged.

While the zombie pirate took another swing, I punched him in the jaw which caused three teeth to fly from his rotten mouth. He fell to the deck. I stomped on his forearm causing him to let go the cutlass. I snagged it and chopped the zombie pirate's head off. I kicked its head across the deck where it rolled under the foot of a much larger zombie pirate.

The basketball player sized pirate zombie charged with his cutlass pointed at my chest. I sidestepped him and chopped off his head off as he went by. I grabbed his cutlass and faced the swarming horde of zombie pirates. Many of the zombie pirates kept busy making short work of the crew and passengers.

Snpgrdxz appeared out of a crowd of zombie pirates. He had transformed into a large, axe-wielding lumberjack. He had shaped both hands into double edged battle axes and let fly at the zombie pirates. Zombie pirate heads flew about the deck.

I worked my way towards him by swinging my two cutlasses. The zombie pirates were no slouches when it came to taking on my amateur swordsmanship, but their swords kept breaking against my arms and legs while my cutlasses proved excellent for the performance of head adjustment services.

When I reached Snpgrdxz, we worked back to back against the zombie pirates. By this time, we heard gunfire on deck. Our gang had returned with their M16s. Jennifer, my bride, charged in my direction, wiping out zombie pirate heads along the way.

Another of those zombie pirate basketball players charged up behind my Jennifer and lifted her over his head. He tossed her overboard. She screamed.

"Jennifer!" I hollered. I charged to the ship's railing and dove in after her. She was gone.

Jennifer's Victorian wedding dress was so heavy with all the layers of stuff underneath that she sank like a rock. I dove under but couldn't find her. I spotted Snpgrdxz dive past me under the water. He was in the midst of morphing into a shark. I popped up for air and dove under again but saw nothing.

While gasping on the surface again, a shark broke through the water and leaped on deck. In its mouth was Jennifer. Gilbert tossed me a rope and I started to climb back on board.

"Where do you think you're going?" said a very loud Turpelator. I feared peeking over my shoulder but the urge to learn what kind of Turpelator monster I was dealing with was too great. I turned. What I saw caused me to exhale more air than I had inhaled.

Paul R. Lloyd

CHAPTER 42

MONSTER OF THE DEEP

The sea serpent was double the size of the Rapid and longer than that zombie pirate ghost ship.

"You appear to be a right tasty morsel for a sea serpent not used to finding humans in his water." The creature snagged me with its shark-like teeth. It flipped me high into the air and positioned itself to catch me into its mouth for the big swallow as I dropped.

Gilbert tossed me an M16. I caught it.

"Grenade," I yelled as I dropped into the monster's mouth. Sea serpent breath was similar to the aroma you inhaled on the wrong side of the beach islands in New Jersey. The sea-facing side of the islands smelled nice, crisp and salty. But the side facing the mainland had brackish, rotting fish smelling air. That was the best I could compare Turpelator the sea serpent's breath to.

Don't even ask about how I know so much about what a New Jersey beach island smelled like. I'll just say that my dad was not the best picker of vacation spots but the house facing the mainland side that he rented was cheaper than the beach front places.

Meanwhile the grenade Gilbert tossed bounced off the sea serpent's teeth. I was on the wrong side of the teeth at the time. I opened fire on the creature's gums at the base of his front teeth. It opened its mouth wide. I yelled, "Pull the pin next time." I dove for the ocean as a better choice than the serpent's belly.

Gilbert pulled the pin on a grenade and tossed it at Turpelator monster. The grenade landed in the creature's mouth just as the brute snagged me before I could hit the water. If you thought about it, hitting the inside of the monster's mouth at the same time as a live grenade was not the best assurance of a long life.

I kicked my feet in an attempt to escape. I felt something against my foot as I kicked. I looked down into the darkness of the beast's throat and spotted the instant of explosion. The creature's mouth was open enough still that I was able to clamber over its teeth and duck in the groove between its teeth and lips.

The jarring effect of the explosion left me bouncing between the soft gummy tissue under the creature's lip area and its teeth. The monster shook its head causing more violent thrusting about of my body. The thing spit a large gush of blood that washed me into the ocean.

"I don't like dentists," said Turpelator the sea serpent. It swam off into the fog.

Gilbert threw me another rope and hauled me back on deck with the help of Tony and Frank. I checked on my Jennifer who battled zombie pirates despite her saturated wedding dress. We embraced while the battle swarmed around us. By this time, the zombie pirates knew to keep away from my Jennifer. Some realized they couldn't kill me no matter how many times they stabbed me with their cutlasses. Instead they attacked Tony, TJ, CJ and Frank.

"Are you okay?" I asked my Jennifer.

"No, we're not married yet."

"I think we are. We said our vows."

"But Captain Jenkins didn't pronounce us."

"That could be tricky, Jen. I think that's his body in the corner there."

My Jennifer screamed as she tore into a swath of zombie pirates. Heads flew left and right as the battle moved in our favor. We were down to about fifty zombie pirates and two Turpelator admirals.

Then the giant sea serpent showed up again. Turpelator the sea serpent was still not on our side.

"I can deal with this monster. Toss me a grenade," I said.

Tony tossed a grenade at me. I batted it with my cutlass sending it to the two Turpelator admirals. It exploded at their feet. Blood and body parts replaced them on the rail of the ghost ship.

"This time don't pull the pin," I said.

"Oh," said Tony. He tossed me another grenade that I caught.

I yanked the pin and tossed the grenade into the sea serpent's mouth. With its mouth closed, it said, "Not again."

The grenade exploded taking the front of the sea serpent's mouth with it. The serpent slunk under the water.

I spun about to take on more zombie pirates, but they had retreated back to their ghost ship. The ship sailed into the fog despite having no sails or other means of propulsion.

***

We buried a dozen sailors and crew that afternoon. Captain Jenkins went over last. First mate McNichols conducted the services. When he finished, my Jennifer, still in her sopping wet bridal dress, sidled up to the first mate. "Are you the captain now?"

"Yes, temporary until we make landfall. The owners will appoint the new captain."

"Are you captain enough to pronounce us?" Tears dibbled down Jennifer's cheeks.

"Pronounce you? Pronounce you what?"

"You know."

"Know what?"

"Man and wife."

"But Captain Jenkins did all that already. We can't be having weddings after so many funerals at sea."

"But he didn't pronounce us. We have to be pronounced."

"Oh, all right." First mate and temporary captain McNichols called all hands to deck. The crew and passengers trudged back from below. We could see their exhaustion.

"What is it?" Tony asked. He sounded peeved.

"We have to finish what Captain Jenkins started so this young couple can move forward in their new lives and this young man can remove this young lady's wedding dress before she catches the chills so now by the power I think might be vested in me as first mate and acting skipper of the Rapid, I now pronounce you two man and wife. May God bless this union now and for all times. You may sign the log."

"Aren't we supposed to kiss first?" Jennifer asked.

"You're married now, missy. You can kiss him any time you like. Right now, we need the book signed all legal and proper like."

We signed the log with our friends as witnesses. Our signatures stood out against the other writing in the log for its modern appearance. Tony had a nice cursive signature, while the rest of us managed to scribble our names as various forms of wavy lines and printed letters. We were keyboarders, not calligraphers.

The odd way our signatures appeared caught McNichols's attention. "English would have been sufficient for your signatures. And I notice the three Miss Hawkinses signed their names with exactly the same scroll. How be that, mateys?"

"We're sisters. Hand writing runs in the family," said CJ.

"Well, if it runs in the family, I would think it would be finer than what I'm seeing here, but no matter. Your X would do for signature purposes and this is more than your X so all is well and all is legal like, I think."

Jennifer pulled me into an embrace. As my friends and shipmates, crew and time travelers cheered our first marriage kiss, Third Jennifer muttered, "They're too young."

CHAPTER 43

FIRST NIGHT

"Ouch!" my Jennifer squealed in a natural enough voice when you consider I didn't know how to undress a Victorian lady with her layer upon layer of material. I began well enough as the clothing removal process involved a mere matter of undoing two thousand three hundred and eighty-seven buttons.

Given the complexity of the task to arrive at bare skin, how did Victorians produce offspring?

Our cabin had been occupied by the pirate captain before CJ ate his crew. A couple of sailors set up a double bed for us to sleep in, not that we needed the extra bed space on our honeymoon night. They shared several off-color wedding night stories with us that sounded very much like the ones you hear at weddings in our home time. The cabin had a porthole window, a closet and a cabin door with a lock that didn't quite catch until I yanked the door hard to the left.

To get to this eloquent bridal cabin, we first had to share a round of rum for all hands. Jennifer had to change into dry but Victorian clothes for the wedding supper. Acting captain McNichols poured the toast. There followed a round of handshakes and kisses for the bride from passengers and crew alike. Dinner was the usual shipboard fare, but meager as supplies were low this close to port. Tony, bless his heart, promised us a steak dinner at a New York restaurant he thought was supposed to be pretty good. He called it Delmonico's.

When the handshaking and kissing of the bridal couple led CJ to take my hand, she smiled with tears down her cheeks. "I'm so happy for you and your Jennifer."

"This must be hard for you," I said. "I found it easy to think of you and Third Jennifer as my Jennifer's older sisters. But you're not. You two are my Jennifer as she roams through time. You attended your own wedding, in a sense. Are you my wife, too? No, my head won't wrap around that. But you are an older Jennifer with my Jennifer's memories up to the time you split off into your own timeline. What I'm attempting to say, and not succeeding at, is if I were in your shoes, I'd be suffering at this moment to gaze upon a younger version of myself marrying someone I once loved."

CJ hugged me. "My tears are not for you, dear Bryan. Yes, you were my first love, but I'm crying for what I have lost in these years of time travel. I have aged and could pass for a college student, but remember, I've been through the time warp twenty-eight times and carry the memory of each round. I've lived with and without you in my life for more than one hundred forty years. I'm a very old lady, and it's been a long time since the day you approached me in Lincoln High School and kissed me. Yes, I am fond of you and will always cherish that awkward, childish moment, but I am no longer your Jennifer and have not been for a very, very long time."

Despite her protestations, CJ kissed me with a taste of tongue work before she backed off with a smirk like a teasing pixie. "You did say we were married, right?"

My Jennifer punched CJ on the shoulder. "Hey!"

When Third Jennifer came up for the handshake, she wore the stern expression that had become her trademark. "You're too damn young, buster." She moved down the line to repeat her one line to my Jennifer. She changed "buster" to "missy."

Little Jenny hugged my knees, stared up to my face and smiled. I lifted her so we were eyeball-to-eyeball. "Don't you want to kiss the groom?" I asked.

"Yes, Daddy." She planted a wet one on my cheek.

"I'm not your daddy."

"I was kidding, Daddy."

I handed her over to my Jennifer. "I didn't know a five-year-old could tease?"

When Tony came through the line, he shook my hand. "Good luck, young man, and take good care of your Wild Thing. She will make you a happy man over the years, whenever in time you two end up."

Frank shook my hand. "I'm next, stud."

Snpgrdxz tried to kiss me, but I pushed him off with a cry, "Yo!" Funny how "yo" resonated so well with the crew aboard the Rapid.

Gilbert grabbed me into a hug. "You dumb somnabitch."

Meanwhile, back at that "ouch" cried by my Jennifer in our honeymoon cabin. I had thought the wedding night bit would be the easiest as it sounded so natural for two persons in love. While we hadn't done the deed before the wedding, we had practiced the setup during our make out sessions while hidden away in the cargo hold.

The first serious indication of an issue with inexperience in matters of mating came when I planted a foot-long scratch down the middle of Jennifer's back, caused when my hand slipped while I unraveled a girdle thingie secured to Jennifer's midsection by tight lacing, like the laces on shoes, except these were larger.

To make amends for the scratch that led to the angry ouch, I planted a series of butterfly kisses down her spine. Goose bumps formed on her skin so she enjoyed butterfly kisses, unless it meant she was cold. I wanted to work on keeping her warm in the future.

After completing my assignment as the officially-designated Jennifer undresser, my Jennifer undressed me.

"I prefer to open my own presents." She worked on my multiplicity of buttons. The ones located where a pants zipper belonged proved the most difficult. I shouted more than a few ouches of my own and danced merrily about the cabin. Well, not exactly merrily, but I did hop about until my privates recovered.

The goose bumps proved more related to cold than passion, although passion played a huge part of our wedding night. We snuggled together under a couple of blankets until our own body heat warmed us.

Under those scratchy woolen blankets, my Jennifer and I became man and wife. You don't need to know the details of our awkwardness or how Jennifer received the other scratch, the one on her left thigh that crossed her dark birth mark shaped like a backwards map of Italy. Nor do you need to know about her teeth marks impressed upon me in a spot where teeth marks don't belong.

We curled up in each other's arms as we sailed towards New York City with half a continent left to cross before we could time travel home. With Jennifer's eyes closed in sleep and mine heavy, I realized I had not solved any of the mysteries from that long ago impossible week before the start of my junior year of high school.

Why did Jennifer Hawkins take a shot at me? Why did Snpgrdxz kill her? Why did Gilbert bury her and then dig her up? How was Jennifer able to help Gilbert and Snpgrdxz dig herself up?

The answers involved time travel, and this road trip wasn't yet over. I had so many questions on our wedding night with no answers. Would we find Maria Gonzalez? Would DaemonTurpelator ever stay dead after we killed him? And what about CJ? Would she always be a werewolf? Could her condition become worse?

I felt bad about abandoning the ghost of Brigitte Wurzburger who hunted for her lost body back in nineteen twenty-three. Would she ever find it? I suspected her cause was lost to history in which case she may be haunting the old Turpelator mansion to this day. Well, not this day in eighteen thirty-eight, but to our home time in the twenty-first century.

With age came experience and with experience wisdom, or so Tony said. My wisdom came with the realization that you can't wimp out when it was time to take on the bullies, wayward teachers and the Daemon Turpelator no matter what hideous form he assumed.

When bullets flew, you had to stand in there with your comrades. And you had to tell the girl you were attracted to how you felt about her. Otherwise you would miss out on someone important. But wisdom had its limits. Like a fool, I thought wisdom begat courage. It didn't. My second mistake was to think I somehow had become courageous on this journey. My third error was to think the worst was behind us.

Despite all the unsolved mysteries in my life, one thing was certain as the good ship Rapid rocked me to sleep. Tony had been correct all along. That night my Jennifer had earned her nickname of Wild Thing.

THE END

Thanks for choosing the Snpgrdxz series.

Purchase more of my books, including **Snpgrdxz and the Time Hunters Book 3 of the Snpgrdxz Series** by searching Snpgrdxz on www.amazon.com.

Or keep reading the Snpgrdxz series now...

SNPGRDXZ
AND THE TIME HUNTERS

BOOK 3
OF THE SNPGRDXZ SERIES

BY PAUL R. LLOYD

CHAPTER 1

MONSTER ON THE LOOSE

I leaped over eighteen-year-old Jennifer Ganarski to block the bright orange and green beast from harming her while she slept. The fiend swiped at my chest with its hand-claw but did not break my skin. I jumped back and fell on my new bride's well-formed, but skinny bottom. My hand shook as I rubbed my uninjured chest.

Jennifer's eyes popped open. She started to yell at me to get off, but as she took in our strange orange visitor with the green racing stripe down its middle, its three-foot long, pointed tail covered in scales, and its bat-shaped wings – well, what would you do? My wife of eighteen hours yanked out a Glock from under her pillow and fired.

The brute backed away from us. The pesky villain pulled the bullet out of his chest with a hand-claw and tossed it on the deck. "Oh, no, Slorm makes mistake. You not queen. Where queen, Bryan Ganarski?"

The critter expressed its displeasure by raising two fist-claws into the air and sharply bending his pointy bat elbows while curling his back and stamping one foot-claw on the deck. It ran to the porthole and flung it open.

The monstrosity took one last gander at us and hissed before it thrust itself out the aperture.

I ran to the porthole and watched the demon flutter into the distance towards the hazy skyline of New York City visible beyond the bow of the ship. The skyline appeared lower than the one you know because the day I stared out of this porthole was in eighteen thirty-eight, decades before architects designed the first skyscrapers.

"What was that?" Jennifer asked.

"How did it know my name?"

"Seriously, what was it?"

I snuggled against her on the bed. "It was one more visible sign of my growing teenage insanity."

"If you're crazy, then so am I."

***

CJ, one of our travelling companions, achieved the minimum required front coverage if she yanked down on her t-shirt, which she did. This naturally made the back of her t-shirt rise up to expose her butt, but that was not visible to my Jennifer and me unless we chose to gaze into the mirror on the wall behind her. I gawped. Jennifer poked my ribs with her sharp elbow. That's when I noticed "Wheaton Fire Department" emblazoned across the front of her shirt.

CJ occupied the cabin next to ours. She matched my Jennifer with the prettiest wild green eyes you ever saw. Her pale complexion complemented her dark brunette hair. Her grin was ear-to-ear, unlike Jennifer's scowl.

"Put something on," Jennifer ordered.

"Don't you like my t-shirt? Frank gave it to me."

While the two young ladies appeared to be twins, they were more. We called my bride and joy my Jennifer, Wild Thing or that Ganarski woman among other things. I usually referred to her as "my Jennifer." Her twin was College Jennifer or CJ. CJ and Jennifer were in fact the same person brought together by their time travel misadventures. CJ appeared five years older than my Jennifer, again due to disparencies in time travel.

Fireman Frank approached the door from behind CJ. He placed a blanket around her. "Let's not catch cold, Darling." Frank had joined our road trip escapades when we found him in the land of the trolls on our first visit there. If you hadn't guessed by now, he and CJ had fallen in love despite CJ's tendency to show off more than most of us wanted to see.

"Spoilsport," CJ said as she covered herself.

"Why don't you guys dress while Jennifer and I check on the others?" I tugged my Jennifer's hand to lead her to the next cabin.

Third Jennifer answered her door. She was dressed in her buckskin outfit. "Time to head out?" We called her TJ when it didn't confuse us with CJ.

"Yes," my Jennifer said.

TJ was also the same person as the other two Jennifers. Wasn't time travel wonderful? You met yourself coming and going. This version of Jennifer was eight years older than my Jennifer, including five years from nineteen eighteen to nineteen twenty-three in our world plus the three years she survived in the troll land wilderness alone before we met up with her. She seemed most at home in rough neighborhoods where she had no problem ending any fight someone else started.

"Let me dress Little Jenny, and we'll meet you on deck," Third Jennifer said. Little Jenny was the five-year-old daughter of a fourth time-travelling version of my Jennifer. This other Jennifer was killed by a brutal rapist in London which resulted in poor Little Jenny being abandoned on the street. We were so blessed to find her.

"Coming Aunt Third Jennifer," Little Jenny called. Even though the many Jennifers were all the same person as the woman who gave birth to Little Jenny, she called each of them "aunt." It made sense when you considered that none of the Jennifers present on this voyage had actually been the version of Jennifer who gave birth to Little Jenny despite being the same person. Don't ask. It's a teenage insanity thing.

At the next cabin, we found the rest of our gang including Tony, our hippie high school art teacher and trip leader, Gilbert, my best friend from high school, and of course, Snpgrdxz. They were dressed and followed us on deck.

Snpgrdxz needed a little explanation. I won't tell you everything right now or we'd be here all day. He or she, depending on his or her mood, was a teenage alien shape shifter trapped on earth as the result of a flying saucer crash that killed the rest of his crew, including his father.

Snpgrdxz appeared as Daniel Brickmaster, his current teenage boy persona. He changed identity and shape every few years to avoid the infamous men in black since his flying saucer crashed back in nineteen forty-six. We weren't sure about running into the men in black in our current time, but you never know whose working for the feds or when the NSA was actually begun as opposed to when the government said they started it up.

Like my Jennifer, Gilbert and me, Snpgrdxz was a teenager when we set out on our journey, except in his case he was a one-hundred-seventy-five-year-old teenager. While he had about another one-hundred-fifty years to go before becoming an adult, the rest of us already had crossed that threshold or we felt like we had what with this road trip of ours taking multiple years. One of the little ironies of a time travel road trip was you lost track of how long you were gone.

With our group assembled on deck, I asked, "Did anyone see an orange guy running around? He was naked and had a green racing stripe down his middle. And he looked like a bat, except for the colors and long, scaly tail."

"Bryan, was it a female or male creature?" CJ asked.

"Male, but that's not important," I said.

"It would be important to him," CJ said.

My Jennifer placed her hands on her hips. "Bryan wants to know if you guys saw this critter. He invaded our cabin this morning and could be dangerous."

"I thought honeymooners were supposed to have sweet dreams," said Gilbert.

"Hey, how was your wedding night?" Snpgrdxz asked. This was a good time to mention that the best way to pronounce his name was to stick an "i" in every place you thought a vowel was needed. His name sounded like Snip-grid-ix.

My Jennifer punched him. "We better watch out for this monster because he knew Bryan's name. He said he was looking for a queen."

"Bryan's not a queen, is he?" asked Snpgrdxz.

We grabbed hold of the deck rail together as the paddle boat shifted hard towards port. We were about to dock.

Tony shook his head. "Jennifer's right. If there's a creature checking up on us, we better take care. We can't afford to have anything or anyone keep us from the Wheaton When Portal and our return home."

***

About half of my steak had vanished when Daemon Turpelator visited our table along with the short, orange-faced tagalong with a green stripe down its middle who had invaded our cabin back aboard the Rapid.

Paul R. Lloyd

True to his word, Tony Romano had treated the team to a steak dinner at Delmonico's after a day of wandering about the streets of old New York. We had booked passage on a riverboat scheduled to leave in the morning for the journey up the Hudson River when Tony announced our next stop was dinner.

While I had never heard of the place, everyone else, including Snpgrdxz, understood that Delmonico's was the finest Victorian restaurant in the world.

We had steaks that were maybe just under two inches thick and weighed a couple of pounds. Our waiter, a Black man named Joe Williams, explained that we could have our steaks "rare, done right or well done." "Done right" appealed to us. He served the steaks with mashed potatoes topped with cheese and breadcrumbs. We drank red French wine, despite our youth. If there was an age limit for alcohol, I never heard about it.

Turpelator smiled enough to indicate peaceful intent but not enough to expose his fangs. "Greetings, chums. Welcome to America."

Take your choice with Turpelator. Was he our physics teacher from back at Lincoln High? As far we knew, that Mr. Turpelator didn't have fangs, except for the time he visited my bedroom to suck my brains out but panicked when he noticed the big crucifix my grandma hung on the wall above my bed board. Trust me, you had to be there. Or was he some sort of vampire and werewolf combination like the Turpelator we ran into in the troll world?

Turpelator was a bootlegger when we visited nineteen twenty-three and a murderous pastor in London this year of eighteen thirty-eight. He bit CJ in the troll world and turned her into a werewolf, something we attempted to cure without success using aconitum which you may know as wolfsbane.

The little fellow with Turpelator wore a long black evening jacket and a tall silk hat. He had fine engraved leather cowboy boots with high heels. He became agitated when he arrived at the table. "Slorm see queen, Daemon Turpelator."

"Of course you do, old boy, but now's not the time to crown her," said Turpelator.

"You have a purpose for your visit?" Tony asked.

"Merely a social call to encourage your little troupe to remain in New York for the present." Turpelator spoke slowly, enunciating each word in an annoying superior manner.

"You want us to remain in eighteen thirty-eight?" Sweat poured down my spine.

"You should have no problem, young Ganarski. You have your bride with you. And I will make it worth your while financially. I will provide for all of you if you choose to remain here." Turpelator's closed-mouth smile covered the entire width of his lower face.

"And if we don't?" my bride asked.

Turpelator revealed his three-inch incisors. He hissed as he dove at my Jennifer's throat. Before his teeth could penetrate her skin, she picked up her silver butter knife and jammed it into Turpelator's chest.

It takes a wooden stake to kill a vampire, but Turpelator was a daemon, a human who evolved into a sort of demon or minor league god. Turpelator was both vampire and werewolf plus a lot more. Our little group wasn't yet certain of all his powers, but we knew enough to want to avoid him as much as possible. Unfortunately, Turpelator had chosen us for his enemies. He already transformed CJ into a werewolf. Was my Jennifer next?

Jennifer's silver butter knife penetrated Turpelator's chest. The werewolf juice in his blood boiled and steamed out. He screamed and lurched towards my throat. Jennifer twisted the butter knife in Turpelator's chest while I shook in place with nothing in hand to defend myself.

Turpelator's fangs pushed against the skin covering my jugular vein, but they did not penetrate. He vanished.

The people sitting around us must have thought they were witnessing a magic act because they applauded.

Slorm shouted, "You attack Master. Slorm attack you." The creature reached for my throat with its claw-like hands. Jennifer held her silver bloodied butter knife to his throat. His claw scraped against my throat but did no damage.

My Jennifer pushed her butter knife into the side of Slorm's neck until blue blood dripped.

He backed off. "But first, Slorm save Master."

My head went fuzzy as Slorm ran out of the room.

My hand shook when I reached for my Jennifer's arm. "Thanks for saving me."

"I've got your back, partner."

Joe, our waiter visited. "Is anything the matter here?"

"A little trouble with the local Turpelator and one of his minions, but we took care of it like we always do," said Gilbert.

"We don't list trouble on the menu here at Delmonico's," said Joe. "But if you want a troubling dish, I'll tell you about this brand new haunted place."

"Haunted?" asked Snpgrdxz, aka Daniel Brickmaster.

"Yes, sir. You see there was a fire some time back that burned the old Delmonico's. Now some of the customers that didn't finish their steaks come around here looking for them."

The Delmonico's we ate at stood at Two South William Street. The restaurant was brand new, as Joe had indicated. The head waiter sat us at a big table to accommodate our entire team, with no pushing little tables together. The solid wood furniture included walnut, mahogany and other woods I didn't know. I guess some things were oak. I could have paid more attention whenever the mother of all fathers, my dad, hauled me over to our local big box home center. Delmonico's didn't sport particle board with vinyl veneer-covered furniture here.

The tablecloths were delicately embroidered, clean, starched and old-fashioned by twenty-first century standards.

The dishes and silver had ornate designs. The plates were especially thin. I'd hate to have to wash them without breaking a few. They owned forks, knives and spoons made out of silver. Maybe it was silver-coated. I couldn't tell for sure. But the surface definitely was real silver. You get to know your silver when you deal with werewolves and other creatures of the night.

While Joe Williams was our waiter, any number of other servers roamed around to assist. They were Black men wearing starched white suit coats and black pants.

Frank returned us to the bit about ghosts. "Sounds like disappointed customers more than ghosts."

"Oh, they are both, sir. They were customers at our old place, but they burned up in the fire. Now they want their steaks and they want them well done, just like at the old restaurant."

"Almost sounds reasonable," said Tony.

"Ain't no reasonable when it comes to ghosts," said our waiter. "You order a well-done steak and chances are one of those ghosts will sneak off with it and we'll have to cook you up another one."

"Let's order a well-done steak and see what happens," said my Jennifer.

"Nothing might happen except you will enjoy a delicious steak," said the waiter. "Or you might find yourself sharing a table with a late dinner guest."

"Late? Get it, gang?" Frank asked.

When my Jennifer's well-done steak showed up, we were busy with our wine. Gilbert especially became tipsy so Joe suggested that our "African friend calm himself before the white folks become dismayed with him eating in a fine restaurant."

Gilbert didn't appreciate the comment, but CJ reminded him that he, like the rest of us, needed to adapt to the nineteenth century because the nineteenth century would not adapt to us. Besides we had to keep a low profile to avoid endangering ourselves or altering the past any more than necessary.

My Jennifer calmed the situation when she said, "I'll take a bite to test it before the ghosts strike, but I'm not really hungry."

"Why don't you share," asked Third Jennifer.

A ghostly face appeared over the steak in the shape of Turpelator. It opened its mouth and swallowed our well-done steak in one gulp. Like the others, I backed away from the table. Turpelator the ghost smiled.

To continue reading, please search **Snpgrdxz and the Time Hunters Book 3 of the Snpgrdxz Series** on www.amazon.com.

ABOUT THE AUTHOR

Paul R. Lloyd writes fiction that explores the monsters and strangers among us. His offbeat characters reveal the horror and humor of the human condition. He investigates themes such as cowardice in the three-book Snpgrdxz series, forgiveness in Amazon top seller HAGS, redemption in Amazon top seller FULFILLMENT, and the nature of love (and hate) in STEEL PENNIES. Paul teaches workshops and speaks on how to reach the next skill level as a writer. He heads the Write Time Writers Group and serves as a member of the DuPage Writer's Group, the Chicago Writers Association and Lively Arts, a group of Christian artists and writers. Paul recently completed a 30-year career as head of a marketing communications firm.

Visit him online at: http://paulrlloyd.blogspot.com

To read more paperback books or ebooks by Paul R. Lloyd, including the next book in the Snpgrdxz series, please search Paul R. Lloyd on www.amazon.com.

FICTION BY PAUL R. LLOYD

NOVELS

Fulfillment

Hags

Steel Pennies

Snpgrdxz and the Time Monsters
Book 1 of the Snpgrdxz Series

Snpgrdxz and the Time Warriors
Book 2 of the Snpgrdxz Series

Snpgrdxz and the Time Hunters
Book 3 of the Snpgrdxz Series

SHORT STORIES

Angel Thorns

Little Miss Forgotten

Egbert

To Dwell Among Us
Prequel to Fulfillment

Paperback and E-Book versions available by searching title or
Paul R. Lloyd on www.amazon.com.

www.ingramcontent.com/pod-product-compliance
Lightning Source LLC
Chambersburg PA
CBHW070343260626
47160CB00003B/1126